BLOOD RUNS CROOKED

WHEN THE LIFE OF ONE
DEMANDS THE DEATH OF ANOTHER

LEVI BRONZE

Black Rose Writing | Texas

ISBN: 978-1-68513-726-7
LIBRARY OF CONGRESS CONTROL NUMBER: 2025946595
PUBLISHED BY BLACK ROSE WRITING
www.blackrosewriting.com

Printed in the United States of America
Suggested Retail Price (SRP) $19.95

Blood Runs Crooked is printed in Garamond Premier Pro

*As a planet-friendly publisher, Black Rose Writing does its best to eliminate unnecessary waste to reduce paper usage and energy costs, while never compromising the reading experience. As a result, the final word count vs. page count may not meet common expectations.

Cover design by eauart.com

To Jena, my Mississippi Queen. If the sun refused to shine,
I would still be loving you. When mountains crumble to the sea,
there will still be you and me.

PRAISE FOR
BLOOD RUNS CROOKED

"If you are a fan of John Grisham or John Irving,
you will love Levi Bronze."
—Bill Schweitzer, author of *Doves in a Tempest*.

BLOOD RUNS CROOKED

CHAPTER ONE

Lane eyed the house from behind an oak tree. He'd checked the place every day since school had let out for the summer three weeks prior. The word around Huntsville County High School was that the new pastor of Soulshine Church was moving into town from Amarillo, Texas. That he'd played a season for the Miami Dolphins before getting "the call" to swap an NFL playbook for the Word of God, a team for a flock, and the gridiron for a pulpit. Whoever he was, one thing was certain: he'd be the closest thing to an actual celebrity Locust Fork, Mississippi had ever had. Sure, there were a dozen or so local bigshots in the bedroom town. Bank presidents, doctors, lawyers (the town had more than its fair share of them since Ole Miss was less than an hour away), business owners, city and county politicians, and a smattering of families with old money and inherited real estate. But this new preacher, whoever he was, had been on television and that set him apart from the rest of the pack of the local Who's Who.

Gunner wouldn't be happy if he knew Lane was wasting valuable daylight spying when there were chores that could be done. Soulshine Church's property began where the tree line ended so Lane wasn't trespassing. He was on family property. Family . . . now there was a word as empty as a suitcase at a thrift store. Wasn't always this way, though. Used to mean something. Used to be real. Fun conversation at the dinner table. Affectionate rubs on the crown of the head by a loving, calloused hand.

Instructions in the backyard on how to throw a fastball. GOOD presents on Christmas morning. Walking the fencerow and inspecting the herd with a real dad, a genuine hero. Seeing his mother smile and hearing her laugh. The house filled with the aroma of tasty meats and vegetables cooking on the stovetop. Cornbread, biscuits, pies, and cakes baking in the oven. Often seeing the two of them embrace when in the same room of the house. The exchange of gentle kisses. Their walks along the edge of the pond, almost always hand in hand. He at the wheel of the big John Deere with her standing next to him riding shotgun. And then there were the vacations. Down to the beach at Gulf Shores, Alabama. Up to Branson, Missouri for the music and attractions. Over to Dallas to watch the big-name cowboys give it their best atop bulls like Sidewinder, Timebomb and Fender Bender. Those were the days. Now it was just Lane and Gunner. Sandwiches and microwave dinners. Canned soups and chili. A house filled with tenseness and awkwardness. Few words and always spoken matter-of-factly. For Lane, reprieve came on Friday and Saturday nights when, in religious fashion, Gunner left the house at 7 PM. Lane didn't know where the man went. Didn't care. Every time he left, Lane hoped he'd just not come back. His hopes, however, were futile. For just as faithfully as Gunner departed, he returned. About 3 AM, a beat-up truck with a rust-cancered exhaust, high beams on and Gunner at the wheel barreled up the driveway. If the headlights and engine noise failed to arouse Lane from his sleep, the slam of the truck door or the crash of the house door succeeded. For the teenage boy, the concept of family had devolved. Once it had been permanent, written in all caps. It was now a lowercase term, written in pencil, then erased. All that remained were shadows and residue.

Lane had a panoramic view of the church's complex, but he was virtually undetectable. That is unless someone really studied the tree line. But who would have reason to? A basketball goal stood in one corner of the parking lot. An unsupervised group of boys whom Lane guessed to be middle-schoolers played a game of three-on-three. A compact Ford sedan, a Toyota Camry, two Chevrolet full-size pickups, and a Dodge minivan flanked the back of the building near two glass entry doors, the words "Church Office" prominent on a placard above them. The house Lane had been watching for the past several days was situated about fifty yards from the church building. It was a two story. Mostly brick, but a considerable amount of wood as well. The wooden portions of the house and the window shutters had new paint. Two weeks earlier, three men spent three days covering beige with stark white. They worked for a company called "Fresh Touch", at least that's what their van said. The full-size patio on the back of the house was furnished with a large cook grill and an eight-seat outdoor dining set. A large umbrella stuck up from the stone floor through the middle of the table. The bricks of the house matched those of the church building. The house was a parsonage. At least that's what the kids at school called it. Celebratory words erupted from the boys shooting hoops. Lane watched as three of the boys gave each other high-fives. One of them must have made a great shot. The roar of a big engine from up the street diverted Lane's attention from the action around the basketball goal. An eighteen-wheeler pulling an enclosed trailer rolled down the pavement. Emblazoned across the side of the light blue trailer were the words "Friends Moving Company," The "M" in the word moving was formed by the image of a twin-peaked house. That's cool, Lane thought. The slogan under the company name read, "Because when it's time to move, you need friends."

The truck slowed to a stop in front of the house. Two men emerged from the cab and headed to the rear of the trailer. They wore khaki shorts and light blue polo shirts. One of the men flipped down a latch and released the lock of a loading ramp. In unison they reached under the trailer bed and grabbed the metal ramp. With each of them on opposite sides, they walked the end of the ramp back and lowered it to the asphalt. They exchanged a few words that Lane couldn't make out. One man walked to the back of the truck and positioned the edge of the ramp even with the bed of the truck. He then raised the back door of the trailer. The second man walked to the parsonage. In less than a minute the garage door began to raise. The man must've entered through the front door. Lane pulled his head further behind the tree when the back door opened. Best not to take a chance on being spotted. The second man exited, took a quick survey of the patio then walked around the house and rejoined his partner at the ramp of the semi. A light blue van pulled up close to the driveway and stopped on the shoulder of the street. It too had the Friends Moving Company logo painted on the side. Two men and two women got out of the van, all dressed like the two men who'd arrived first. The team of six began unloading the furniture from inside of the trailer. Two of the men carried an oxblood leather sofa end to end down the ramp and into the house. The other members of the crew joined in and unloaded a recliner and a coffee table. A pearl-colored GMC Yukon pulled into the driveway and parked at the back edge where the concrete met the grass of the backyard. The passenger door flew open and a boy hustled out. Lane guessed the boy to be twelve or thirteen. He wore a Miami Dolphins tee-shirt, jeans and Air Jordans. Lane recognized those shoes even from a distance. The boy ran to the back of the house and entered through the back door, his thick blonde locks bouncing on his head. The driver emerged. The new pastor no doubt. He wasn't as big as Lane had imagined. Actually, he was really kind of normal-sized. Fit but not muscled-up. Dressed like a tennis player minus a headband. The man walked to the back of the moving truck and peered inside. The two men who'd carried in the sofa returned to the truck. The man met them with handshakes and what looked to be cordial greetings. The arrival of a late model silver Mercedes sedan caused Lane to turn his attention away from the man and the movers. The car came to a stop next to the SUV at the back edge of the driveway. Both doors opened at the same time. The driver got out. A lady. *Must be the pastor's wife.* Like the man, she was fit. She didn't close her door. Her blonde hair barely touched her shoulders. She removed her sunglasses and positioned them on top of her head. In one hand she held a large foam cup. She took a drink from the straw as she walked into the garage, the hem of her cotton summer dress sashaying with each step. Though the passenger door was open, the passenger remained in the car. *Why?* The sun's brightness against the car's windshield made it difficult for Lane to make out anything about the passenger. He stepped from behind the tree a bit in hopes of getting a better view. A black and butterscotch Yorkie jumped out of the car from the driver's side and hurried into the garage to join the woman. *Okay, she must be the dog's favorite master.* Lane saw the passenger's white sneaker touch the concrete drive. The leg was tanned. Then the other sneaker. A girl exited the car. She was older than the boy . . . noticeably older.

The evidence of her early womanhood was unavoidable. Her straight hair was blonde like her mother's, only longer, reaching halfway down her back. The bottom of her burnt orange sleeveless Texas Longhorns shirt hung just below the waistline of her denim cutoffs. She opened the back door of the car and pulled a carry bag from the back seat then shut the door. With the strap of the bag on one shoulder, she walked around the front of the car and onto the patio. She inspected the dining set and sat down in one of the chairs. The boy joined her on the patio and encouraged her to come into the house. She rose from the chair and walked to the grill. "Come on!" the boy said, his voice loud, his tone demanding, the typical communication tactic of a kid in want of something. The girl raised the lid of the grill and checked it out. He tugged on the strap of her bag. "Come on!"

"Alright! Alright!" she said and lowered the grill's lid. As she began to follow his bidding, the boy released the strap and ran to the back door of the house. It was a large piece of glass with a metal frame. The kind of door annoying marketing people at big box stores and outdoor events are always wanting to talk to shoppers about. He flung it open and darted inside. The girl took her time. By the time she reached it, it had closed. She pulled it open but hesitated. She looked back toward the woods and raised an opened hand toward Lane. She'd seen him.

CHAPTER TWO

Lane jerked back behind the tree and leaned his back against it. He shot his hands into the hair above his forehead and interlocked his fingers on the top of his head. How could she have noticed him? He clinched his eyes shut and inhaled a belly full of air. *She probably thinks I'm a freak, a peeping Tom or something.* He shook his head and drug his palms down his cheeks, his heart thumping. *Lane, you're such an idiot. You knew better than to step out where you could be seen.* He turned and pounded the trunk of the tree a few times with a hammer fist, then paused and shook his head, his hands on his hips. Oh well. What was done was done.

When Lane arrived back at home he went straight to the barn. Gunner would be home before too long and if the grass wasn't cut Lane would hear about it . . . or possibly feel it. The front yard and backyard combined made up just over an acre. Inside the lean-to portion on the end of the barn sat two mowers. A Grasshopper 52" zero turn and a 22" economy brand pusher. The zero turn could knock the job out in thirty minutes. With the pusher, however, the job would take three hours, maybe more. Lane's dad had purchased the zero turn five years prior and taught Lane how to drive it. Cutting the yard with it was fun. Lane would just sit in the seat, work the levers and, like magic, the beast would transform ankle-high grass into a lawn comparable to a golf course fairway. When the job was done, Lane could see the result. A great sense of accomplishment. And he wasn't all sweaty and covered with grass shavings. Two years ago, the Grasshopper broke down. When it came to getting it fixed, Gunner said, "I can't afford it." Instead, he bought the low-budget 22" pusher from a trade-day event in neighboring Union County. The mini speech he gave Lane when he unloaded it from the back of his truck still rang in Lane's mind: "It'll take you a little longer and you'll have to work a little harder, but you're young and strong. You'll be fine. Besides, it'll be good exercise." Lane didn't need the exercise. He was almost six feet tall. No love handles. Defined biceps. He drug the pusher from the barn with one hand and lugged the gas can in the other. Halfway between the house and the road he stopped along the driveway and filled the tank of the meager mower. He made his way to the blacktop, intentionally leaving the gas can behind. He'd performed the arduous ritual so many times that he knew the places in the yard where refilling the tank would be necessary. Why carry the can to the road just to have to come get it later? Might as well leave it close to where he would need it next. When he reached the end of the yard where the grass met the shoulder of the road, he pulled the ripcord and the small engine chugged to a start. He began making the first narrow swipe across the massive yard. Hundreds more to go.

An hour and twenty minutes later Lane sat on the back porch, a half-full bottle of water in one hand, an empty one next to a leg of his chair. The Mississippi heat index clung to his body like a blanket soaked with hot water. He could've timed the job better. Could've had the front cut before ten o'clock. Taken a six-hour break and started the back at four. Lane would've had the yard cut well before Gunner got home from work and avoided the sun's vengeance. But he didn't want to miss the arrival of Soulshine Church's new and much talked about pastor, so he opted to push the mower in the middle of the day, endure the heat and deal with the sunburn that was sure to follow. He finished the last half of the second bottle and stood to his feet. A familiar, horrifying sound came from the road and grew louder as it got closer to the house. Gunner's raggedy pickup truck. He was home two hours early. *Why, for crying out loud?*

The truck slowed to a stop in the well-worn spot in the dirt driveway just past the back of the house. Gunner got out and slammed the door shut as if he was trying to hurt the rusty heap. He looked up at Lane, his brow drawn down, his eyes mingled with question and hatefulness. "It's over a hundred degrees. They sent us home early because of it. You shoulda had this grass cut by ten or ten-thirty. What'chu been doing, Headlight?"

Headlight. Lane recoiled. It was the belittling, insulting nickname Gunner concocted and assigned to Lane shortly after Lane's mother had died. The term ignited a fire in Lane's veins every time Gunner spoke it.

Lane clinched his teeth behind closed lips then relaxed his bite. "I spent some time out on the property this morning. You know, checking the fence and stuff like that."

The tension in Gunner's face eased a bit. Perhaps the excuse had worked. He began shaking his head. "Well, if you die of a heat stroke out here, it's your own stupid fault. I'm gonna take a nap, something I don't normally get to do. Then, we need to go to the grocery store. Be leaving in a couple of hours. And you'll need a shower before we go." Gunner wrenched his face. "Now, hurry up and finish this grass. If it ain't done and you're not cleaned up and ready when I wake up, I'll whoop you good. You got me, Boy?"

Lane lowered his head and answered in a defeated tone. "Yeah, I got you."

"What'd you say. You smart-mouthing me?"

"No, Sir. I just said, 'Yeah, I got you.'"

With lips pressed, Gunner raised his chin a bit and adjusted the cap on his head. It had a patch above the bill with the words North Mississippi Electric Cooperative, his place of employment since before he entered Lane's life. He walked to the back porch and ascended the steps, his Igloo lunch box in tow. Lane kept his head down as Gunner passed by the chair where he sat. Gunner entered the house through the back door. Lane raised his head and studied the landscape. Why had things come to this? A barn once filled with farm equipment and stocked with hay and livestock feed, now stood vacant and hollow. The area around it that once resonated with an ensemble of bird noises—chickens, peacocks, ducks, and guineas—was now as quite as a cemetery. A pasture once home to more than a hundred head of Black Angus cattle, three quarter horses, and four donkeys was now just acres overgrown with weeds and thistles. If running away to his grandparents were an option, Lane would catch a bus and be gone. But he had no grandparents. He didn't have an aunt or an uncle either. Just Gunner. Which meant he had . . . no one.

•   •   •

Gunner wheeled the truck into the parking lot of Oscar's Cupboard, a regional chain that specialized mostly in obscure branded groceries and household goods. The raw, unmuffled exhaust of the truck's engine hijacked people's attention outside the store. Lane felt their eyes as Gunner drove between the rows of vehicles in search of an empty space. It was embarrassing, but what could Lane do? Gunner pulled into a space toward the back of the lot. He turned off the obnoxious machine and Lane got out, careful not to bang the maroon mini-van that Gunner had parked beside. A man sat in the van's driver's seat. Lane cut a glance at the numerous tattoos on the man's forearm as he rested it on the seal of the lowered window.

"Evening," the man said.

"Evening," Lane replied and cut his eyes to the man's face. The man's eyes were bright and kind. His wide grin revealed that he'd perhaps never been to a dental office. Young voices came from the behind the man. Two children sat in the second seat: a boy and a girl. Both had disheveled hair, their facial features strikingly similar. The girl looked to be a couple of years older than the boy.

"You like Elvis?" the boy asked.

Odd question for a young kid to ask, Lane thought.

"Well, I guess I like a few of his songs."

"He loves Elvis," the girl said. "He can even sing like him. Go ahead, Donnie. Show him."

Without waiting for Lane's approval, the boy raised one side of his upper lip and, as if suddenly endowed with a mature, baritone voice from heaven, belted out, "I'll have a blue Christmas without you. I'll be so blue just thinking about you."

Lane's eyes shot open. "Wow," that's really incredible."

The little boy winked at Lane and smiled. "My name's Donnie Newhouse and you'll hear me on the radio one day."

The man in the driver's seat turned and looked back at the boy. "If the Good Lord wills it and you don't get on a high horse about it." The man looked at Lane. "He's loved Elvis since he was three years old."

"Well, he's got some real talent, Sir."

"Thank you," the man said.

"Would you like to hear another one?" the boy asked.

"Now, Donnie. The man's got shopping to do. Don't bother him."

"Maybe some other time," Lane said. "I've got to be going for now. But thanks."

Lane started toward the store, in no hurry to catch up to Gunner who was standing near the front door motioning with one arm for Lane to "come on." When Lane joined Gunner, he was met with a question: "What was that all about?"

"A man and his two kids are in the van next to your truck. The boy has an amazing singing voice. Sounds like Elvis."

"Elvis, huh?" Gunner pulled his head back and wrinkled his brow. "I'd have to hear that for myself."

The glass automatic doors slid open as they approached them. They walked in and Gunner raised a hand toward two long rows of shopping carts. "Grab a cart and let's get started."

Lane obeyed and pulled a cart from one of the rows. He walked slowly behind Gunner as his antagonist began shopping the store's inventory. Their first stop was to the soda section. Various flavors of a soft drink brand called Gusher were organized on wooden pallets. Gunner pulled a twelve pack of regular cola from one of the stacks and dropped it in the cart followed by a twelve pack of grape flavor. "Remember, you can have three cans of each," he said and started walking. "The others are for my work. If you drink up your six before we come back next week, you'll just have to drink water."

Lane shook his head as he followed, his lips pressed in angst. They rounded the corner and entered an aisle, shelves of chips and crackers to one side, dry cereal on the other.

"Hey, Harley Ray!" Gunner called out to a man a short distance up the aisle.

The man paused from pushing his shopping cart and looked back. The woman that accompanied him stopped and looked back as well. Atop the man's head was a North Mississippi Electric Cooperative cap. "Well, hey, Gunner," he said, a friendly grin on his pudgy reddish face. He walked back to Gunner and extended a beefy freckled hand for a shake. Gunner obliged. Harley Ray's female companion walked up next to him.

"This here's my wife, Joanne," Harley Ray said, his pride unavoidable for he'd definitely married above himself. "Honey, this is Gunner."

"Nice to meet you, Joanne," Gunner replied. "Harley Ray and I work on the same line crew."

Joanne's eyes twinkled the way those of happily married women do when introduced to others by their husbands. A kind smile stretched on her face. "Nice to meet you as well." She turned her attention to Lane. "And is this your son?"

Lane ratcheted his grip on the handle of the cart. Gunner lifted one hand and rested it on Lane's shoulders. "Yes. This is Lane."

"Hello, Lane," she said in a polite tone that reminded Lane of his mother. "And how old are you?"

"Eighteen."

"I bet all the girls go crazy over you. You're a handsome young man."

A compliment. Wow! Lane felt warmth in his cheeks. He smiled. "Thank you. You're very kind."

These were regular people. Nice people. Why couldn't Lane live with folks like them instead of Gunner.

"Oh, Joanne, you're gonna make him get the big head telling him things like that," Gunner said, tainting Lane's moment of encouragement.

Harley Ray tugged at his belt line and adjusted his pants around his fleshly midsection. "It was nice to knock off three hours early today, wasn't it?"

"It sure was," Gunner said. "And we got paid for the full day anyway."

"It was hot as blue blazes today."

"Man, you ain't kidding. I thought I was gonna pass out up in that bucket lift today. When Charlie told us we were knocking off early, I just thanked God," Gunner said, an open hand raised in a worshipful fashion.

Lane clinched his teeth behind closed lips at the remark. Gunner thanking God? Right.

Joanne nudged her husband on the elbow. "Harley, we need to finish up here. The Porters are coming over later you know. The roast is in the oven."

Harley concurred with a nod and looked Gunner in the eye. "I guess I'll see you tomorrow." The friendly big man cut a look to Lane. "Good meeting you, Lane."

"You too, Sir."

Harley Ray made a one-eighty with the shopping cart and he and his wife resumed their shopping. Lane imagined the spread Joanne would be putting on the table for the Porters. He was certain it'd be delicious and that the conversation that accompanied it would be much like what he and his mom and dad's used to be like.

"Alright, Headlight, let's get a move on," Gunner said, his command as blunt as a lead pipe. "I want to finish up here. That new TV series I've been looking forward to watching starts tonight and I don't plan on missing a single minute of it." He tossed a couple of large bags of potato chips into the shopping cart followed by a box of unsweetened whole wheat flakes. Lane knew better than to protest Gunner's choice of the cereal. Gunner wouldn't be eating it. He never did. The cereal had the texture of dry magnolia leaves and tasted like cardboard. It'd be Lane's breakfast until the following week's grocery run. Sugar helped make it a little more appetizing, but Lane had to use discretion. Two teaspoons per bowl and no more. Gunner purchased a five-pound bag at the beginning of each month, and he didn't purchase it with Lane and the concentration camp cereal in mind. No, he bought it for his coffee which he liked to be as sweet as syrup. If the five-pounder started depleting too quickly, Lane would hear about it. Might even feel the back of Gunner's hand because of it. They made their way between the rows of groceries then turned and headed up the next aisle. The sight hit Lane like ice in his face. A fit, teenage girl. Long blonde hair. Cut off denim shorts and a Texas Longhorns shirt. Lane's heart thumped in his chest. Gunner increased his pace enroute to the sliced bread at the far end he was after. Lane would have to keep up or get scolded. He kept his head down as he tailed Gunner. As he hurried, the front right wheel of the cart began to squeak. Heck! That might get her attention, but he couldn't slow down. Gunner might turn back and bark at him. She'd witness the ordeal, notice Lane and then really think he was a weirdo. He'd want to jump off a bridge or step in front of a train. She began shopping a rack of bagels, her back turned. Great! Lane could just roll past her. With her eyes on the bagels, she'd never notice him. He clamped his grip hard on the handle of the cart and fast walked, his heart rate jumping like a fish out of water. Just as he rolled passed her, a little girl, no more than four years old, darted from her mother's side and out into the aisle in front of Lane. Like hitting an invisible wall, Lane stopped the cart. The little girl raised an opened hand toward a display of donuts. "Mama, Mama, can we get some of these? I love Kispy Kemes," she said, the Rs absent from her pronunciation of the famous brand.

The mother turned on her heels and looked Lane in the eyes. "I'm sorry, Sir," she said. "I should have been holding her hand."

"No problem, Ma'am," Lane replied.

The lady stepped into the middle of the aisleway and took the little girl by one hand. "Now, Catherine, you stay close to Mama."

In his peripheral, Lane could see the Texas girl turn and take note. He wanted to look at her. Wanted to see if her face was compatible to her golden blonde hair, as attractive as her tanned legs. She'd waved at him when he stood at the edge of the woods. Would she smile if their eyes met? Would she speak? And the one question that jacked his nerves like an electric shock—would she recognize him? Lane focused on the little girl and her mother. When they were clear of his path, he wheeled the cart up the aisle, his eyes fixed forward. Gunner turned toward him, a package of Oreos in his hand.

"Three rows in the pack," he said, "Same deal as always. Got it?"

"Yeah."

The "deal" was two rows for Gunner, one for Lane. Gunner would pack them in his lunch box for work and graze on them as a snack when he was home. He'd keep up with the count of his two rows and, though he'd probably take a few out of Lane's row before they returned to Oscar's Cupboard the following week, Lane was to leave Gunner's well enough alone or be prepared to encounter his wrath.

In sinuous fashion they made their way through the rows of groceries. In less than an hour they were standing behind a lady customer at the checkout. Lane watched as she unloaded her selections. A wide black conveyor belt transported the items to the slender female cashier who stood behind a register. The streaks of gray in her black hair and the lines of her small, pale face caused Lane to guess the woman to be in her mid 60's. The fingers of her left hand were ringless. Not even a wedding band. Divorced, no doubt. Or, worse even, a widow. Lane wondered about the lady's life. Why was she having to work a menial, low-paying job at this stage in her life? She should be home digging in her flower bed. Watching her favorite game shows. Baking cookies. Playing with her grandchildren. Life must've been hard on her too. She scanned the groceries at a breakneck pace, the register keeping time, never missing an item. Lane envied the lady customer's collection of food. Steaks. Chicken legs. Breaded fish. Apples. Bananas. Strawberries. Orange juice. Canned biscuits. Bacon. Raisin bread. Chocolate bars. Pastries. Ground beef. Taco shells. Three different flavors of ice cream. Cheese and various other appetizing foods. He looked down at the choices Gunner had made. Two cases of Gusher soda. A case of beer. Sandwich bread. Mayonnaise. Frozen dinners. Sandwich meat. A package of Oreos. And that bland, sugarless cereal that could substitute for slithers of cardboard.

"Lady, would you take me home with you?" Lane wanted to say.

Her bill came to almost $300. Gunner's less than $100.

Aside from the cases of Gusher soft drinks, it took only two brown bags to hold the results of Gunner's shopping venture. Lane and Gunner picked up their goods and exited the store. Gunner carried the lighter bags, Lane the heavier cases of soda. The typical protocol.

As Lane labored past the maroon mini-van, Donnie Newhouse, without a prompt, offered up another Elvis rendition.

"We're caught in trap. I can't walk out. Because I love you too much baby. Why can't you see? What you're doing to me. When you don't believe a word I say. We can't go on together with suspicious minds. And we can't build our dreams on suspicious minds."

Lane lifted the cases of Gusher over the side of the truck bed and set them down in the back. He looked over at Donnie. "Atta boy, Donnie. Keep on dreaming. You'll be on the radio one day. I'm sure of it."

"Thank you. Thank you very much." Donnie replied in a voice unmistakably Elvis-like.

Then, Lane did something he rarely did—he smiled.

CHAPTER THREE

For Lane, it would be another grueling day. With a garden hoe he'd roam throughout the pasture portion of the 120-acre property and dig up thistles. "You need to get'em while their flower heads are purple. If you let'em turn brown, they'll go to seed and take over," Gunner had barked before leaving for work. When Lane's father was still in the picture, Lane would ride shotgun on the tractor with him as the two of them sprayed the property with herbicide. It was a yearly late spring ritual. The pesky weeds never had a chance. In those days, the landscape of the family farm was worthy of a feature article in The American Cattleman, Farm World or The Progressive Farmer. Not now, however. The thistles would have to be dug up by hand because the tractor was no more. Like everything else of value, Gunner sold it shortly after Lane's mother passed. The once picturesque farm was now little more than an overgrown eyesore void of any semblance of its former beauty. So, what difference would it make if thistles took over? None, really. Digging them was just another one of Gunner's unnecessary, burdensome chores dreamed up to keep Lane from having any measure of a normal, happy teenage life. But for the moment, the thistles could just wait.

Lane made his way through the woods. The open yard of the Soulshine Church complex began to come into view as he drew closer to the tree line. Would he get a glimpse of her today? Like before, he took his position at the same large oak tree. No Friends Moving Company truck. The crew must've gotten the family moved in in a single day. The Yukon and the Mercedes were parked at the edge of the back of the driveway where the concrete met the grass. Surely that meant she was home. No kids shooting basketball at the back of the church's parking lot. No cars parked near the door of the church office. Everything was quiet. Lane wondered if it was like this every Friday at Soulshine Church.

Now if Lane were Tyler Frost, he'd just walk up to the house, knock on the door and introduce himself. The new preacher would greet him with a big smile and a firm handshake. He'd invite him in and offer him a glass of iced tea or a soda. For the next two to three hours, he'd help unbox some of the family's belongings all the while asking questions about the preacher's professional football career, life in Texas and any other conversational matters that'd endear him to the family. The preacher's wife would order pizza and breadsticks to be delivered. Then he'd sit down at the table and eat lunch with the preacher's family. By the time he left, he'd have the Texas blonde's phone number and a date for Saturday night. And just like that, a relationship would begin between the town's most popular boy and the town's newest babe. It'd be that simple. Afterall, Tyler was the varsity quarterback at Huntsville County High School. Tyler's father owned the lumber yard in town. Tyler drove a late model Jeep Wrangler and all the popular girls at school loved to ride in it, especially during the summertime when Tyler took the rag top off. But Lane wasn't Tyler Frost. He didn't play football. Didn't have a cool vehicle or any vehicle for that matter. And he didn't have a resourceful father. In fact, he didn't have a father at all. Just a male interloper who'd turned out to be an antagonistic brute.

Lane leaned against the trunk of the giant tree and stared at the parsonage. The yard was vacant. The doors of the house were closed, the garage door down. No sign of her. Even if she was outside and Lane was able to screw up his nerve enough to step out from the woods and meet her, disappointment was sure to be the eventual result? No doubt, sooner rather than later, she was certain to meet Tyler Frost or one of the other "cool" guys of Locust Fork. She'd forget about Lane and that would be the end of it. When school started back, she'd be the talk. A hot commodity on campus. Social osmosis would happen quickly. In no time, she'd be assimilated into the "in" crowd, involved in the clubs and activities that were "their" turf. Lane would see her, and she'd hardly speak to him. Heck, she'd probably just ignore him. So, why kid himself? She probably waved at him the day before just to be nice. And at the grocery store, if he would've spoken to her, she probably wouldn't have recognized him from Adam. Oh well. Might as well get after the thistles. No need to provoke Gunner. He acted like a jerk even when Lane did what he said and didn't do what he forbade. If he came home and a significant number of the thistles had not been dug up, it'd be World War III and Lane was no match for Gunner. At least it was Friday and Lane would have the house all to himself tonight. He turned to head back through the woods and reality struck him like lightning.

"I was hoping you'd come back this morning," she said, standing next to a tree not twenty feet from him. "You walked right past me at the grocery store. Didn't you see me?"

Her hair hung down from a prominent part in the middle of the crown of her head, its sun kissed blonde hues accenting her tanned face. Large brown eyes. High cheek bones. Perfect teeth.

Lane felt a knot in his throat. "Ah . . . yeah . . . I saw you."

She cocked her head to one side and drew down her brow. "Well, why didn't you speak to me, then?"

Lane's cheeks grew warm. "I wasn't sure you recognized me."

She smiled. "Well, I did."

Lane looked toward the house and then back at her. "How? It's kind of a long way from here to your house. It was easy for me to recognize you because you had on the same clothes, but I was dressed different."

"Binoculars."

Lane shot his head back, a look of confusion on his face. "Binoculars?"

She started walking toward him. "Yeah. When my mom and I drove up in the driveway yesterday, I saw something move out here in the woods, so I grabbed my binoculars. Turned out, it was you." As she drew closer to him, her eyes rounded. "Wow! Your eyes are amazing! I've never seen any like them before."

Lane looked away and breathed in through his nostrils.

"No. No. I mean they're beautiful. Like REALLY beautiful. It's called heterochromia. It's very rare. Henry Cavill has it."

Lane slowly turned back to her. "You mean that? Or you just saying it?"

"No, Henry Cavill a-k-a Superman definitely has heterochromia."

Lane lowered his chin to his chest as he slipped his fingers into his front pockets. "No. I don't mean Henry Cavill. I mean the part about mine being beautiful."

"Absolutely!"

"The only person who ever told me that was my mom."

"Well, see there. You should always listen to your mother."

"I wish I still could," Lane said in a tone just above a whisper.

"I'm sorry. What'd you say?"

Lane looked up at her. "Oh, nothing. Why would you come out here?"

She raised her open palms and cocked her head to one side. "Because I'm new in town and you are the ONLY person my age that I have met. Well, not that we've met. We've just seen each other. I came out here to meet you." She motioned toward the tree she'd emerge from. "Been standing behind that tree for nearly an hour."

"You. All alone out here in the woods. Waiting for me. I could be a freak or an axe murderer or something?"

"But you're not. You're a nice guy."

"And how do you know that?"

A broad smile stretched out on her face, dimples on each cheek, her eyes filled with warmth. "Because you're shy. And shy guys are kind . . . honest . . . real."

Who was this girl? Beautiful. Outgoing. And she wanted to meet Lane.

"That word you used. About my eyes. Hetero . . . whatever it was?"

"Heterochromia."

"Yeah. Who knows words like that?

She raised her eyebrows, her eyes rolled upward, a look of sarcasm on her face. "Ah, people that read and think knowing stuff is an important life skill."

Wow! The girl has brains too, Lane thought. *This must be a dream.*

"What's your name?" she asked.

"Lane."

She nodded. "Okay, Lane. Mine's Abigail."

"Abigail!" came a loud male voice from the house.

Lane jerked his head around to look.

"That's my dad," she said.

"Your mother needs your help so come back inside!" he called out.

"Okay! Coming!" she yelled toward her father and turned back to Lane. "You like hamburgers and hotdogs?"

"Sure. Who doesn't?"

"We are going to fire up the grill this evening. I'd like it if you could come over and eat dinner with us? My family is cool. Even my little brother."

Lane couldn't believe his ears. If his heart had an accelerator, she'd just pressed it—to the floor. No, she'd stomped it. The last time Lane had this sense of thrill was when he got to meet and get his picture made with three-time world bull riding champion Rowdy Humbuckler at the Professional Bull Riders Finals in Dallas. That was five years ago. For sure, this had to be a dream. Lane stood speechless, searching for words as if they were diamonds that had been dropped on a beach.

"If you already have plans, I understand. After all, it is Friday night."

Her words helped him. The last thing he wanted to do was decline her invitation.

"Oh, no. Not at all. I'd love to. What time?"

"How's six?"

"Six it is. Should I bring anything?"

That was a stupid offer. Lane had nothing to bring. What if she suggested drinks or chips or a dessert? Why had he let the question come out of his mouth?

"No, we have everything."

Praise God.

"Just bring an appetite. My dad is a real grill master. Well, I gotta go. See you tonight."

"Yeah. See ya."

Abigail trotted out of the woods then broke into a jog when she got past the tree line and onto the grass. Lane stood and watched her make her way to the house. When she got to the back door, she pulled it open and looked back at him. She waved, then went inside. And Lane, well, he did it again . . . he smiled.

CHAPTER FOUR

With motivated vigor, Lane waged war on the multitude of thistles that stood like knee-high enemy soldiers. By the time Gunner got home from work, the front eleven acres of pasture was populated with the uprooted, purple-bloomed nuisance weeds. They lay vanquished, drying and shriveling in the scorching sun.

Gunner got out of his truck and scanned the scene. "Well, Headlight, looks like you got a lot done today."

"Yeah. I figure I can have the job done by Monday."

"If you want to be something in life, you gotta work hard. Success don't come to the lazy. I give you chores to do so you don't get lazy."

Gunner slammed the truck door shut and started to the back door of the house, his lunch box at his side. Lane fell in behind him.

"I was wondering if one day next week you might take me to the courthouse so I can take my driver's test. I turned eighteen last month you know."

Gunner kept walking. "We'll see. I can't promise you nothing. Means I'll have to take off work early. That'll cost me money."

Lane drew up closer to Gunner. "I sure would appreciate it if you could make it work out."

Gunner kept his stride and waved him off with his free hand. "Like I said, 'We'll see.'"

"If I don't get my license before school starts back, I'll be the only senior who doesn't have theirs. Most of them will be driving their own cars too."

Gunner stopped like he'd hit a wall. He turned to Lane, venom in his eyes. He raised an extended index finger to Lane's face. "Back talk me again, Boy, and I'll take the strap to you."

The "strap" was leather. Four inches wide. A quarter of an inch thick. Four feet long. Shortly before Lane's mother died, she made Gunner promise he'd never sell the tractor. "It's sentimental to Lane. He and Roy made many memories on it," she'd informed him. "I want Lane to have it." Less than three months after her passing, Gunner sold it to a coworker. When the coworker came to trailer it, Lane protested, reminding Gunner of his mother's dying wish and Gunner's promise. Gunner, however, would not be persuaded. When the coworker drove away with the tractor, Gunner went into the tack crib of the barn, pulled the "strap" from an old saddle and waylaid Lane with it. Now, the strap was kept inside the house in Gunner's closet for quick, easy access. And he'd beaten and bruised Lane with it on several occasions since the tractor episode.

Gunner's half-complimentary sentiment to Lane about the job done on the thistles had been voided by the question of the driver's license. Gunner was now in a foul mood and that meant Lane had to be careful. No doubt, he'd question Lane if he was aware of Lane's leaving the house in time to be at Abigail's by six o'clock. Best to play it safe. Lane showered, put on his nicest shirt and slipped out the back door. Perhaps Gunner would just head out at seven o'clock like he always did on Friday nights and not even notice Lane's absence. If he did, however, there could be consequences the next day. A risk Lane was more than willing to take, even if the consequences involved the "strap."

Lane stood at the edge of the tree line and observed the activity on the back patio of the parsonage. Abigail's little brother held a large platter as her father transferred beef patties and hotdogs to it from the grill. Lane looked at his watch. 5:56. Abigail was not with them. What should he do? Just stroll up to the house and introduce himself to the preacher? Wait until they went back into the house and then make his approach? If he did wait, then should he go to the back door and knock or go to the front door and ring the doorbell? Lane wanted to do the best thing. But what was the best thing? One thing he knew—being late was not the best thing. He'd take his chances and meet her dad on the patio. As he stepped out of the woods and onto the grass, Abigail's father looked up and saw him. The minister threw up a hand and waved, then motioned for Lane to come. The friendly gesture eased Lane's anxiety and he picked up the pace. When he got halfway to the house, the back door opened and out walked Abigail. She shot him a big smile, struck out in a trot and met him in the yard.

"I'm glad you came," she said.

"Thanks for inviting me," Lane replied.

"You'll love daddy's burgers. They're the best. He has his own secret seasoning."

Side by side they made their way to the house, Abigail talking, Lane's heart thumping.

When they reached the patio, Abigail motioned to her father. "This is my daddy. Daddy, this is Lane."

The minister offered a big smile, his teeth remarkably similar to Abigail's. He moved the large grill spatula from his right hand to his left then extended his right hand to Lane for a handshake. Lane obliged. Though the man's stature was not that of a linebacker or a running back, his hand was powerful, the result of the weight room and practice field, no doubt.

"I'm Will Weston," he said.

Lane recalled a lesson he'd learned from his mom and dad: When meeting someone older for the first time always refer to them as Mister or Missus. It's a show of respect.

"Nice to meet you, Mister Weston. I'm Lane."

"Nice to meet you too, Lane. We're glad you could join us for dinner."

Evidently Abigail's father concurred with what Lane's parents had taught him as he didn't correct Lane by saying, "Oh, please call me Will."

Abigail motioned to her brother. "This is my brother, Brodie."

Brodie set the platter of meat on one shelf of the grill and reached out his hand. "Hey, Lane," he said, the same cordialness in his demeanor as that of Abigail and his father. *This must be a fine family*, Lane concluded.

Brodie picked up the platter again and Will Weston finished transferring the remaining burgers and hotdogs to it.

"Alright, that's it. Let's head inside," Will Weston said.

He pulled open the back door and held it as Brodie carried the platter inside. Abigail and Lane followed. Abigail's mother stood at the kitchen counter mixing potato salad. "You must be Lane," she said as she worked the ingredients inside the large, green plastic bowl with a wooden spoon.

"Yes, Ma'am. Thanks for having me over."

She looked at him with caring eyes. "I'm Erica and we're glad to have you. Would you like something to drink? Coca Cola? Tea? Water?"

"Nice to meet you, Missus Weston. Coke would be great."

"Coming right up," Abigail said and opened the refrigerator door. It was stainless steel with the energy sticker still on it—an update to the parsonage in light of the Westons' arrival to Soulshine Church.

Abigail retrieved a can of Coca Cola. "Would you like a glass?"

"Can's fine. So how do you like Locust Fork so far?" Lane posed to no particular member of the Weston family.

"It's hotter than Amarillo. I can tell you that," Brodie said as he set the platter of burgers and hotdogs on the island in the middle of kitchen.

"Yeah. It can really get hot here. We haven't had rain in two weeks. I know you just arrived in town, but have you had an opportunity to look around at all?"

Will placed the spatula in the sink. "Last month we came and spent a week here," he said and began washing his hands under the faucet. "It was an opportunity to get to know the place a bit. We stayed at The McAllison Mansion B&B. One day, we drove over to Oxford to check out Ole Miss. Abigail's thinking about going there."

"We went to First Monday over in Ripley," Brodie chimed in. "It's like the biggest yard sale ever. It was so cool. I got a helmet from the Vietnam War. I love military stuff."

Abigail began setting the table with plates.

"Brodie, you help your sister," Erica Weston said.

Brodie pulled open a drawer. With one hand he grabbed a fistful of forks. A fistful of spoons with the other. Will Weston took a bottle of ketchup from the refrigerator along with a jar of mustard and a jar of mayonnaise. He sat them on the island countertop next to a large bag of potato chips. Abigail began putting ice cubes in the glasses on the table.

Lane looked on, envious at the sight of the way the Westons functioned. A real family. It brought back memories that were a mixture of both fondness and pain. He turned away and pinched the wetness from his eyes, hoping no one had noticed.

"Okay, let's pray." Will said.

Each member of the Weston family reached for the hand of the other. Lane stood between Will and Abigail. He followed the family's protocol. Abigail's delicate hand felt nice in his. Lane hoped this night would never end. His mind drifted as Will Weston prayed but the words "In Jesus' name. Amen" snatched him back to reality. He opened his eyes.

"Lane, we're not gonna be real formal tonight. It's every man for himself. So, just grab a plate and dig in," Erica said.

Abigail insisted that Lane go first. He made a burger and loaded his plate with chips and potato salad. Lane took a seat at the table, Abigail sat beside him. When the rest of the Weston family had seated themselves, Will brought up the one subject Lane hoped would NOT come up in the night's discussion.

"So, Lane, tell us about your family."

How should Lane respond? Should he tell them the "story" or just say that he lived with Gunner who happened to be his stepfather. And what if they probed further about Gunner? He couldn't really be honest with them and tell them Gunner despised him and he despised Gunner. No, he couldn't. Not yet.

"My real parents are both dead. I live with my stepdad."

Awkwardness hung in the room like a night fog on a lake.

Will relaxed his shoulders and pressed his lips. "Lane, I'm so sorry. I feel terrible for asking."

Will Weston looked like he'd just totaled his car. Lane could see the regret in his eyes. He knew the minister wished he hadn't brought up the subject.

"No need to feel bad," Lane said. "No way you could've known. It was bound to come up sooner or later."

"What's your stepdad's name?" Brodie said.

"Gunner."

"Gunner. That's a cool name. What does he do for a living?"

"He works for the electric company."

Lane looked at the food on his plate, hoping someone at the table would somehow salvage the moment. Erica Weston did just that.

"That's enough questions for Lane. Why don't we let him ask us some," she said.

Abigail turned to Lane, her eyes filled with sympathy. "Yeah, Lane, ask us anything you like," she said and took a bite out of her burger.

Lane scanned the Westons' kind faces. He focused on Will. "Well, word around town is you played football for the Miami Dolphins before you became a preacher. Is that right?"

Lane took a bite of his burger. Abigail was right. It was incredible. Will Weston's secret seasoning was the bomb.

Will shoved a fork of potato salad in his mouth. "Yeah, I played for Miami for one season. After that, it became clear to me that God wanted me to focus on souls instead of goals. We then moved to Dallas where I went to seminary."

Lane wrinkled his brow. "Goals?"

Will cracked a tight smile. "I was a field goal kicker."

Now, that made sense. A player didn't have to be huge to kick field goals. Lane remembered that a few years ago the kicker for Mississippi State was the smallest guy on the team.

The conversation around the table continued to be about the Westons which was the way Lane preferred it. Will and Erica met at the University of Texas (UT). He was from Corpus Christi. She was from Abilene. Will was an All-American at UT his senior year and got drafted by the Dolphins. Fourth round, tenth pick. Abigail had been born while they lived in Miami. They left Miami and moved to Dallas so that Will could attend seminary. They were there for three years. During that time Brodie was born. Will's first church assignment was in San Antonio. They stayed there six years then moved to Amarillo. Lived there for seven years. Loved it and never thought they'd leave. But when Soulshine contacted Will, the entire family prayed about it for two weeks and believed God wanted them to move to Locust Fork. Will spent most of his time preparing sermons. He was still an avid football fan and seldom, if ever, missed watching the Longhorns on television. Erica loved to cook. She'd been taught by her mother who'd published a cookbook when Erica was a teenager. Erica also loved oil painting. Her specialty was outdoor scenes and wildlife. Abigail and Brodie got along well but had different academic tastes. Abigail preferred math and chemistry. For Brodie it was history and literature. Abigail loved kids and wanted to become a pediatrician. Brodie was undecided about his future (something entirely common for a boy of fourteen), but for the time being was satisfied to play video games, read classic novels and anything military related. By the time Lane finished his second burger, the awkwardness caused by the subject of his family had evaporated. When the evening had begun, Lane wondered why Brodie had placed spoons on the table. Two things resolved the question in Lane's mind: two cartons of ice cream—one strawberry, one chocolate. When the table was cleared, a game of Clue commenced. The murder was committed by Professor Plum in the study with the rope. Lane proved to be the evening's Sherlock Holmes.

"It's past ten o'clock and it's dark outside," Will said as they returned the game pieces and cards back to the box. "Abigail and I will drive you home."

Will was right. It was dark and Lane hadn't thought to bring a flashlight for the walk back home. Will turned to his son, "Brodie, you stay here and help your mother clean up the kitchen."

"Yessir," Brodie said.

Will rose from his chair and pulled a ring of keys from one of the wooden pegs on the wall next to the door by the refrigerator. "We'll go through the garage," he said and opened the door. He reached his hand around the door frame and pressed a button. The garage light illumined, and the automatic roll-up door began its squeaky ritual. Lane followed Abigail through the doorway and into the garage. Boxes filled the two-car area. Each box had been written on with a black permanent marker. Most of them had the word "Books" written on them, but others had different words. Kitchen. Art Supplies. Abigail's Bathroom. Brodie's Bathroom. Master Bathroom. Erica's Shoes. Will's Neckties and Socks. Christmas Decorations. Lane noticed a stack of boxes near the back of the garage. They were factory sealed. Each had a logo: Mason. The factory description read "Canning Jars."

"We're going in the Yukon," Will said.

"I'll ride in the back. You ride up front with Daddy," Abigail said.

Lane opened the front passenger door. The clean car smell and the smell of upholstered leather filled his nostrils. The interior of the SUV was perfect. A large stainless steel drinking cup with a burnt orange capital "T" sat in one of the cup holders of the console. Lane slid into the passenger's seat. Will took his place behind the wheel. Abigail sat behind her father. Lane looked back at Abigail and was greeted with a smile.

"Tonight was fun. Thanks again for inviting me," he said.

"It WAS fun," she replied. "We'll have to do it again sometime."

"I'd like that."

Abigail pulled her cellphone from a back pocket. "What platforms are you on? Let's follow each other."

Lane felt his blood cool in his veins. He couldn't believe it. He'd almost made it through the entire evening with his family being the only awkward subject to arise. Now, he had to reveal another embarrassing truth about himself.

"I'm not on social media," he said. "I don't have a cell phone."

There it was. Abigail Weston now knew that she had just spent her Friday night with the only eighteen-year-old boy in America who didn't have a cell phone. He felt like crawling into the glove box of the SUV.

"That's cool," she said and returned her phone to her pocket. "Sometimes I wish I didn't have a cell phone. It is a time-robber. And social media can be just TOO much drama. The good thing is we're neighbors so we can talk face to face. That's better than technology any day."

This girl is amazing. She could've totally written me off as the world's biggest loser. But no. What does she do? She spares me.

In less than ten minutes the two reflectors of Lane's mailbox were glowing in the beams of the SUV's headlights. "That's my driveway up there," he said.

Will slowed and turned left onto the gravel driveway. The lights of the Yukon lit up the house and front yard.

"Wow," you have a beautiful home," Abigail said.

"You really do," Will agreed.

What they saw was a house. Not a home. A home was filled with laughter, communication, reinforcement, support, and love. A home was where good memories were made, where feelings were shared, where individuals valued each other and did life together. What Abigail and Will Weston were seeing was just bricks and wood and paint. Just a house. Nothing more.

As they made their way further up the driveway, a knot tied in Lane's stomach; he felt like a bowling ball had been dropped on his chest. There was another vehicle in the driveway—Gunner's pickup truck.

What! Gunner at home! It was Friday night and not even eleven o'clock.

Will Weston drove closer to the house. The front porch light came on. Gunner stepped out. He gazed at the SUV, a look of seriousness and question on his face. When the Yukon stopped, Lane opened the passenger door to get out.

"Headlight, where on earth have you been?"

Gunner's hateful words stabbed Lane like a knife. He lowered his chin, closed his eyes, inhaled deep then exhaled.

"Is that Gunner?" Will asked.

"Yes."

"I'll talk to him."

Will Weston got out. "Hi. I'm Will Weston," he said and started walking around the front of the truck toward Gunner. "My family and I just moved into town. I'm the new pastor at Soulshine Church. We had Lane over for dinner."

Like an actor switching into character, Gunner's expression turned cordial. He started down the porch steps to meet Will. Lane got out of the truck. So did Abigail. Gunner and Will shook hands.

"I'm Gunner Hubbard. Sorry if I sounded unfriendly. I've been worried sick about Lane. Didn't know where he was."

"My apologies. He's been with us. We had a great time tonight."

Abigail drew close to her father. Will motioned toward her. "This is my daughter. Abigail. She and Lane met yesterday."

Gunner extended his hand to Abigail. "Nice to meet you, Abigail."

"Nice to meet you as well."

Lane approached them with trepidation. Gunner reached out and pulled Lane close to his side. He wrapped his arms around Lane's shoulders and clapped him on the back a few times. "Son, I was so worried. You left and didn't say a word."

Lane didn't respond to Gunner's embrace. He just stood there, his shoulders rounded, his arms at his sides. Gunner released him and turned to Will.

"I heard Soulshine was getting a new pastor. Nice to meet you. Locust Fork is a great town."

"We like what we've experienced so far," Will said. "Do you have a church home?"

"We don't. But I've been thinking about looking for a church for me and Lane."

What a load of bull crap. Getting together with people who believe in God and do good for others was the absolute last thing Gunner would consider. Lane's mother and Gunner frequently argued. Lane remembered a few occasions when his mother suggested church as a possible help to their marriage. Each time Gunner pushed back at the idea declaring the church to be just "a group of Bible-thumping do-gooders out to get people's money."

"Why don't you and Lane come this Sunday and we'll have something in common," Will said.

Gunner drew down his brow and pulled his head back. "What would that be?'

"We'll all be new at Soulshine."

Gunner let out a laconic laugh. "Well, Preacher, I guess you'd be right about that."

"Service starts at eleven. Hope to see you then."

"You might. You just might. It was nice of you to have Lane over for dinner tonight."

Will cut his eyes to Lane and grinned. "We enjoyed his company." He looked back at Gunner. "Hope it's only the first of many. We'll be on our way. Nice to meet you, Gunner."

The two men shook hands again and Will turned to Abigail. "Abigail, we'd better be going."

She nodded and began walking to the Yukon. Lane followed close. "I'll be around the house all day tomorrow unpacking. It'd be nice if you dropped by and said hello."

"Wish I could but I have a lot of work to do around here tomorrow, and he'll be home all day," Lane said, his voice low.

When they reached the truck, Lane opened the passenger door for her, something he'd seen his father do for his mother many times. Abigail climbed into the seat and fastened her seat belt.

"Come on, Lane, and let these fine folks get back home. It's late," Gunner said, phony politeness in his tone.

Lane looked back over his shoulder at Gunner. "Of course. Just saying goodbye." He shut the door. Abigail lowered the power window. Lane looked her in the eyes and smiled. "Tonight was great."

"Ditto that. I'll be at the tree at noon and I'll have an extra sandwich," she said.

"Deal."

Will got into the truck and closed his door. "Goodnight, Lane. Take care of yourself."

Lane cut his eyes to Will. "Yessir, Mr. Weston."

He fixed his eyes on Abigail's once again.

"See ya tomorrow," she said.

Lane nodded. "Absolutely."

He turned and began walking toward the house. Will turned the Yukon around and he and Abigail headed down the driveway.

Gunner stood at the bottom of the steps, the light of the front porch enabling Lane to see the cast iron look on his face. Lane prepared himself for a firestorm and stopped a few feet from his arch enemy.

"Boy, you know I don't like it when you keep things from me."

"I didn't think you'd mind. They're our neighbors."

Gunner raised one side of his mouth. "Yeah. Living all close and convenient to us."

"They're really nice people."

"Uh huh. Well, don't you let that pretty face of hers cast a spell on you."

"What do you mean?"

Gunner drew in close to Lane. "I mean don't you go telling her about our family affairs. Ain't nobody's business but ours. You got it?"

Lane hesitated.

Gunner punched Lane on the chest with an index finger. "I said, 'You got it?'"

"Yeah, yeah, I got it. I got it."

"Good. You open your mouth, and it could cause us trouble. If that ever happens, I'll take the strap to you like never before."

They went in the house. Gunner resumed his place in front of the television. Lane retired to his room. He laid on his bed, gazing at the ceiling, Abigail's face etched in his mind. The window seal of his bedroom whistled a high tone as the wind outside began to kick up. Gunner didn't beat him or even smack him for going to her house. Lane found it pleasantly surprising. He'd chalk it up to good fortune, something rare in the recent years of his life. Lunch tomorrow—he couldn't wait.

CHAPTER FIVE

Lane sprinkled two teaspoons of sugar over the top, poured in the milk and huffed down the flakes. He checked the clock. 7:30 AM. Gunner's normal Saturday morning routine was to sleep in until ten or eleven. Lane guessed that today would be different seeing that the brutish man had deviated from his usual routine and spent the previous evening at home. He'd heard the television go silent just before midnight the night before. Lane figured Gunner could walk into the kitchen at any minute. If he did, it'd mean the day would start out like a grenade exploding. The best thing for Lane was to get out of the house early. He pulled a sheet of paper from the pad next to the wall-mounted telephone and scribbled a note. *Got an early start. Digging thistles all day.* He took two bottles of water from the refrigerator, hurried out the door, grabbed the hoe from the barn, and headed to the pasture. A flowing creek with a rock bottom snaked through the property. His father had told him the creek was the reason Lane's great grandfather had purchased the land more than a hundred years ago. Lane crossed it at its narrowest point. To ensure his drinking water stayed cold, he positioned the two bottles in the loose rocks near the stream's edge. In an hour or so he would come back. His shirt would be wet; his throat would be dry. Before him lay sixty acres of rolling pastureland. He scanned the battlefield. Legions of knee-high thistles stood at attention in the early morning sun. Lane clamped his grip on the wooden handle of the hoe and launched into his violent assault, leaving slain enemy weeds in his wake.

At 9:30 Lane downed the first bottle of water. He returned to the creek's edge at 10:30 to do the same to the second. He removed his shirt and washed the sweat out of it in the stream's cool water. The cool, wet cloth felt good to his heated skin as he wiped his face and the back of his neck. He plunged the shirt back into the water, then wrung it over the top of his head. His scalp welcomed the water and his body temperature began to decrease to a more pleasant degree. Lane pulled the second bottle from the edge of the creek, twisted off the cap and began sucking down the water, his chin pointed toward the sky, his eyes closed in satisfaction as he drank.

"Headlight!" came the voice he appalled.

Lane ceased drinking and looked.

"Come on," Gunner said. "I got a call from a buddy I work with. He's got a tree down at his house and needs some help. I told him we were on the way."

Lane lowered his chin to his chest and exhaled. He'd rather be left alone, but he knew better than to say a word.

"Come on, now! We gotta get going. Besides, you look like you could use a break."

Lane slung the drenched shirt over one shoulder and crossed the creek, the half-filled bottle of water in one hand. He looked at his watch as he walked behind Gunner. It was getting close to eleven. Lane hoped this co-worker of Gunner's, whoever he was, lived close by and that the tree could be taken care of in minutes instead of hours.

Gunner's work buddy was a man named Desi Pritchard. And Desi, as it turned out, lived just over the line in neighboring Union County, a mere twelve-minute drive. Thank God for that. Gunner turned off Highway 45 and drove down an unmarked, weathered county road for a couple of miles. They came to a red mailbox mounted on top of three metal car wheels welded one on top of the other. Gunner made a hard right into Desi Pritchard's driveway. Unique mailbox creations like Pritchard's were not unheard of in north Mississippi, especially in the rural areas. When school was in session, Lane passed by one two times each weekday, once while he rode the bus to school and once while he rode the bus back home from school. It was painted gold and attached to a welded stack of horseshoes, each shoe painted one of three colors: red, white or blue.

Desi Pritchard's driveway was flanked close on each side by large hardwoods, so close, in fact, that Lane could've reached out and touched one as they rolled pass. A handmade sign nailed to a tree read, *"We Don't Speak to Strangers. We Shoot Them."* A bit past it another one read, *"We Provide No Cost Funerals."* About fifty yards further, still another one. *"Next of Kin Will Not Be Notified. Sorry."* One thing was for sure. Desi Pritchard and his family didn't want any uninvited visitors. Lane wondered if, at any moment, someone might step from the trees into the driveway and greet them with a twelve-gauge shotgun. The narrow dirt drive bent sharply to the left and Desi Pritchard's house came into view. One final handmade sign affixed to a tree read, *"Good Luck. You've Taken Your Life Into Your Own Hands."*

Gunner pulled up in front of the house and parked next to a blue carbon fiber Ford F-150 Raptor. The outside of the rugged, sharp-looking truck was free of any sign of dirt whatsoever. Either Desi Pritchard had just washed it or he was anal to the fifth degree when it came to his pick-up. Desi's house looked relatively new. Not big. Appealing to the eye. Stained cedar siding. Metal roof. A red entry door was in the middle of the front of the house, two large windows on either side of it. Each trimmed with dark green shutters. Lane got out of the truck and looked around. No sign of a fallen tree. The front door opened and a petite red-haired woman stood in the doorway. Bare footed. Faded jeans with the knees out. A tee-shirt with the world-famous Rolling Stones' mouth and tongue image on the front.

"You must be Gunner," she said.

Gunner grinned. "I am." He motioned toward Lane. "And this is my son, Lane."

Lane gritted his teeth behind his lips. *Your son. Yeah, right! Why don't you just tell her the truth? Just say, "My unwanted stepson."*

"I'm Becky. Desi's out back. The tree's on the shop. Just walk back there and you'll see."

On the shop. That doesn't sound encouraging.

Gunner walked to the back of the house, Lane following. The shop was a metal building almost as big as the house. The top of the tree covered the roof. A red, banged up Ford 4WD was parked in front of the shop, its tailgate lowered. A man used the tailgate as a work bench as he sharpened the chain of a Stihl power saw with a file.

"How's it going, Desi?" Gunner said.

Desi Pritchard paused and looked up. "Thanks for coming, Gunner. I'd been meaning to take down this tree. It was hollow at the bottom." Desi shook his head, one side of his mouth crimped. "Buuut, I messed around and put it off and put it off. And now look what I've got. Woke me and Becky up at two thirty this morning when it fell. About scared us to death."

Gunner gazed up at the top of the shop. "Well, it don't look like it did any real damage. Just need to get the top cut off the roof is all."

Desi inhaled and exhaled, shaking his head. "Wait till you see the back."

He resumed sharpening the chain. Gunner and Lane walked to the back of the shop. Thirty feet from the back of the metal building the roots of the great tree reached into the air. At its base, the tree was as thick as a 55-gallon drum. It leaned forward toward the building, its massive trunk resting on the crunched back wall of the metal structure.

Lane wanted to spit. The rest of his day would be spent with Desi Pritchard and Gunner. Yes, Gunner of all people. Lane wouldn't be there when Abigail showed up at the tree line with the sandwiches. What would she think? Would she understand when he explained why?

•　　•　　•

Lane placed the last limb on the brush pile. It was past 5 PM. Job accomplished. Hallelujah. The once hulking tree was now a collection of fireplace-length logs of various diameters. Logs that didn't need splitting had been stacked in Desi Pritchard's woodshed. The ones that did lay where they'd been cut. Desi's plan was to rent a wood splitter the following weekend and finish up the job himself.

Lane chugged down a bottle of water. The fourth one since he and Gunner's arrival. Earlier in the day, Becky Pritchard had laid out a southern spread for Lane, Gunner and her husband. Fried chicken. Mashed potatoes. Fried okra. Pinto Beans. Cornbread. Brownies for dessert. And for the beverage, the preferred drink of all true southerners: sweet tea. Lane's glass had to be refilled two times. As delicious as Becky's cooking was, however, Lane would have gladly forfeited it for one of Abigail's sandwiches.

Desi set the Stihl on the tailgate of the truck and looked at Gunner. "I need to get something out of the house. I'll be right back. Don't leave." He went into the house and returned in less than a minute.

"I really appreciate your help. Gunner," he said and handed Gunner a hundred-dollar bill. Gunner nodded and took the money. Desi turned to Lane. "You too, Lane. You worked every bit as hard as we did. Here," he said and gave Lane a hundred as well.

Lane looked at the bill, his eyes rounded. "Thank you, Mr. Pritchard. I didn't expect this, but I really appreciate it."

"You deserve it. From time to time I need a hand around here. Would you be interested?"

"Sure. Just give me a call."

Desi offered a kind smile then turned his attention to Gunner. "Well, I guess I'll see you on Monday," he said and the three of them started walking to the front of the house.

"Weatherman says it's gonna be another hot one."

"Well, maybe we won't have a lot of line work to do Monday."

Becky walked up to them just as they reached Gunner's truck. "Here," she said and handed Lane a brown paper bag, a smile on her face, her blue eyes filled with kindness. "It's leftovers from lunch. No rush on the plastic containers. You can return them whenever you're back this way."

"That's really kind of you, Becky," Gunner said.

"It sure is." Lane added.

"Y'all really helped Desi. I would've been a nervous wreck if he'd been by himself. It was dangerous work. Would have been REAL dangerous for just one man."

Lane and Gunner got in the truck and headed away from the Pritchard's house. Lane guessed those signs on the trees next to the driveway were just for fun. The Pritchard's were nice people . . . really nice people. On the drive back home, Gunner didn't say a word which was completely fine with Lane. The silence gave him time to think about what he might buy Abigail with the hundred dollars he'd earned.

•   •   •

Lane sat on the edge of the bed, his hair still wet from the shower he'd just taken. He starred at the image of Benjamin Franklin for a few seconds, then read the words. *Federal Reserve Note. One hundred dollars. The United States of America. This note is legal tender for all debts, public and private.* The last time Lane had held a hundred-dollar bill was his thirteenth birthday. A gift from his parents. He'd used the money to buy a pair of Justin cowboy boots. All the big-name bull riders on the PBR circuit wore Justins.

Lane continued to study the bill. He wondered what kind of gift Abigail might like. Flowers? No. They didn't last long. An Ole Miss jersey? That might be good. But then again, she probably already had one. A piece of jewelry like a necklace or a bracelet? Both were real possibilities. If only his mama were still alive, she'd know what the best gift would be. Becky Pritchard kind of reminded him of his mama. She didn't look like his mama, but she was a good cook like his mama. And she was kind like his mama. And she smiled a lot when she spoke. His mama used to smile a lot too when she talked . . . before she married Gunner.

In a split second a hand reached in and snatched the money from Lane's fingers. Lane jumped to his feet. He was face to face with Gunner.

"What are you doing?"

Gunner shoved the bill in a front pocket of his jeans. "I need this for bills and stuff."

"I earned it fair and square!"

Gunner leaned forward, his eyes like those of a serpent. "WE earned it. Remember, I'M the one who drove you over to Desi's. We rode in MY truck. And MY truck runs on gas that I pay for. You eat food that I pay for. You wear clothes that I pay for. You live under MY roof."

Fire ran through Lane's mind. "It's not your roof! My daddy built this house!"

Before Lane could jerk his head out of the way, Gunner backhanded him on the right side of his face. Lane's head rocked to the left and his right cheek felt like a thousand needles suddenly stabbed into it.

"Why are you so ungrateful?"

Lane looked him in the eyes. "I hate you."

Gunner sighed and rolled his eyes. "You can always leave." He raised his hand toward Lane's bedroom door. "Just walk out and never come back . . . Headlight."

Lane stood ram rod straight, his eyes fixed on Gunner's but said nothing.

Gunner clicked his tongue and cocked his head to one side. "Oh. I know. You don't have anywhere else to go. Do you?"

Lane's eyes welled.

"You need me. So, I guess that means you're gonna have to get used to doing things my way."

Gunner turned and walked out of the room. Lane fell back on his bed, cussing Gunner under his breath. He heard the truck engine start and the gravel crack under the tires as Gunner drove down the driveway. It was Saturday night. He wouldn't be back until early Sunday morning.

Lane went to the kitchen and opened the bag of food Becky Pritchard had given him. He took out two pieces of the chicken, two pieces of cornbread and two brownies. He placed them in separate bag and added two cans of Gusher soda. There was still an hour of daylight left. He grabbed a flashlight and bolted out the door. He could be at the tree line in less than ten minutes.

•   •   •

Both the Yukon and the Mercedes were parked in the driveway. Lane sat down just inside the tree line. *God, let her look out and see me*, he prayed. *I have to tell her why I wasn't here at noon today. I just have to.* A stout car motor roared in the distance. As the vehicle got closer, Lane felt his stomach drop. He recognized the big V-8, the sound of power accented by large tail pipe tips. Lane watched, his blood cool in his veins, as a familiar Jeep Wrangler turned into Abigail's driveway. The garage door rolled up. She came outside, got into the passenger seat and they drove off into the evening. Abigail and Tyler Frost.

●   ●   ●

After he'd combed his hair and brushed his teeth, Lane checked himself in the mirror. He wore a teal golf shirt (his best shirt) and his darkest blue jeans. Hopefully his dress attire would be sufficient. He pulled open the bottom drawer of the nightstand and retrieved the hardback Gideon Bible. Everyone would have a Bible. Wouldn't they? Lane had never read it. He got it three years ago. A man at a booth at the county fair was giving them away for free. He insisted that Lane take one. So, Lane did. He brought it home and put it in the drawer. He'd tried to throw it in the garbage a few times, but something just wouldn't let him. And, on top of that, the man's words seemed to be stored away in a closet in his mind somewhere. When Lane thought about getting rid of the Bible, the man's words would crash open the closet door and remind him. "Son, this is the Word of God, the only book God ever wrote."

Lane grabbed a bottle of water and the last three Oreos from his row in the package. Gunner had a full row plus an additional six left. Lane walked out the back door. Today, he'd do something he'd never done before—go to church.

●   ●   ●

"Good morning and welcome to Soulshine Church. We're glad you are here today," a lady said from across the entry room, a small stack of papers in her hand. Smiling all the way, she walked over to Lane. She was the age of a grandmother and had done something to her hair to make it look full on her head. An abundance of hairspray kept it from moving when she walked. She extended one of the papers to Lane. "Here's one of our bulletins for today."

Lane nodded and took it. "Thank you."

She motioned to two large wooden doors. "The worship center is through those doors." The doors were held open wide by brass kick stops at their bottoms. "Come on in," the doors seemed to say. Two men stood at their jams. They smiled at Lane when he looked their way. "Okay. Thank you," Lane said to the lady.

"Feel free to sit wherever you like," one of the men said as Lane walked into the large, cavernous room. Lane saw an empty seat. Second row from the back. Next to the aisle along the right-side wall. A good spot to avoid being noticed and a good spot in case he decided to get up and leave. He sat down and began examining the bulletin. The front panel was a picture of a small wooden boat floating in the middle of lake. Two men stood in the boat pulling on a net. In large words under the image were the words: "*And Jesus said unto them, Follow Me and I will make you fishers of men.*" What did fishers of men mean and how could someone fish for men? Lane opened the bulletin, his attention focused immediately on the prominent announcement on the left side.

"We are excited today to welcome our new pastor, Dr. Will Weston. Dr. Weston comes to us after having served for seven years as the pastor of Grace Church in Amarillo, Texas. Before that he served for six years as the pastor of Mount Moriah Church in San Antonio, Texas. Dr. Weston is a graduate of the University of Texas. He received his Master of Divinity from Southwestern Baptist Theological Seminary and his Doctor of Philosophy from Dallas Theological Seminary. Before surrendering to the call of God, he played professional football for the Miami Dolphins. Dr. Weston is married to Erica. They have two children, Abigail age 17 and Brodie age 14. Please welcome them into our family today and pray for them as they settle into Locust Fork. *Wow. Mr. Weston must be a smart man. Should I call him Mr. Weston or Doctor Weston?*

The service schedule was listed on the right inside panel of the bulletin. Four songs would be sung. Lane recognized only one. Amazing Grace. He'd heard it often from Big Pop. Big Pop was the high school janitor. Singing the song and pushing a dust mop seemed to go hand in hand for him. He wore blue overalls and brogan boots every day. He was a tall man, bald with a protruding belly. Kids at school loved the always-smiling gentle giant. His handwriting was nicer than any of the teachers'. Kids often asked him to write their names on the boards of their classrooms. He always obliged and no teacher complained. Ever! Big Pop had graduated from Huntsville County High School many years before, but passionate team spirit continued to live in his heart. The coaches gave him an honorary jersey each year. Always the same number: 00. He wore them to every game he attended. And he attended EVERY game, even the away games.

The back panel of the bulletin informed everyone that a meal would be held in the fellowship hall immediately following the service. It also stated that a deacons' meeting would be held in the pastor's office at 4 PM. At the very bottom in smaller letters were the church's office hours and the staff members' names as well as their cell phone numbers and email addresses.

The worship center had four sections of chairs and aisles between each section. Between the two middle sections the aisle went from the back doors all the way down to the platform where the pulpit stood. Only a sparse number of seats remained vacant in each section. Five people stepped up on the platform. A skinny man with a beard, long black hair and dressed in khaki pants and a black shirt took his place behind a drum kit. A woman in a jean skirt and a red blouse sat down at a keyboard. A muscled man strapped on a Martin twelve string. He wore gray dress slacks, a light blue button-down shirt and had a military-type haircut. The fifth man wore jeans, a white oxford shirt and snakeskin cowboy boots. He stood behind the acrylic pulpit and spoke into a hand-held microphone. "Okay, Church. Let's lift up our voices to the King of kings." The instrumentalists began to play, words appeared on a large overhead monitor, the leader began to sing, and all the people joined in. It all sounded great. Lane had to admit.

After the third song, a man rose from a chair on the front row and walked to the pulpit. He challenged the members to donate to the church's food pantry and clothes closet and exhorted them to come to the Wednesday night prayer meeting. "There's power in prayer," he remarked. He then reminded kids that vacation Bible school would be starting the following month and encouraged everyone to stay for the lunch that was to follow the service. He looked down at a man seated in front of the pulpit. "Brother James Babcock, would you come lead us in prayer before we sing our final song and hear the message God has laid on Dr. Weston's heart for us today?" A tall man stood to his feet and walked to the platform. As he ascended the steps, Lane recognized the man. Big Pop. So, Big Pop's real name was James Babcock and he attended Soulshine church where Abigail's father was the new pastor. Lane concluded that if Big Pop was a member of Soulshine Church then it must be a good church. And he wondered how many other people he knew were members as well. Big Pop thanked God for the number of people in attendance. He asked God to use every member to reach someone else. Finally, he thanked God for bringing Dr. Weston and his family to Soulshine and asked the Holy Spirit to give Dr. Weston unction to preach. Lane wondered what unction was and how the Holy Spirit could give it. Who or what was the Holy Spirit? Big Pop closed his prayer by saying, "In Jesus' Name. Amen." He then stepped away from the pulpit and the band began to play and sing Amazing Grace. Lane noted that people sang louder than they had on the other songs. He concluded that the song was everyone's favorite. When it was over, Abigail's father rose from one of the chairs at the front and took his place behind the pulpit. Will Weston wore a dark blue suit, a white shirt and a bright red tie. After expressing his optimism about Soulshine's future and his family's anticipation of fitting in well in Locust Fork, he gripped each side of the pulpit and said, "Open your Bibles to Luke chapter ten." He paused. Lane heard pages turning as the people turned to where Dr. Weston had told them. Lane had no idea where Luke chapter ten was. Thankfully, the Gideon Bible had a table of contents. After scanning the names of the Old Testament books, he began scanning those of the New Testament.

Ah, Luke. There it is. Page seven eighty-eight.

Lane turned to the passage.

"We'll begin at verse 30 and read down through 37," Will Weston said.

He began reading the passage, his voice now transformed. It commanded attention. It was like he was speaking on the radio or something. And when he came to the very last verse he said, "Go and do the same," in a way that made Lane feel like he was being challenged personally to do just that. After reading the verses, Will Weston said a brief prayer, and launched into his message. The man was totally different than he was on the patio at the barbeque grill. Different than he was at the dinner table Friday night. Different than he was when he drove Lane home. It was like Will

Weston had become a different man before Lane's very eyes. He spoke as if his words were the last, most important words he'd ever say. Lane looked around. People were locked onto the preacher like watching a movie in a theater. Some nodded. Others said, "Amen!" Lane saw tears on the cheeks of two men. Yes, two MEN! He wasn't accustomed to seeing a man cry. What was going on? Was this the "unction" that Big Pop had prayed and asked the Holy Spirit to give Will Weston? Lane didn't know. One thing he did know. Something was happening. It was obvious, Will Weston's words were doing something in the people. Lane could tell by the expressions on their faces. Lane could feel something in the room. It wasn't like a teacher lecturing in a school classroom. It was serious. Heavy. Thought-provoking. Lane continued to listen as Will Weston spoke about caring for other people. Being kind. Giving. Serving. Reaching out to those in need. Having good character. And then he brought everything together at the close of the message by challenging people to go and do the same because Jesus said to do so.

After he finished the sermon, Dr. Weston asked people to respond the way the Holy Spirit would have them respond. What did that mean? Dr. Weston had spent the last forty minutes talking about obeying Jesus and now he was telling them to do what the Holy Spirit wanted? Lane was confused. Dr. Weston prayed a short prayer again. After he said, "Amen," Lane looked up to see more than twenty people walk to the platform and get on their knees. Others joined hands with people close to them. Lane felt a tap on his shoulder. He looked up into a man's smiling face. Big Pop.

"God bless you today, Lane," he said. "It thrilled my soul to look out over the congregation and see you. I hope you'll come back." He handed Lane a card. "Here's my phone number. You call me if I can ever help you in any way."

"Yessir."

Big Pop walked to a man seated several rows from Lane, put one hand on the man's shoulder and began talking to him.

Minutes later the people were all back at their seats. Dr. Weston gave a last encouragement for all to stay for the luncheon that was to follow and then prayed the blessing on the meal. People began filing out of the auditorium. Several gathered around Will and Erica Weston. Lane stood to his feet and began looking for Abigail.

"Young man, you're going to stay and have lunch with us, aren't you?" came a female voice.

Lane turned and saw a woman. She stood next to a man. Both smiled. Both had waistlines that strained their clothes.

"Well, I guess so."

"Good. My name is Alice."

"I'm Floyd," the man said. "We're headed to the fellowship hall. You can walk with us."

The couple waddled their way from their seats to an aisle. Lane followed them.

"Is this your first time to visit Soulshine?" the woman said.

"Yes, ma'am."

"This is a sweet church. You'll meet some fine people here. We have a good youth group too," the man said.

Lane noticed three girls standing and talking next to the grand piano at the edge of the stage. One girl wore a light blue dress and had long blonde hair. Abigail. He raised his hand to get her attention. It worked. Her eyes lit up. She excused herself from the two girls and started toward Lane.

"Nice meeting you," Lane said to the portly couple. "I see someone I need to speak to."

"Of course," the man said.

"Absolutely," the lady added.

Lane and Abigail met each other in the main aisle.

"Hey, you made it. I was hoping I'd see you today."

"Abigail, I'm so sorry. I came here to tell you. Gunner got a call yesterday morning and we had to go help one of his friends. A big tree blew down on his shop and we had to help cut it up. Took me all day basically. I promise I didn't mean to bail on you."

"No problem. I figured something happened."

"So, you're not mad at me?"

"Not at all."

Lane exhaled. "Thanks for understanding. I was afraid you'd—"

"Well, I'm not. Are you staying for lunch?"

"Yes."

"Great," she said. She cocked her head to one side and looked at him through the corners of her eyes. "Then we can sit together?"

Lane slapped his palms to the tops of his legs. "Of course. Of course."

They made their way to the spacious fellowship hall. Lane could tell from the floor that the space doubled as a gymnasium when people were not eating in it. On one side of the room was a large kitchen area. People formed a line single file in order to be served in buffet fashion. Women from the church filled people's plates with barbeque, coleslaw, fries, baked beans, and sourdough rolls. Just past the servers was three eight-foot-long folding tables filled with various desserts the church members had brought for the celebratory occasion. Lane and Abigail stood at the back of the line.

"What are you planning to do tomorrow?" Lane asked.

"I've still got some unpacking to do and then Mom and I are supposed to go shopping in the afternoon."

"Think you could break away for a few hours?"

"I might be able. What's up?"

Big Pop interjected before Lane could answer. "The two of you are not going to wait in this line. Come on. Follow Me."

He led them to the serving station. "Oliver," he said to the man at the front of the line just about to be served. "Let the kids cut in front of you. This is the pastor's daughter, and this is Lane. This is the first service for both of them. They need to be up here at the front of the line."

"Yes, of course. You kids jump right in," Oliver said.

"Absolutely," the man behind Oliver said.

Lane and Abigail thanked them and picked up plates and silverware.

"Hey, Lane," a woman said as she put a generous helping of pulled pork barbeque on his plate.

"Oh, hey, Miss Cotler."

Mary Cotler was a server in the lunchroom at Huntsville County High School. She called every student by name as she put food on their trays.

"And you're the preacher's daughter. Aren't you?"

"Yes ma'am," Abigail said.

Lane and Abigail continued through the serving area and then to the dessert table. Abigail chose a piece of strawberry cake. Lane, a slice of blueberry pie. A man at a drink station gave each of them a glass of iced tea and they sat down at a table.

"I'd like to take you on a walk."

"Where to?" Abigail said and shoved a fork filled with barbeque in her mouth.

"I'd like to show you around the farm. It's nice. Not as nice as it used to be but it's still nice."

"Sounds cool, like an adventure. I'll get the unpacking done later this evening. What time tomorrow?"

"How about we meet at nine?"

"The usual place?"

"Yeah. I'll meet you at the oak tree and we can start from there."

Abigail grinned. "Okay, nine it is." She took a bite of her roll.

•   •   •

Lane entered the house through the back door, the roaring of car engines and the voices of sports commentators blaring from the television. To get to his bedroom he'd have to walk through the den. Gunner was there glued to whatever NASCAR race was airing. Lane hoped he could slip past him unnoticed, get to his room and shut the door. Maybe Gunner didn't know that Lane had been gone for the past four hours. Lane eased the door closed. He walked with his head down. Maybe keeping his eyes fixed on the floor would give him more stealth. He breathed in deep through his nostrils and entered the den from the kitchen. Careful not to make heavy steps he walked across the hard wood floor to the bottom of the stairs.

"Where you been?" Gunner said, never looking away from the television screen.

Lane stopped and looked back. "I went to church. Thought it might do me some good."

"Uh huh, right," Gunner replied and took a long drink of his beer. "Remember what I told you. Don't go telling her or her daddy any of our business."

"Yessir."

Gunner raised a hand toward the television. "No! When he's drafting, you can't let him drop down to the inside on turn three! He'll pass you every time! You gotta block him. You should know that already! Now, you gotta burn more fuel to catch him!"

Lane hurried up the stairs and into his room. He put a Johnny Cash album on the turntable. His dad had loved Johnny Cash. Lane laid down on the bed. He opened the Gideon Bible in the place where he'd inserted the church bulletin. Luke chapter ten—the parable of the Good Samaritan. The needle of the turntable touched down on the LP. Lane began reading. Johnny began singing. *I hurt myself today . . .*

CHAPTER SIX

Lane had been at the oak tree since ten minutes before nine o'clock. He checked his watch, something he'd done so many times he'd lost count. It was 8:58. Abigail exited the house, looked toward Lane, threw up a hand, and trotted out to the tree line. She wore a pair of red athletic shorts, lace-up boots and a white tee-shirt with a prominent Nike swoosh screen-printed across the front. Lane wanted to tell her how great she looked.

She offered her perfect smile. "Good morning."

"Good morning."

"Okay, I expect a complete tour with commentary."

Lane smiled and nodded. "Well, okay. I'll do my best."

He led her through the woods and showed her the place where he killed his first and only buck four years ago. "Got it with a 30-30," he said. "Wasn't a big deer. Just a five point. But the meat was good."

They came to the widest spot of the creek where it curved like a crescent moon. It had a tall bank on one side where the water was deepest, a rocky shoal on the other. Abigail began untying her boots. "Let's get our feet wet."

"Cool," Lane said and began taking off his shoes.

They walked in the shallow water on the shoal side.

"This is beautiful. How deep is the deepest part?" she asked.

Lane pulled down his brow and squinted his eyes a bit. "I'd say . . . six feet . . . or so."

"You ever gone swimming in it?"

"No."

"Well, it's deep enough."

As they continued on Lane glanced down at her feet several times. She had pretty feet. Suntanned. Toenails painted crimson. Lane spotted a pointed stone in the water. He leaned down and picked it up. An arrowhead. About two inches long. He held it up. "Abigail, look at this."

"How cool is that?" she said and stepped close to him.

Lane handed it to her. "It's a nice one. No chips. Kind of rare to find one tri-colored like that. Probably worth something."

"No kidding," she said studying it and turning it over in her hand. "What tribe do you think it's from?"

"Chickasaws lived in this part of Mississippi."

She offered it back to him. "Here you go."

"No. Keep it. It's yours."

"You sure?"

"Absolutely. You might could get couple a hundred for it. Maybe more."

She shook her head. "I'll never sell it."

Would she never sell it because she thought it was cool or because Lane had given to her? Did she value it simply because it was a unique artifact? Or did she have an emotional attachment to it because she felt like she and Lane were connected?

"There's something else I want to show you."

"Sure."

"It requires a little walking so we'll have to put our shoes back on."

They stepped out of the water and slipped their feet back into their shoes.

"I don't have a pocket. Will you hang on to this for me?" she said and held the arrowhead out in an open palm.

"Yeah. Of course,"

As Lane took the stone from her hand, his fingers drug across the skin of her feminine hand. His heart seemed to jump, the sensation of her skin to his made his face tingle. What if he clasped her hand? Would she welcome it? Or would she think he was being too forward? What if it scared her and she stopped meeting him at the tree line? He couldn't risk it. He slipped the arrowhead into a front pocket of his jeans. He pointed an index finger. "We need to head this way."

They continued through the woods until they came to a broad and long opening. The terrain was flat with grass reaching above the knee.

"In springtime, when my dad was alive, there'd be corn here for a far as you could see. We'd harvest it in the fall, and it'd feed more than five hundred head of black angus cattle the entire winter."

"You like cattle?" she asked.

"I do."

"Me too."

"You do?"

"Of course. I'm a Texas country girl. I can ride a horse. Bait my own hook and take my own fish off."

Lane perked up. "No kidding!"

"Heck yeah. You probably thought I was the prissy cheerleader type. You know, the kind that's afraid to get her hands dirty or scared she's gonna break a nail."

"Well . . . ah . . . I."

"I can shoot too. When does dove season open in Mississippi?"

"First part of September."

"Alright. Come September, I'll prove it."

Abigail's remark sent a thrill to Lane's heart, not about dove hunting with her or seeing her shoot a shotgun, as exciting as those two things would be, but the very fact that it was July and Abigail planned to be in Lane's life come September.

"I'll be looking forward to it."

"You do that." She turned her attention toward the grassy field and motioned a backhand in front of her like she were opening a curtain. "So, is this what you wanted to show me?"

"No." Lane threw his head back and pointed into the boughs of the large tree they stood under. "What I wanted to show you is up there."

Abigail looked up. Her eyes shot open as she rounded her lips. "Is that a tree house?"

"It is."

"Can we check it out?"

"The ladder's on the other side."

"Well, what are we waiting for? Let's climb it," she said and walked around to the other side of the tree.

Lane followed her. "It's been a while since I've used it. Let me make sure it's safe first."

The ladder was numerous two-foot lengths of treated two by fours secured to the trunk of the tree with deck screws. Lane checked for stability and solidness as he cautiously climbed it. Once he reached the floor of the treehouse he looked down at Abigail. "Alright, it's safe. Come on up."

With the enthusiasm of a child running to Santa Claus at a department store, she hurried up the ladder. Lane pulled himself up into the treehouse and got down on his all fours. He watched her come up to him. He extended his right hand to her. She took it and he pulled her into the treehouse with him.

Though its boards had been grayed by time and weather, and its extended period of not being used was apparent, the treehouse was solid. A rigid floor. Firm walls. An old Daisy Red Ryder BB gun leaned in one corner. A row of books stood on a small wall shelf.

Abigail inventoried the books, moving her hand across their spines. "Aw, look at these. Sounder. Where the Red Fern Grows. The Hatchet. The Adventures of Tin Tin. The Red Badge of Courage. The Chronicles of Narnia. The Lord of the Rings. Treasure Island. Have you read all of these?"

"My mother read every one of them to me," Lane said as he unlatched a hasp and pushed open the little house's large wooden window. "Check this out."

Abigail turned to see. She brought her hand to her mouth and drew up next to him. "Oh, my word. It's breathtaking."

"Yup. You can see for miles." He pointed an index finger. "There's the Locust Fork town square. And over there is Oscar's Cupboard grocery store. There's the high school football stadium." He raised his hand a little higher. "Does that look familiar?"

Abigail studied for a moment. "Is that the Ole Miss Campus?"

"It is. You see that triangle shaped top?"

"I do."

"That's the front of Vaught-Hemmingway Stadium."

Lane moved his hand to the right. "You see that tower way out there."

"Yeah."

"That's the fire tower over in Marshall County. And that large body of water over there is Sardis Lake."

"How long has this tree house been here?"

"My parents and I built it when I was thirteen."

"Tell me about your parents."

Lane felt her eyes on the side of his face. He turned and looked into them. They were asking him to let his guard down, to trust her.

"It's hard for me, Abigail. I haven't really talked to anyone about them. Heck, I don't even know if I can. I get choked up just thinking about them."

She reached out one hand and gripped one of his wrists. "It's okay. I'm a good listener."

Lane pushed up one side of his mouth and nodded slowly. "I believe you. What if I—"

"I like it when a guy has the courage to cry."

Courage to cry. Lane had never heard it put that way. But then again, he'd never met anyone like Abigail. He felt like he'd known her not just for days, or weeks or even months. But for years.

He sat down on the floor and leaned his back against a wall. Abigail did the same opposite him.

"Abigail, I had the most amazing parents. They were good people. They loved each other and they loved me. We did all kinds of things together. Even went to New York City one time. Can you believe it? Three hicks from Mississippi going on vacation to New York City just so we could say we'd been there."

Abigail grinned, hanging on Lane's words.

"My dad was a man's man. Strong but kind. Tough as saddle leather on the outside. Soft as rabbit fur on the inside. He worked hard and I worked right alongside him . . . well, as best as a kid can, I guess. I never minded. I loved it. WE loved it. It was a Saturday afternoon in August. Must've been a hundred and five degrees in the barn. We were stacking hay bales in the loft. I was up in the rafters. He was down on the floor. He went to toss me a bale and the widow-maker hit him." Lane's voice cracked. He swallowed a hard lump and closed his eyes to regain his composure. Abigail placed a hand on top of Lane's and gave it a comforting squeeze. "I'm so sorry," she said.

Lane continued. "The doctor said he was dead before he hit the floor. Mama was awesome. Tender. Supportive. Said things in ways that made me feel like I could do anything. Be anything. She was a good cook. Real good. I'm talking better than any restaurant in the county good. She laughed a lot. I can still hear her sometimes at night when I'm lying in my bed with the window open. The crickets chirping. The bullfrogs croaking. After daddy died, she stopped laughing. Worried about me with no dad around. Worried about the farm with no man around. Six months later, money started getting tight, so she started waiting tables at a diner in town. One day she came home and told me she'd met a man. Told me she wanted me to meet him too. So, we had him over for dinner."

"Gunner?" Abigail asked.

Lane shook his head, a look on his face like he'd just tasted sour milk. "Yeah. Gunner. Said his wife had died a few years earlier and that they'd had no kids. Said he wanted to have a family and that he loved my mama. Before long he was coming over every day. Doing things with me like daddy used to do. Fishing. Hunting. Working the farm. Six months later he and Mama got married. As soon as that happened, he changed. Mama started acting depressed. One day at school the principal pulled me out of class. Said it was a family emergency. Two police officers drove me to the hospital. Doctors had machines hooked up to Mama and tubes coming out of her. She wasn't able to talk. Gunner was there. Told me they were working in the barn. Said Mama was climbing the ladder to the loft." Lane's voice cracked again. He sniffled. Tears rolled down his face. He wiped them away with the back of his forearm. Breathed in and out a few times.

"It's okay, Lane. It's just me and you."

Lane wrestled to regain his composure. "Said she fell and landed on the turning plow. The doctor said the trauma of the impact caused a blood vessel in her brain to burst. I was standing next to her when the machine flatlined."

Lane broke down and began to weep. Abigail moved in close beside him. She put one arm around his shoulders and leaned her head against his. In response, Lane leaned his head against hers, his shoulders and torso began to quake.

"It's time to let it out, Lane. Let it out. Have the courage to cry."

For several minutes Lane couldn't speak. Abigail maintained her embrace. Lane slowly collected himself. He looked at her face. It was compassionate and sympathetic, and her eyes were moist too. Lane pressed his lips tightly and sniffled again. "Thanks."

"You bet. Show me something else cool."

They stood to their feet. Lane pinched the remaining wetness from his eyes, and they climbed back down to the ground. They crossed the broad field of tall grass then hiked through a patch of woods. The woods ended and a terraced pasture populated with purple-bloomed thistles began. In the middle of the pasture was an oblong pond the size of two football fields. At one end a pier reached from the bank twenty yards into the water. Turned upside down on the bank near the end of pier was a pale white wooden boat.

"Is that a rowboat?" Abigail asked.

"Yup."

"Does it float?"

Lane shrugged his shoulders, a slight grin stretched on his face. "Ain't but one way to find out."

Abigail nudged Lane with an elbow. "Well, come on then. What are we waiting for?" She broke into a jog. Lane smiled as he watched her go. After a few seconds he struck out in a jog too. When they reached the boat, they turned it over. A large brown water snake slithered into the water like it'd been hit with a bolt of electricity. Abigail held her composure and reached down to pick up one of oars that had been under the boat.

"I expected to see a cottonmouth," she said. "But that was just a harmless water snake."

Lane shook his head in amazement and picked up the other oar. "Most people would have freaked out, especially girls."

Abigail started inspecting the inside of the boat. "In Texas, you see rattlesnakes on a regular basis, copperheads too. If you just leave them alone, you're fine." She checked the boat's board seat. "Seat's fine. Not rotted."

They drug the boat into the water and got in. They sat down next to each other and began rowing the vessel toward the middle of the lake.

"What kind of fish are in this tank?" she asked.

Lane wrinkled his brow and raised one side of his mouth. "Tank?"

"Yeah. In Texas we call ponds tanks."

"Hmm. Okay. Yeah, it's got bream, catfish, largemouth bass and some carp."

"Think we could try our luck sometime?"

"Of course. I've got some fishing gear in the barn."

"The barn near your house?"

"Yeah."

"Will you show it to me? Barns are cool."

"Sure. When we leave here, we'll head that way."

They made a couple of circuits around the pond then returned the boat to this place on the bank and flipped it upside down like it was before. On the way to the barn, they came to a six-strand barbed wire fence. Lane pulled one strand up with his hands and pushed the one below it down with his foot so Abigail could slip through. She returned the favor for him. When they reached the barn, Lane gave her a tour and informed her of the things that his family USED to have before Gunner sold them. A John Deere tractor. A Bushhog. A combine. A corn crusher. Quarter horses. Saddles and other tack. A conveyor that transported bales of hay from the flatbed trailer to the hay loft on the second floor of the barn. Chickens, ducks, guineas, and emus.

Finally, Lane showed her the collection of fishing rods, the big zero turn mower that didn't work and the knock-off brand push mower that did. As he was wrapping things up, Abigail inquired about a lone farm implement under the equipment awning.

"Is that it?" she asked.

"Yes. That's the turning plow."

"Gunner chose not to sell it?"

Lane sighed and shook his head. "Heck no. Gunner's tried, believe me. Just about everyone in Huntsville County knew my dad or knew of him. And the circumstances of mama's death are well known. Out of respect for them, no one will buy it. So, it just sits here."

"I would've loved to have met your parents."

Lane's eyes welled again. "They were the best."

"Show me your house."

"Like everything else around here, it's not what it used to be."

Lane gave her a tour of the inside of the house. As he did, he relayed the unique facts about the house's history. How his mother had drawn the plan for the kitchen out on a napkin at a restaurant in Memphis before she and his dad were married. That the ceiling beams in the den were chestnut and had been harvested and stored in the barn when Lane's dad was a teenager. That the mantle over the fireplace had once been in a plantation mansion in Locust Fork during the Civil War. And how the Union Army had firebombed the mansion, but somehow the mantle had survived. He told her about his dad killing a bear in Montana when Lane was six years old and that the bear's pelt used to hang on the wall above the mantle before Gunner sold it. That the bookcase in the hallway came out of the old Citizen's Bank building before it was turned into the Locust Fork Chamber of Commerce. When Lane showed her his bedroom, he told her how much his dad loved Johnny Cash. He showed her his dad's extensive music album collection and played his dad's favorite Johnny Cash song on the turntable: *One Piece at a Time.*

Abigail checked her cell phone for the time. "I need to be getting back home. Mom wants me to go with her to Memphis to shop for new furniture for the den and dining room."

"Sure," Lane said. "Mind if I use the bathroom real quick before we head back?"

"Not at all."

"Feel free to look around some more if you want. There's some bottled water and sodas in the fridge if you're thirsty."

Lane stepped to the bathroom. When he was finished, he searched the books on the bookshelf until he found the title he was looking for. When he returned, he found Abigail in the kitchen, her head back and a can of Gusher soda turned up as she was finishing it off. She tossed the empty can in the garbage. "That was good. Thanks."

Lane handed the book to her.

She studied the cover. "Hmm. Selous Scouts Top Secret War. Lieutenant Colonel Ron Reid Daly as told by Peter Stiff."

"It's a book about the special forces of Rhodesia before it became Zimbabwe," Lane said. "I thought your brother might enjoy it."

Abigail looked up at Lane. "It's sweet of you to think of him, Lane. He'll love it. Moving here hasn't been easy for him. Or me, for that matter. We left all our friends back in Texas, people we loved. When we decided to move here, I started praying that God would let me make some special new friends. I can't imagine anyone in this town being more special than you."

Lane felt warmth in his face.

"I wrote my phone number on the pad next to your telephone," she said and swiped her cellphone. "What's your number?"

She keyed in the number as Lane recited it.

•　　•　　•

They stood at the big oak tree at the edge of the tree line. Dr. and Mrs. Weston and were standing outside the garage talking.

"I guess I better get going. I bet Mom's finalizing things with Dad about our shopping trip."

"Thanks for letting me show you around. It was fun."

"No, Lane. It was amazing! It was the most fun I've had in a long time."

"Me too. And what happened in the treehouse." Lane paused and gazed up into the treetops for a few seconds then looked back into her eyes. "Let me just say it was SO helpful."

She smiled.

"You want to hang out some tomorrow?" Lane said.

She shook her head, a look of regret on her face. "I can't. I have some family stuff going on tomorrow and Wednesday. I'm sorry."

Lane's countenance fell. Was she pulling back already? Was the "I just want to be friends," conversation on the near horizon? Was Lane in for another huge disappointment?

"No, no need to apologize. I understand completely."

Not exactly true. He didn't understand completely. How could she say that she'd had an amazing day and the most fun she'd had in a long time and then ghost him?

"I'm free on Thursday, though," she said. "Can we make it Thursday?"

Lane's heart leaped inside his chest.

"Of course. Thursday's great."

She grinned. "Okay. Thursday it is. What time?"

Okay. What should he say? If he picked a time in the morning, she might think he was trying to smother her. If he picked a time in the afternoon, he might disappoint her. He looked at her through the corners of his eyes. "Nine?" he said, sheepishly.

"Okay. Nine. Under one condition."

Uh oh. What kind of condition? That she be able to bring her brother along because her parents would be away? That they no longer spent time alone on his property or in the treehouse because she was concerned he'd get the wrong idea? That she be back home by eleven because she had promised to do something with some of the girls at church? Or even worse, Tyler Frost?

"Okay. Whatever you say?"

"You have to wear shorts. No jeans."

Whew! Disaster avoided.

He raised an open palm and gave her an expression like he was agreeing to go to with her to a beauty salon. "Well, then. I'll leave my jeans in the closet. Shorts it is."

"Excellent," she said and started walking toward her house. Then, she stopped in her tracks, turned on her heels and walked back to him. She drew in close to his face. "Aren't you forgetting something?" she said and tweaked her eyebrows.

What! Was she wanting him to kiss her? He certainly wanted to. More than he ever wanted to do anything in his entire life.

"Ah . . . do you mean . . . you . . . ah . . . would like . . . ah . . . for me to—?"

"Yes, Lane. I want you to—" She nodded slowly, her eyes fixed on is. "Give me my arrowhead back now." She grinned and held out an opened palm.

"Oh, yeah," Lane said, reaching one hand into a front pocket of his jeans. "Of course. I totally forgot."

He placed the arrowhead in her hand. She quickly clutched it, catching his fingers before he could pull them back. "Thank you," she said and released his hand deliberately, keeping her eyes fixed on his. "I'll see you Thursday."

She turned and started toward the house again, the arrowhead in one hand, the book in the other. Lane stood and watched her. "By the way, Lane," she said without looking back. "I stole something from you today."

"What'd you say?"

She stopped and turned back to him. "I said, 'I stole something from you today.'"

He shook his head, a confused look on his face. "Stole what?"

"I stole some of your Oreo cookies while you were in the bathroom. Hope you don't mind. I couldn't help myself. Oreos are my favorite." She made a crazy face, then turned and trotted to the Mercedes where her mother was waiting. She opened the passenger door and got inside. The horn of the Mercedes honked and then began backing out of the driveway.

CHAPTER SEVEN

The first thing Lane did when he got home was check the package of Oreos. Only a full row was left which meant Abigail had eaten six. Gunner would blow a gasket. What could Lane do? The closest store was Felston Baker's Quick Stop. Five miles away. Lane had no car. Not even a bike. He could walk but he wasn't certain that Felston carried Oreos. Besides, Lane had no money. He WOULD'VE had money had Gunner not taken the hundred bucks that Desi Pritchard had paid him. The only hope Lane had was to somehow put Gunner in a good mood. That'd be a feat one step shy of a miracle in and of itself. And then, Lane would have to come up with a schmooze-job reason why the cookies were gone. It was a long shot. No, a near impossibility. But, if Lane could pull it off, maybe . . . just maybe, Gunner would let him slide. If not, it'd be the strap for sure. Unsure but hopeful, Lane grabbed two bottles of water and headed to the barn. He knew there was one thing he could do that might grant him favor in Gunner's eyes. It was going to be a long, hot day.

Like a machine, Lane chopped the thistles out of the ground. He was driven to get as many as possible uprooted before sunset. Normally he'd pace himself. There was no need to get a chore done in rapid fashion because every time he completed one laborious job, Gunner would give him another. It seemed that Gunner was forever coming up with them. One time he had Lane sling blade the grass of the right-of-way on the opposite side of the road from the house. "Hoodlums could use it for cover and then break in the house while we're not at home," he'd said. And Lane's well-being seemed to be of little concern. Once a water pipe burst under the house. When Gunner crawled under the house to fix it, he discovered a mother fox and her three pups. He told Lane to remove them saying, "I fixed the pipe. You get rid of the foxes." So, wearing a pair of welding gloves and using a fish net, Lane managed to relocate the angry varmint and her young. An even more dangerous assignment occurred earlier in the year. The week before school let out for the summer, Gunner made Lane tar over all the nail heads on the barn roof. "A preventative measure," he told Lane. "To keep the nails from backing out of the tin and causing leaks." So, Lane spent four afternoons when he got home on the structure's slick roof, a can of black roof cement in one hand, a putty knife in the other. Lane suggested a safety harness given that the peak of the barn was so high. "Aw, just be careful and you'll be fine. Ain't as high as it looks," Gunner replied.

It'd been three weeks since it'd rained. The Mississippi heat had baked the surface of the ground into a hard, pottery-like crust. Uprooting the thistles with the garden hoe required extra brawn. Lane anted up to the task, driven by his affection for Abigail and his dread of Gunner and "the strap." By dusk not a single thistle stood on the pasture around the pond. Lane had done the work of two men. His aching body affirmed it. Beaten to a frazzle, he lumbered back to the barn, his shirt soaked in sweat, his arms and face red from the sun. A water spicket stuck out of the ground next to a watering trough. The trough, now dry and unused, once was the water source for the goats and emus during the days when the farm flourished. Lane leaned the hoe against the trough and turned on the spicket. He cupped his hands and drank for several seconds, then doused his face and hair. The cool water made his shirt stick to his heated torso as it dripped down his back and chest. Slap! Instantly, Lane felt a stinging pain that reached from the top of one shoulder down to just above his beltline. He fell forward to his all fours. Slap! The pain came again along the same part of his back, this time more intense. He fell to his stomach and rolled over, wincing, his eyes clinched, his lips stretched open, his teeth gritted.

"Ah!" he cried out.

He opened his eyes to see Gunner standing over him, the strap in his right hand.

"You know better than to eat my food or drink my drinks, Boy!" Gunner's words were hard, Nazi-like. "And what do I find when I come home? That you've eaten some of my cookies. The next time, I'll beat you till you bleed! Got it!"

"Yeah. I got it."

"You know, Headlight, I'm always clear about things with you. You do what I say and we'll get along just fine. You disobey me or sass me, and they'll be hell to pay. Remember?"

"Ah . . . yeah. Yeah, I remember."

"Well, it seems like you needed reminding. So let this be a reminder to you."

"Okay. It won't happen again."

"You better hope it doesn't."

Gunner gritted his teeth and wrenched his face with hatred as he raised the strap to strike Lane again. Before he could follow through with his intention his cell phone chirped in his pocket. He relaxed himself, lowered the strap and retrieved his phone.

"It's Desi," he said and accepted the call.

"Hey Desi. What's going on, Bro?"

He paused and nodded as he listened. "Oh. I'm sure he'd be interested. He's always looking for ways to make some extra spending money. I'll tell him. He'll be ready when she gets here. Alright. I'll see you tomorrow."

Gunner ended the call and looked down at Lane. "He's got some work for you. Becky'll pick you up in the morning at nine."

Gunner turned and started toward the house. Lane pulled himself up to his feet, his back still stinging from the beating. He turned off the spicket and picked up the hoe. As he walked back to the barn, he replayed in his mind the day he'd had with Abigail. Wading in the creek. Rowing the boat on the pond. Her head leaned against his in the tree house. And her final words as the two of them parted. "Oreos are my favorite." He smiled as he returned the hoe to its place among the other farm tools. Heck, he was glad she ate them. Too bad she didn't eat every one of them. If she had, then

Gunner wouldn't have any for his lunchbox the next day. And that would've given Lane a great sense of pleasure.

•   •   •

Lane sat in a wooden rocker on the front porch and watched Becky Pritchard make her way up the driveway in the Ford Raptor. She threw up a hand and waved. Lane raised his hand in response. She stopped the truck near the house and Lane descended the steps. He pulled open the passenger door. "This is a beautiful truck."

"Wanna drive it?"

Lane wanted to say yes. He would've loved to have driven the fine vehicle. "Thanks. That's nice of you but maybe some other time."

Becky pushed the shifter up into the park position and unfastened her seat belt. "Oh, come on. You drive."

Lane felt the heat in his face like he did when he informed Abigail that he didn't have a cell phone. "Miss Becky, I can't."

"Sure you can. I insist," she said and opened her door.

"Miss Becky. Really. I can't. I don't have a driver's license."

She pulled her door shut and looked at him. She narrowed her eyes and pressed her lips. "How old are you?"

"I'll be nineteen in October."

"Can you drive?"

"Oh yeah. I can drive. I can even drive a stick."

She drew her head back and raised her brow. "Then why don't you have a driver's license?"

Lane rolled his eyes and stared through the windshield, shaking his head. "Gunner never seems to have the time to take me." In an instant it hit him. He'd spoken without thinking of the consequences should Gunner find out that he'd opened his mouth. He shot his palms to the sides of his head. "I shouldn't have told you that. If Gunner finds out he'll—" Lane caught himself.

"He'll what?"

Lane lowered his chin to his chest and closed his eyes. He paused for a few seconds. "He'll what?" she said again, this time with a measure of passion.

Lane turned and looked at her. "Let's just say he'll be mad--real mad."

She turned away from him. She nodded her head slightly as she gazed toward the barn. She turned back again and looked at him the way his momma used to when she was about to tell him something important. "You got a school ID and a social security card?"

"Yes ma'am. In the house."

"Go get'em," she said.

"You serious?"

"As a loaded shotgun. Go inside and get'em."

"But Gunner—"

"Don't you worry about Gunner. I'll handle him," she said with a wink and motioned toward the house. "Now, you go get'em."

Lane returned, his school ID and social security card in hand. He got back into the Raptor. Becky Pritchard pulled the shifter down into reverse. She backed the truck into the grass at a ninety then pulled onto the driveway. On the way to town, she began inquiring about Lane's homelife. Lane played it safe. As best he could, he avoided anything he thought might set Gunner off. By the time they reached the Department of Motor Vehicles, she knew that Gunner was Lane's stepfather. That Lane loved and missed his parents. That he knew most everything when it came to farming and that he, like his father, loved country music. Especially Johnny Cash. And that was about it. Lane had successfully evaded and dodged all of her questions that might lead to an episode with Gunner and the strap.

Lane scored a 98 on the written portion of his driver's test. Once behind the wheel of the Becky's flashy pickup truck it took him less than fifteen minutes to demonstrate to the testing officer that he was indeed a qualified driver. Just before noon he and Becky exited the Department of Motor Vehicles office, Lane's driver's license in his pocket. Becky paid the fee.

Becky pushed on her sunglasses. "Okay, Lane, I'm hungry. How does Bertha May's sound?"

"Ain't never been there but I hear it's good."

"Best banana pudding in north Mississippi," she said. "You're driving."

For thirteen years straight Bertha May's had garnered the "Best Plate Lunch in Mississippi Award" by the state's beloved *Magnolia Magazine*. The famed eatery was closed on Sundays and Mondays. Tuesday through Saturday, however, it was open from 11 AM to 2 PM. Rumors routinely circulated around Locust Fork that the acclaimed restaurant was slated to be a filming location for an upcoming movie adaptation of a John Grisham novel. Lane navigated the Raptor into a parking space between two other pickup trucks. Though it was not payday Friday, Bertha May's teamed with hungry patrons. Lane and Becky walked between the cars, making their way to the entrance. A vehicle caught Lane's eye. A white Chevy truck. The words North Mississippi Electric Cooperative painted in large green letters on its doors. *Oh, God. Surely Gunner is not here.*

They walked through the front door. The tantalizing aroma of fine southern cooking inside the place made Lane's empty stomach growl. Extended on her toes with her chin raised, Becky scanned the room. She motioned with a hand and nodded, acknowledging Desi near the back wall. No sign of Gunner. Thank the Lord. Becky and Lane scissored through the crowded tables. When they reached Desi, he rose from his chair and pulled one back from the table for Becky.

"Hey, Baby," Desi said and gave her a quick kiss on the lips.

"Glad you could meet us for lunch," she said.

Desi slid her chair up for her. "Yeah. My crew's not out in the county today." He sat back down. "We're in town running new cable on Market Street. So, it worked out great." He turned his focus to Lane. "So, I hear that congratulations are in order."

Lane perked up. "Yeah, I got my license today. Should've gotten it over a year ago."

"I was planning on taking off this Thursday so we could get it done," came a voice from behind Lane. The voice stole Lane's appetite like a purse snatcher.

Gunner patted Lane on the shoulder as he brushed past him, pulled a chair from the table and sat down. "It was gonna be a special surprise."

"I hope you don't mind me helping him," Becky said. "I didn't mean to spoil anything."

"Oh, no. It's perfectly fine. It was very thoughtful. Lane and I appreciate it." Gunner nudged Lane's elbow with his. "Ain't that right, Son?"

Lane swallowed a hard lump. "Yes, Ma'am. For sure."

Desi jumped in. "As I said the other day when we were getting that tree off my building, I've been needing an extra hand. Lane's a great worker. So, I figure on hiring him pretty regular." He shrugged his shoulders and turned opened palms upward. "Heck, I'm surprised someone hasn't hired him already. There'll be times when he'll need to drive places. You know, the parts house. The hardware store. The Co-op. Et cetera. Becky can't always stop what she's doing and run errands. She has her online business to run."

"How are you folks today?" a friendly female voice interjected.

The four of them looked up at the waitress.

"My name's Tracy. Our special today is meatloaf, mashed potatoes, pinto beans, and coleslaw. And it comes with our famous banana pudding. Will you be needing menus?"

The four of them ordered the special. Gunner dominated the table conversation. Desi paid the check. Lane left with a to-go box. He barely touched his food.

•   •   •

Using the splitter Desi had rented, Lane turned the numerous logs in the Pritchard's back yard into hundreds of fireplace compatible wedges of firewood. He tossed the last chunk on the stack and looked at his watch. 6:24 PM. Desi emerged from the shop, a welding shield pushed up on his head. "Good job, Lane. I wasn't sure you'd finish it all today. But you dang sure did."

"How about some dinner?" Becky asked.

Lane turned and looked toward the back deck of the house to see Becky setting a plate of sandwiches and a pitcher of iced lemonade on a table.

"I think I'll take her up on that offer. What do you say, Lane?"

Lane and Desi sat down at the table as Becky was adding a bag of potato chips, a package of chocolate chip cookies and drinking glasses to the collection. This time Lane's appetite was just fine. He ate two sandwiches, a pile of the chips and ten of the cookies. When the meal was over, Desi pulled three bills from his pocket—a fifty, a twenty and a ten. "Here you go, Lane. Wanna work tomorrow?"

"Sure."

"Great. I'll need you to take the splitter back. Do you know where Rent Right is?"

"Yessir."

"You can pull it with Becky's truck. Do that first. When you get back, wash and vacuum her truck." Desi looked at Becky and gave her a wink and a smile. "I can't have the best wife in Mississippi driving around in a dirty truck."

Becky returned the wink and smile. "Well, she's married to the best husband in Mississippi."

Desi cut his attention back to Lane. "A contractor is coming on Thursday to repair the damage the tree caused. He said he could do it in a day if the shop was cleaned out. So, I need you get everything out." Desi motioned toward the back yard. "You can just put everything out on the grass. The weatherman says it's not gonna rain this week so everything should be fine. You'll have to use Becky's truck to pull the Cutlass out of the shop. I don't have it running yet." He looked to his wife again. "Can you pick him up at eight in the morning?"

Becky paused from chewing. "Sure."

•　　•　　•

When Desi and Lane pulled up next to Lane's house Gunner came out on the porch. Lane got out of the car. Gunner started down the steps. Lane walked past him without saying a word. Behind him he heard his persecutor and Desi exchange greetings. Desi commented on what a good worker Lane was. Lane opened the door and entered the house. He'd derived a strategy on the way home. Gunner was not getting ALL the hard-earned cash Desi had paid him. Once in his room Lane opened the drawer of the nightstand and pulled out the Gideon Bible. He slipped the fifty-dollar bill between the pages and returned the Bible to the drawer. There'd be an ice storm in Key West before Gunner would open a Bible so the fifty would be safe. He placed the twenty and the ten in plain sight on top of the night stand next to his bed. Lane pulled his bedroom door open wide then retreated to the bathroom. After doing his business, taking a shower and brushing his teeth, he returned to his bedroom. He heard the television blaring from the den. The twenty and the ten were gone. Lane closed the door and locked it. He took the Bible from the nightstand and sat on his bed, his back against the headboard, his ankles crossed. The Bible fell open where the fifty was. Lane studied the bill. What should he buy Abigail? He'd ask Becky. She'd have some ideas. Lane took note of the large, bold words at the top of the page of the Bible. *The Gospel According to John*. Lane's dad's name was John. Lane began to read.

CHAPTER EIGHT

At 7:59 AM the blue Raptor turned off the road and rolled up the driveway. Lane descended the steps. Becky got out and walked around to the passenger side.

"You're chauffeuring again," she said with a grin on her face and got in the truck.

Lane climbed in under the steering wheel and his workday began. He made a U-turn in the yard and headed toward the blacktop. He'd get straight to what was on his mind. Becky seemed like the type that played all her cards face up.

"I need some advice," he said.

Becky kept her focus forward. She pushed up her top lip with her bottom lip and nodded. "Alright. Shoot."

"There's this girl . . . and I . . . um."

She turned and peered at the side of his face. "I got you, Honey," she said with a tight smile. "I'm an expert when it comes to girls. I've been one all my life. So, you just let it rip."

Becky's words stilled Lane's nerves a bit. "Well, we just met but I think we have a connection. Actually, I'm pretty sure we have a connection. I want to get her something. As a gift you know. But I want it to be right. Something she'll like but not something that will make her—." Lane searched for the right words.

Becky began nodding and making a rolling motion with one hand. "Freak her out. Come across too strong. Scare her off. Yeah, I get you."

"Exactly," Lane said.

"Alright, tell me about her. What is she like?"

"She's awesome."

"I figured that. Be more specific."

"Well, her parents are cool. And she's got a younger brother who seems to be a great kid."

"Not her family. Her."

"Well, let me see . . . ah. She likes science and chemistry."

Becky clicked her tongue and shook her head. "That's not helping me. What kind of things does she like to do? If you've been in her house, what does she have in her room?"

"She says she can shoot and fish and stuff. Her room is full of boxes and stuff because she just moved here."

"Where'd she move here from?"

"Texas."

Becky squinted one eye. "Um. That's helpful."

"I think she's a Texas Longhorn fan. First time I met her she was wearing a Texas jersey. I know her father's a Texas fan. He used to play football for Texas. He played for the Miami Dolphins too."

"A yellow rose."

Lane cut a glance Becky. "A yellow rose? Just a yellow rose? You sure? That's not very much. I've got enough money to buy way more than a yellow rose."

Becky turned and looked at him, her expression displaying the confidence of trial attorney in a courtroom. "A single yellow rose. Trust me on this, Lane. It'll be perfect." She relaxed her peaked eyebrows. "The state flower of Texas is the bluebonnet, but it ought to be the yellow rose if you ask me."

"Okay, I'll get her a single yellow rose."

"You know where the library's at?"

"Yes."

"Davidson's Florist is right across the street."

"When do you plan to see her again?"

"Tomorrow."

"After you return the wood splitter to the rental place, go by there. Tell Stella I sent you."

•   •   •

A brass bell jingled as Lane pulled open the door and walked in. Flower arrangements and figurines were perfectly placed throughout the small, quaint store. Music that was not too loud or too soft accented the scene. Lane recognized the popular song, the newest release of the latest pop sensation. A girl with a first name only. An odd name, one that seemed made up. Lane tried to recall it, but it escaped him. A large, double-glass door refrigerator filled with fresh flowers stood against one wall of the shop. Lane walked over and began surveying the various specimens.

"Good morning. What can I do for you today?" came a polite, female voice.

Lane turned to see a petite lady with a prominent smile. He guessed her to be older than Becky Pritchard, but not by much. Ten years at the most. Her black hair bristled on the top of her head. It was cut close on the sides and formed short sideburns that pointed toward her cheekbones. Gold hoop earrings dangled from her lobes. Her brown eyes seemed to twinkle behind the lenses of her black rimmed eyeglasses.

"Ah . . . yes, I'd like to buy a yellow rose."

"Long stem?"

"I guess so. Is that what you'd recommend?

"Who's it for?"

"A girl."

"I assume that this is a special girl. Correct?"

How did this woman know that? Was it that obvious? Like painted on his forehead obvious?

"Yeah. You could say that," Lane said, feeling his cheeks getting warm.

The lady walked up beside Lane and pulled open one door of the refrigerator. "Long stem. Definitely. And I'd put it in a box if I were you."

"Sounds good."

The lady pulled a single long stem rose from the fridge and walked to the checkout counter. She reached under counter and produced a narrow, white box approximately 18 inches long. The box had a clear plastic window on its front the size of a credit card. Under the window was the golden image of a long stem rose and, below the image, written in gold calligraphy were the words *Especially For You.* Lane looked on as the lady meticulously formed a small cylinder with a large piece of tissue paper. She slid the stem of the rose inside the cylinder up to where the leaves grew. She gently placed the rose inside the box, the held it up for Lane to see. "What do you think?"

Lane grinned. "That looks great."

The lady made some punches on the cash register. "That'll be ten sixty-nine."

Lane reached into his front pocket and produced the fifty-dollar bill. He handed it to the lady. "Are you Stella?"

The lady cocked her head in surprise. "I am. How did you know?"

"Becky Pritchard told me to come see you."

Stella looked as though she had just won something. "How do you know Becky?"

"I work for her and Desi some. I had to return a wood splitter to the rental place this morning. I'm headed back to their place now."

Stella motioned toward the front of the store. "You know I thought that looked like her truck when you pulled up. She must really think a lot of you."

"They're great people," Lane said. He started to tell Stella that Becky had helped him get his driver's license and that the rose was her idea, but he figured it might be too much information to share.

"Here. Don't break this," she said and handed the fifty back to Lane. "It's on the house."

Lane pulled his chin back and drew down his brow. "You sure?"

"Absolutely. Tell Becky hello for me."

"Thank you, Stella."

Lane picked up the box and slipped the bill back into his pocket. The brass bell dinged again as he exited Davidson's Florist.

When Lane arrived back at the Pritchard's, Becky put the rose in the refrigerator. "It'll keep it from wilting," she'd said. Her truck had some brake dust on the front wheels and dirt on all four fenders behind the wheels. The carpet needed a little vacuuming and the front floor mats had some light debris. The rest of the truck, however, was near spotless and, in less than an hour, Lane had the truck spit shined.

The workshop looked like a bomb had hit it. When the fallen tree crashed through the back of the shop it demolished a large shop table, broke the motor off of an air compressor, smashed a portable generator, and waylaid two large tool chests. Wrenches, sockets, nuts, bolts, washers, screws, and nails covered the concrete floor like leaves on a lawn in November. In uncanny fashion, however, Desi's 1971 Oldsmobile Cutlass convertible remained unscathed. It was as if an angel from the Almighty had hovered over the desirable muscle car and protected it. Nothing about the car's exterior or interior indicated that its surroundings had been the victim of nature's wrath.

With the deliberateness of a pediatric surgeon, Lane secured one end of the tow rope to the front of the Cutlass. He tugged on the rope several times and rechecked the hookup to reassure himself that the tension would in no way damage the beautiful old car. He sat down in the driver's seat, shifted the car into neutral and called out, "Okay, Becky, ease it out!" Becky drove the Raptor forward at a snail's pace until the tow rope tightened. She turned and looked back at Lane. He gave her a "go ahead" motion with one hand and the two of them navigated the Cutlass out of the mangled shop and onto one shoulder of the driveway. Lane then began the tedious process of clearing the floor of the tools, nuts, bolts, and screws. He expedited his efficiency by using a wheelbarrow. After several trips back and forth, the floor was clear. Lane used a hammer and crowbar to wreck the damaged shop table into smaller, more manageable pieces and piled them on the stump of the fallen tree. He used a furniture dolly to move the welder, the generator and the air compressor. Though Desi's two up-right tool chests were both mangled, their wheels were still good, so Lane rolled them out of the shop and onto the back lawn. When Desi arrived home from work, Lane was finishing off the clean-out project by sweeping the shop with a push broom.

Desi got out of his truck and walked up to Lane, a grin on his face. "Looks like you got the job done."

"Yeah. Wasn't complicated. Just took a little time. I assume you're planning on burning the tree stump, so I piled the scrap wood on it."

"Hadn't planned that far ahead. But I like your idea. Smart thinking."

Lane reached into a front pocket of his jeans and pulled out two one-hundred-dollar bills. "I found these in a coffee can."

"You're a good man, Lane," Desi said. He took the bills and handed one back to Lane. "This is for what you did today."

Desi's complimentary words were like medicine to Lane, antivenin, as it were, that helped neutralize some of the toxins of Gunner's berates and insults. Lane wondered why Desi and Becky had no children. They sure seemed like the parenting type. Based on Lane's experiences with them thus far, Desi would make a great dad and Becky would make a great mom.

Lane shoved the money into his pocket. "Thank you, Desi."

Desi shook his head. "No. Don't say that. When I get paid, I don't say, 'Thank you.' When Becky's clients pay her, she doesn't say, 'Thank you.' You know why?"

"Why?" Lane replied, his eyelids narrowed, his brow pulled down.

"Because it's business. Understand?"

Lane pondered a moment and pressed his lips together. "Yeah. Makes sense."

"Always remember that."

Lane gave an affirming nod.

"Now, when someone gives you something or does something for you that's when you say, 'Thank you.' Always. Got it?"

"Got it."

Desi bumped Lane on one shoulder with a fist and gave a firm look with kind eyes. "Good job today. I'm impressed. Real impressed. Hop in my truck and I'll take you home."

"Sure thing. But I need to get something first." Lane raised a hand toward the back door of the house. "It's in the house. Becky put it in the fridge for me."

"Alright. You run inside and get it and I'll be waiting in the truck for you." Desi started for the truck and Lane started for the backdoor. Desi stopped and changed directions. "On second thought, she might want to ride with us," he said and began following Lane.

They walked through the backdoor and into the kitchen. All was quiet. No sign of Becky. "She's probably in her office," Desi said and stepped out of the kitchen. In less than two minutes he was back, Becky with him. She walked to the refrigerator. Pulled open the door and retrieved the boxed rose. She handed it to Lane. "Here you go. I can't wait to hear how she responds."

"Oh, a rose for a girl, huh?" Desi said.

Lane grinned. "Yup."

"Good play, Lane."

"Well, Becky helped me decide."

Desi shot Lane a nod of certainty. "Well, then, your girl's gonna love it." He looked at Becky. "By the way, Babe, guess what Lane found cleaning out the shop?"

"What?"

"Not one—" Desi raised a peace sign. "But two hundred-dollar-bills."

"Where were they?"

"In an old coffee can," Lane interjected.

Becky looked at Desi and winked. "Where else are you hiding money from me?"

Desi shrugged. "I'll never tell," he said, his words seasoned with humor.

•   •   •

Gunner was home but didn't come outside when Desi, Becky and Lane drove up.

"Let me know when you have some more work," Lane said.

"I will," Desi said, looking at Lane's image in the rearview mirror of the truck.

Lane opened his door to get out. "And thanks again, Becky, for the advice. I wouldn't have thought of a yellow rose."

Becky turned and looked back at Lane. "Anytime. Don't forget to let me know how it goes. Maybe the four of us can do something together sometime. Movie and dinner or a ballgame or something."

Lane felt a thrill well-up inside of him. "Yeah, that'd be awesome. I'll talk to y'all later."

Desi and Becky both made parting remarks and Lane got out of the truck. As he walked up the sidewalk, he heard them drive away.

Lane walked into the house. Gunner sat in front of the television, a Taco Bell bag on the coffee table in front of him, a can of beer in his hand.

"Welcome home," he said without looking up from screen.

Welcome home. Yeah, right. You're only glad I'm home because you know I have money in my pocket and you want it. You're a loser. I wish you would die. Maybe you'll get electrocuted on the job or get broadsided by an eighteen-wheeler.

Lane replied to Gunner's insincere greeting with a simple, "Yeah." He walked to the kitchen and placed the boxed rose in the refrigerator then made his way to his room. The plan had worked the day before, so Lane decided to try it again. He pulled the Gideon Bible from the nightstand drawer and replaced the fifty inside it with the hundred that Desi had paid him. He then placed the fifty on top of the night stand next to his bed, pulled a change of clothes from his chest-of-drawers and headed to the bathroom, leaving his door standing open.

When he returned to his room, much to Lane's surprise, the fifty was still on the nightstand. No television sounds from the television. Strange. Lane walked to the den. The TV was off. No sign of Gunner. Lane heard voices outside. Maybe Desi and Becky had returned. He walked to a window and pulled back the curtains for a view. Gunner and a tall, fit man stood in front of a black, late model Lincoln Navigator. Gunner pumped both hands in the air indicating his concurrence as the tall man appeared to speak matter-of-factly to him. The man turned his back to Gunner and stepped to the driver's side of the SUV. With his hands on his hips, Gunner watched the man make a U-turn in the yard and drive away. Gunner lowered his head as if exasperated or confused then he turned to walk to the house. Lane quickly let go of the curtain and quick stepped to the bathroom again. After a few minutes, he flushed the toilet though he'd not used it and walked back to his room. The fifty was gone. Standing at the threshold of his bedroom, he eyed Gunner once again sitting in the den. Instead of watching the television his nemesis pressed cartridges into the magazine of the semi-automatic pistol that lay in front of him on the coffee table. Lane eased his door shut and locked it. He flipped through his LP collection and found the one he wanted. He removed the record from the sleeve and placed it on the turntable. The needle burped through the speakers when he touched it to the vinyl. The instrumental introduction commenced and then came Johnny Cash's voice. *This yellow rose of Texas I'm going home to see...*"Lane cracked a smile and sat down on his bed. He pulled the Gideon Bible from the drawer and opened it to the place where the C-note was hidden. The year on the crisp bill was current which meant Desi had placed it, along with the other one, in the coffee can just recently. After studying it a few seconds he picked up reading where he'd left off in the Gospel of John the night before. Tomorrow was going to be a big day.

CHAPTER NINE

Lane was uncertain as to why exactly Abigail had told him to wear shorts. Did she want them to shoot basketball or kick a soccer ball around on Soulshine's property? Was her plan that they go play tennis somewhere? Lane had never played tennis. Boy, would he look like a buffoon. Maybe she wanted the two of them to spend their time walking the track at Faulkner Park? Well, whatever she wanted to do was perfectly fine with Lane. Didn't matter to him one bit. They'd be together, doing what she wanted to do. It'd be heaven to him.

Lane emerged from his room donning a pair of Huntsville County High School gym shorts, a Bass Pro Shop tee shirt and Converse All Stars. The shorts and the sneakers were required attire for his previous year's Physical Education class; the tee shirt was a twenty-five-cent find at a yard sale the summer before. Lane's breakfast plan was a bowl of the bland, paper-like cereal and the last one of Becky Pritchard's brownies. That is, unless Gunner had found where Lane had stashed it away in the back of the pantry. Lane reached behind a stack of pinto beans and, to his delight, grasped the small brown bag of tasty treasure. Lane grabbed the cereal and a bowl from the cabinet, a spoon from a drawer and tore off a paper towel from the roll that sat on the countertop. He put the items on the breakfast table and pulled open the refrigerator door. In an instant ice shot through his veins. Lane gritted his teeth. The boxed rose was NOT there. Gunner had wronged him again. Lane slammed the door and reached for the kitchen garbage pail. Like looking for a lost diamond, he rummaged through the trash. No sign of the rose. Perhaps Gunner tossed it in the big, green one outside. Lane darted out the back door and rushed to the can. He threw open the hinged lid. Laying on top of the collection of trash was the box, bent double, the stem of the rose broken inside it.

•   •   •

Lane made his way through the woods. As he drew closer to the tree line, the Soulshine property came into his view. When he reached the edge of the woods, he looked down on the parsonage. A knot formed in his stomach at what he saw—Tyler Frost's Jeep parked in the Westons' driveway. What the heck? Would the two of them come out of the house and drive off together like lovebirds? Would she ghost him and stay inside with Tyler? They were probably laughing and having fun. Maybe playing video games or sitting at the table and having a great breakfast. No doubt, Abigail's parents were becoming more impressed by the day with Tyler Frost. And, why not? Tyler's family was part of the "in crowd," the upper crust of Locust Fork. Lane stood there in agony, the yellow rose in one hand. He looked down at the once elegant flower, now damaged, just a lone blossom with a three-inch bruised stem. It typified everything about his life. He sighed in sorrow, one side of his mouth pushed up.

The mechanical sound of the parsonage's rising garage door interrupted Lane's thoughts. Could he bear to watch it? Should he just toss the rose and walk back to the house. Do his best to forget about Abigail and his incredible experiences with her in the short time he'd known her. He turned to walk back into the woods but caught himself. She seemed so genuine . . . so real. Certainly not like the type that would lead him on and lie to him. He turned back again and leaned against the big oak tree, his eyes fixed on Abigail's driveway. Tyler Frost walked out from the garage, a pair of sunglasses positioned in the thick hair on top of his head. Abigail followed him. She wore cut-off jeans, a University of Texas cropped jersey and carried a wicker basket by its handles. Would the two of them go on a romantic picnic? Lane felt like he'd been punched in the gut. He continued to watch as Abigail followed Tyler out to the Jeep. Tyler opened the driver's door and got in. Abigail approached him. They exchanged some words. What exactly, Lane couldn't hear. The door made a loud "Wham" when Tyler jerked it shut. Abigail backed away from the vehicle a few steps. The big V-8 roared when Tyler cranked it. Abigail stood and watched him as he backed out of the driveway and onto the road. She raised a goodbye hand. Tyler pulled the sunglasses from his head and positioned them on the bridge of his nose. He motioned to Abigail with a raised index finger and drove away. Abigail turned and looked toward the tree line. She raised her hand waved a big wave over her head. Lane could see her smile even from the edge of the woods. His heart leaped inside his chest. He took a few steps forward and returned the wave. Abigail started walking to him, purpose in her steps.

She approached him, her cheeks piqued below her eyes, her smile radiant. "What's up?"

"Oh, nothing much. It's good to see you," Lane said, holding the rose in one hand behind his torso.

"Good to see you too. You ready?"

"Yup. What are you wanting to do?

"I want to go to the creek where you found the arrowhead."

"Cool," Lane said and paused.

Abigail lowered her chin a bit and raised her brow. "Okay, let's go then."

Lane raised an open palm. "Ah, wait. I've got something for you?"

He held up the rose in front of her face. Becky was right. Abigail liked it. Lane could tell by her sudden inhale and rounded mouth.

"It's beautiful. Here. Hold this," she said and handed him the basket.

Lane took it and she took the rose. She fingered its petals gently and smelled it. Then, she pulled her hair back on one side and stuck the rose's short stem between the top of one of her ears and the side of her head. "What do you think?"

What did Lane think? He thought she looked absolutely gorgeous. The rose was more beautiful next to her face than it ever was in the box, even before Gunner broke it. Lane stared into her eyes a moment. Speechless.

"Well, are you going to say something or what?" she said.

"Yeah . . . ah . . . yeah. It looks great." Lane said, awkwardly. He shook his head and stated his real genuine sentiment. "No . . . I mean YOU look great."

She smiled. "Well, okay then. I guess we'd better get going."

"Yeah, sure." Lane raised the basket a little. "I'll carry it."

"Okay, lead the way."

Lane looked into the woods and motioned with a hand. "This way," he said and began walking. Abigail followed.

Lane looked back at her without stopping. "So, what's in the basket?"

"Do you like picnics?" she asked, her attention focused on where she was stepping.

"Of course. Who doesn't?"

"Then you'll like what's in the basket."

As they walked, Lane used the opportunity to prepare Abigail for when he would ask her to go on a double date with Desi and Becky. Lane told her about how he'd been working at their house for the past two days. That they lived in the next county over back in the woods. How Desi worked with Gunner and that Becky ran some kind of internet business. How they were the nicest people imaginable, and that Desi had a really cool old muscle car.

Once Lane and Abigail reached the bend in the creek where Lane had found the arrowhead, Lane set down the basket. He scanned the scenery. "Well, here we are. Where do you want to sit down for the picnic?"

"The picnic is for later. It's not even ten o'clock yet. We're going swimming," she said and started slipping out of her shoes and removing her socks. Lane followed her lead. She tossed her shoes and socks on the ground at the base of a tree. Lane felt his heart quiver when she pulled off her jersey. Underneath it she had on a red bathing suit top. She left on the jean shorts and waded into the water. "Come on in, Lane. The water's great," she said and plunged in. Lane added his shoes and socks to hers and stepped into the water. He watched her frolic and splash for a few seconds then shallow dove into the stream. Abigail did a breaststroke up the creek for about twenty yards and then freestyled back close to Lane.

"You're a great swimmer," Lane said.

"I was on the high school swim team back in Amarillo. I've loved the water since I was a little girl. Does Huntsville County have a swim team?"

Lane shook his head. "Naw. Sorry. We don't have a pool. We're just a 4A school."

"Oh, well. It's not the end of the world," she said and bolted under the water. In thirty seconds, she emerged at Lane's back. She made fanning motions with her arms, throwing sheets of water on him. He pushed water in her face with his palms. They laughed and waged water war at each other till they both were winded. Abigail stepped and stroked her way to the shallow bank of the creek. She sat down and leaned back on her elbows. Lane drew up close to her and sat beside her. He pulled his knees close to his torso and folded his arms on top of them. He wanted to ask her about Tyler Frost but felt it'd be prying and might cause her to pull away from him. Eventually, the subject of the star quarterback who drove the coolest vehicle in town would come up. But not today.

"You're a Mississippi country boy. Right?" she asked.

"Born and bred right here in Locust Fork," Lane said.

"Okay, then. There's something I want you to do."

"You name it."

Abigail sat up straight and moved close to his side. She pulled herself up on her knees and leaned her head closer to his. Gazing into his eyes with a solemn look on her face she spoke deliberate, calculated words. "I . . . want . . . you . . . to . . ."

Lane's heart pounded. Could it be? Was she about to ask him to kiss her. In a flash, she grabbed the bottom of his tee shirt and pulled it up and exclaimed with a laugh. "Take off your shirt and let's swim some more!" When she did, the humor in her expression washed away like a sandcastle crashed by a wave. She let go of his shirt tail and shot a cupped hand to her mouth. "Oh, my goodness. What happened?"

Lane felt his cheeks warm. He dropped his chin to his chest. He didn't want to speak. Didn't want to look at her. She placed a hand on his shoulders. "I'm sorry, Lane. Please don't be upset. I would never want to upset you. I promise."

The genuineness and compassion in her words helped erase some of Lane's embarrassment. Abigail knew he didn't have a car and didn't seem to think less of him. She'd witnessed him cry and hadn't thought him weak for it. She'd spared him great humiliation when he had to confess that he didn't even have a cell phone. Though he hadn't known her long and didn't know her deeply, something inside him told him he could trust her. The whole Tyler Frost thing was a question in Lane's mind—a big question. But thus far, her relationship with Tyler Frost hadn't posed an issue between her and Lane.

Lane inhaled a belly full of air then exhaled and turned to her. "Gunner."

There. He'd told someone. In defiance of Gunner, he'd told someone. What would transpire because of it? Lane wasn't sure and didn't care. If Gunner beat him to a pulp, so be it. Divulging the secret was therapeutic. Lane felt like a great stone had been lifted from his back.

Abigail looked at Lane in horror. "Really?"

"He hates me, Abigail." Lane turned away from her and lowered his chin again. "Ab-so-lute-ly hates me. No telling what he'll do if he finds out I've told you, or anybody for that matter. The man's a monster. Worse than a monster even. He doesn't even call me by my name. Calls me Headlight to make fun of me because my eyes are two different colors. Says I look like a car with one headlight on high beam and the other on low beam." Lane rested his forehead on his folded arms.

Abigail sat down facing Lane. "Look at me, Lane."

Lane raised his head and looked her in the eyes.

"I know we haven't known each other very long," she said. "But I don't believe it's any coincidence that we met. I feel like we have known each other for a LONG time. And I want you to know that you can talk to me. You can tell me anything."

Lane saw a fire in her eyes. He didn't know what to make of it exactly, but it seemed to be one of fearless loyalty.

"I want to hear ALL about you and Gunner," she continued. "And I want to know why your back is all bruised up like it is. You can trust me, Lane. I'm on your side."

CHAPTER TEN

Lane leaned against a post of the front porch. He was tired. Didn't sleep well the night before. The previous day started out great. Looked like it was going to be a thrilling day spent with Abigail topped off with a picnic. Instead, the day turned out to be a day of reliving the painful years Lane had spent sharing the house with Gunner. Abigail listened attentively as Lane informed her of everything related to his miserable home life. From Gunner's rules for groceries to his numerous brutal responses with "the strap" and everything in between. At times, Abigail wept with Lane as he talked. Other times, she boiled in anger.

Lane waited for Becky to drive up. Desi had called the night before. As promised, the construction guy was able to repair the back of the shop in a single day. Now, Desi needed Lane to put all the stuff back in the shop that he'd removed two days prior. The weatherman was predicting much needed rain showers starting at 2 PM so time was crucial. Desi couldn't do it himself because he couldn't take off work. Two of his crew members were out. One had the odd misfortune of having a case of the flu in the summer. The other was at his wife's bedside at a hospital in Memphis. Breast cancer.

Just after 8 AM the Raptor headed up the driveway. Lane got in. Lane and Becky exchanged morning greetings and, five minutes later, they were making good time on Highway 45, Lane gazing through the passenger side window.

"You gonna tell me or do I have to ask?" Becky said.

Lane turned to her with a confused look. "Ask what?"

"Come on. How'd she like the rose?"

Ever since he'd awaken, Lane had been replaying in his mind the tell-all he'd had with Abigail the day before. He'd forgotten about his pact to share with Becky about Abigail's response. "Oh, I'm sorry, Becky. She liked it. A lot, actually. I think. She wore it in her hair just over her ear most of the day."

Becky smiled. "She wore it in her hair just over her ear, huh? Okay. Okay," she said, nodding as she spoke. "That's a good sign. I'd expect you to be all excited. But you're drab. What's up?"

"I've just got some things going on. That's all."

"It's called life. Happens to all of us. Anyway, cheer up. The rose was a success. Trust me. By the way, what's her name?"

"Abigail."

Becky turned her attention to the road. "Well, I look forward to meeting Abigail."

•   •   •

As they rolled up in the Pritchard's driveway, Becky pushed the button on the remote clipped to the driver's side sun visor. The shop's roll-up door began to raise. Three large boxes sat in the middle of the shop floor. Becky pointed an index finger toward the boxes. "Those are tool chests and a rack system. Desi bought them at Lowe's yesterday. He said you'd have to put the wheel assemblies on the chests."

"No problem," Lane said.

Becky stopped the truck. "I'll be in the house if you need me. How do tacos for lunch sound?" she asked as she reached behind the console and grabbed her purse.

"Sounds good. I love tacos."

"Me too." She opened her door and stepped out of the truck. She looked back at him. "Bet she keeps it."

Lane wrinkled his brow. "What?"

"The rose. I bet she keeps it. Probably in a book or journal or something."

•   •   •

Becky slowed the Raptor to a stop in the driveway of Lane's house. 2:25 PM. The weatherman was right. The rain on the hood and roof of the truck sounded like falling marbles. Becky had the wipers slapping back and forth on the windshield at rock 'n' roll speed. She shifted into park and pulled eighty bucks from a pocket of her jeans. "Here. This is for today."

Lane took the money.

She pressed the brake with one foot and shifted the truck into reverse. "Desi'll probably call you when he gets home. He's planning on pulling the engine out of the Cutlass tomorrow. I'm pretty sure he could use your help."

"Cool. I, uh . . ." Lane hesitated a couple of seconds then completed his statement. "I'm sorry for acting out of sorts today."

Compassion filled Becky's eyes. "No problem. We all have stuff we have to work through from time to time."

"What do you do when it seems like there's no way to work through something?"

Becky placed a hand on top of Lane's. "Hang in there. Do the best you can and take it one day at a time, Honey. And, just at the point when you think all hope is lost and the storm will never pass—" She squeezed his hand. "Something unexpected will happen and cause the sun to shine again."

Lane felt like she was his mother talking to him. Lane gave an agreeing nod. "Thanks, Becky."

"Keep your chin up. Whatever you're going through, it'll all work out."

"I sure hope you're right," Lane said and opened the truck door. He got out in haste and ran to the front porch, fisting the cash he'd been paid, the rain coming down in buckets. Standing at the front door, he watched the taillights of the truck move down the driveway.

•   •   •

Gunner was not yet home from work, but he'd be home soon, no doubt. His boss would have his crew knock off early because of the rain. With it being Friday, Lane would be Gunner-free from evening until early the next morning. That is, IF Gunner kept to his usual routine. Lane picked up the landline phone and did something he'd not done up to this point. He called Abigail's cell.

She answered on the second ring. "Hello."

"Abigail, this is Lane."

"Hey! How's it goin'?"

"All good. I just got home from working at Desi and Becky's and was thinking maybe your parents could drop us off on the square. There's an Italian restaurant. It's called Bartolini's or Gambolini's or something like that. Supposed to be really good. My treat of course. The city park is close by. Has a lake in the middle. You can even feed the fish."

"Sounds nice but I have plans with my family already. Mom's cooking crab legs. We're gonna watch a movie on the new big screen TV we got today."

Lane's heart sank. He longed for Abigail. To see her. To talk to her.

"Hold on a second," she said.

The phone went silent. Had letting his guard down about life with Gunner and bearing his soul to her caused her to push back? She'd said that he could talk to her, and he did. But was Lane's drama too much for her? Was she pulling back? Was it all about to end? Would there be no more meetings at the tree line? No more walks in the woods? Or picnics at the creek? Or talks in the treehouse?

"Why don't you come over and join us tonight?" she said.

For Lane, her question was more valuable than gold.

"That'd be great. I'd love to."

Lane heard voices in the background. Something about the rain and it being too wet to walk.

"Yeah, you're right," she said. Lane could tell she was replying to whoever it was that had commented. "Okay. I'll tell him."

"Lane, even if the rain stops, it's going to be soaking wet outside. What do you say if we pick you up about six thirty?

"Sure. I'll be ready."

"Okay. See you then."

They both said, "Bye," and ended the call.

Lane heard a door slam outside. Gunner was home. Lane hustled to his room. He pulled the four twenties from his pocket, placed two on the nightstand and slipped the other two into the pages of the Gideon Bible. He grabbed some clean clothes, headed to the bathroom, intent on staying longer than necessary. Best to give Gunner time to settle in, and more importantly, steal the forty bucks so Lane wouldn't have to deal with him. The sound of the television exterminated the silence from the house— Lane's cue that it was a good time for a stealthy walk to his room. Like a cat burglar he stepped on the balls of his feet. Gunner sat in the recliner that used to be Lane's dad's, his eyes glued to the screen. He gripped a glass of milk on top of one arm of the chair as he munched on some Oreos. As Lane slipped through the den on the way to his room, he noticed the Remington shotgun laying on the couch. Gunner didn't say a word. *Thank God.*

Lane closed his bedroom door behind him and locked it. The two twenty-dollar bills were gone, of course. He pulled Johnny Cash's *Live at Folsom Prison* LP from his dad's collection and placed it on the record player. He assumed his reading position on the bed and retrieved the Gideon Bible from the nightstand. One hundred forty bucks. Should've been twice that, but there was no benefit to dwelling on the loss. Johnny's words demanded his attention. *And I ain't seen the sunshine since I don't know when.* Lane wondered when the day would come that Becky said would come, the day when his sun would shine. It certainly wasn't today. Oh well. In a little over two hours Abigail and her dad or mom would be pulling up in the driveway. He didn't know what they'd eat in addition to the crab legs nor what movie they'd watch. Didn't matter to Lane. He'd be with Abigail and that meant everything would be perfect. It'd be utopia.

A few minutes after six the sound of the locked doorknob being tried interrupted Lane's reading. Gunner beat on the door. "Open the door, Headlight."

"Alright. Just a second."

Lane closed the Bible and returned it to its place in the nightstand. He got up and unlocked the door. Gunner pushed it open. "I've told you a hundred times. There ain't no reason to lock the door. Ain't no women in the house. Just us. Anyway, I'm about to go out for the night. Desi called and asked if you could help him tomorrow. I told him, 'Yes.'"

"Sure. Working for Desi's cool."

"Good because we need to make a grocery run in the next day or two and the money will sure come in handy. It's about time you started doing your fair share to help pay the bills around here anyway."

Gunner's words were like soured milk. Lane did his best not to let his disgust show.

Gunner curled one side of his upper lip and drew back one hand as if he would strike Lane. "And you can get that look off your face, Boy, or I'll knock it off. When are you gonna start showing a little gratitude for all I do for you."

Lane raised his palms as if he were being confronted by a cop. "I'm sorry. I'm sorry. You're right. I'll do better."

Gunner relaxed his expression and lowered his hand. "Desi says he'll pick you up at seven in the morning, so you make sure you get in the bed early tonight. Desi's my friend. It'll be embarrassing if you go over there and are too tired to work hard because you stayed up too late. You get what I'm saying?"

"Yessir."

When Gunner turned and walked out of the room Lane saw the semi-automatic pistol sticking in the back of Gunner's pants. In less than a minute, Lane heard the obnoxious sound of Gunner's engine. Lane stepped to the den and watched through a window as Gunner drove away to do whatever it was he did almost every Friday and Saturday night.

Lane walked to the bathroom, brushed his teeth again and checked his hair in the mirror. A car horn sounded outside. Lane fast-stepped to the den.

Will Weston's pearl-colored Yukon was parked in the driveway. Lane scurried to his room. He pulled the two twenties from the Bible and slipped them into his wallet. If, by some chance, the evening's affairs involved going out for anything, Lane wanted to make sure he could pay for Abigail's whatever. He bolted out the front door. The rain had stopped but water was still puddled in the low places of the walkway. Lane stepped over them as he trotted to the SUV. He pulled open one of the back doors of the truck. He was met with Abigail's smiling face.

"No, you sit up front with Daddy," she said.

Lane concurred and sat down in the front passenger seat.

Will Weston reached his right hand over the console for a handshake. "Hello, Lane. How's it going?"

Lane obliged the pastor's gesture with a grin. "Fine, Mr. Weston. Thanks for picking me up."

"Glad to," said the preacher.

Lane looked back at Abigail. She looked great as always, her smile accented by the dimples in her cheeks.

"Hey," Lane said.

"Hey."

During the handful of minutes it took to travel from Lane's house to the parsonage, Lane told Abigail and her father about his day at Desi and Becky's and how he was going back the next day to help Desi pull the engine out of the Cutlass.

"I like old cars and trucks," Will Weston said.

"Me too," said Abigail. "They have personality."

They arrived at the parsonage. Will Weston pressed the garage remote, and the door inched up. The garage was clear of boxes except for the canning jars which sat stacked against one side wall. The Westons had made great strides in settling in. Lane followed Will and Abigail through the garage and into the house. The savory aroma inside testified to the fact that Erica had been busy in the kitchen. On the kitchen island sat a dish of corn on the cob, a bowl of baked potatoes, a bowl of coleslaw, and a basket of dinner rolls. The sight caused the cavern in Lane's stomach to grow even bigger. He couldn't wait to dig in. Erica Weston hovered over a large stock pot that sat on the stove, a pair of tongs in hand. She shot Lane a big smile. "Glad you could make it tonight, Lane."

"Thanks for having me."

"You bet." She turned her focus from Lane to her family. "Okay, everybody, we'll be in the dining room tonight" she said and began lifting steaming crab legs from the stockpot and placing them on a large platter. "Abigail, you put out some plates and silverware. Brodie, you start putting ice in glasses. Will, you can start putting the food on the table. We'll eat when Tyler gets here."

What! When Tyler gets here! What the heck was he coming over for? Lane's appetite curbed. He began preparing himself for the obvious. The night would be torture. Lane would be nothing more than a spectator, looking on as Tyler and Abigail fanned their romantic flame and strengthened their relationship. When it came time to watch the movie, they'd probably hold hands the entire time. And it would only be a matter of time before she would inform Lane that she needed to talk to him. It'd be the dreaded "I just want to be friends" talk. Lane heard a sound outside. The sound stabbed at his heart like a switchblade knife. It grew louder as it continued to get closer. In seconds the sound was just outside the house. Tyler Frost shut off the big V-8 engine. Lane heard him slam the door of the Jeep. He waited in mental humiliation for the doorbell to ring. It did. Brodie paused his ice duty and walked to the door that opened into the garage. Tyler Frost stood at the threshold. He looked taller than Lane remembered, his smooth complexion perfectly tanned, probably from hours spent basking in the sun on his family's ski boat. It was common knowledge at school that the Frosts not only owned a house in town but also a second one that looked out over the Mississippi River.

"What's up, Brodie?" he said.

"Hey Tyler. Good to see you."

The Westons may have thought it was good to see Tyler, but Lane didn't. Not AT ALL.

Tyler walked into the kitchen with the confidence of a movie star. With each step he made, the muscles in his toned thighs flexed underneath the hems of his Nautica shorts. The top button of his Columbia short-sleeved shirt was unbuttoned and showcased the gold chain he wore around his neck. The thick TAG Heuer watch on his left wrist was unavoidable.

Erica set the large tray of crab legs on the kitchen island and fixed her attention on Tyler. "I made brownies for dessert per your request."

So, Erica Weston was even utilizing her cooking skills to help Abigail win the heart of Mr. Huntsville County High School. Could things get any worse? Lane wished he was back home locked away in his bedroom.

"Ah, great! I'm your slave," Tyler said. "Oh, by the way," he continued. "Mom wanted me to tell you that Camelot Estates is having their yearly neighborhood yard sale tomorrow. It's a huge deal in Locust Fork. There'll be all kinds of great stuff. Mom said she'd love it if you and Abigail could go with her. Said she could pick y'all up at six."

Erica perked up. "I would love to."

"Me too!" Abigail said.

Forget being back home in his bedroom. Lane now wished someone would just shoot him and put him out of his misery. Would someone go ahead and call the coroner!

Abigail moved an index finger back and forth in the air. "I assume you two know each other."

Lane nodded.

"We've never hung out together, but we know each other, kinda," Tyler said and offered Lane a handshake.

Lane obliged, feeling like he was shaking hands with the devil himself.

"By the way, Lane," Abigail said. "We're cousins. Our moms are sisters."

Lane's spirit resurrected. He felt his heart flutter inside his chest. "Oh, okay. I was wandering what the connection was."

"I tried to convince Estella to be a Longhorn," Erica said, shaking her head, her eyes rolled to the top of her skull highlighting the humorous sarcasm in her tone. "But she chose to be a Rebel. Ole Miss offered her a better scholarship and off here to Mississippi she went." Her expression turned somewhat serious. "It worked out okay in the end though. She met Phillip her senior year. They got married after they graduated and had Tyler, my favorite nephew."

"I'm your only nephew."

"I know, but you're still my favorite," she said and chuckled.

The evening passed like the blink of an eye. A bond even began between Lane and Tyler. "You gotta come out to the river house before summer's over," Tyler had said. "I'll teach you to water ski." The two strategized about the first day of deer season as well. Tyler had never killed a buck, but Lane would see to it that he got his face bloodied (a southern tradition in which the new hunter's face is marked with the blood of the first deer he kills). The food was great and so was the movie. The latest production of Alexandre Dumas' *The Count of Monte Cristo*. Lane and Abigail sat next to each other on the sectional sofa as they watched it. They didn't hold hands, but they sat so close that Lane could feel her body next to his the entire time.

CHAPTER ELEVEN

Gunner drug his carcass out of the bed at 11 AM and zombied to the kitchen in nothing but a pair of Fruit of the Loom briefs. He pulled open the refrigerator door, studied the sparse collection of perishables a few seconds as he rubbed his matted scalp and took a can of beer from a shelf. With the beer in one hand and the near empty package of Oreos in the other he lumbered to the den and sat down on the sofa. The can hissed as he popped it open. He took a long swig and shoved one of the cookies in his mouth. The television jumped into action when he pressed the remote. He chewed, then washed it all down with another gulp and continued channel surfing the numerous less-than-appealing Saturday morning options. A car horn sounded outside. He walked to window and pulled back the curtain as if he were spying. What he saw parked in the driveway hit him like shot of electricity—the black Lincoln Navigator, its front passenger window lowered. Gunner opened the front door and leaned his head out. "Let me put my drawers on and I'll be right out."

He shut the door, locked the deadbolt and scurried to his bedroom. The jeans in the floor reeked of liquor and cigarette smoke but they'd have to do. The man waiting outside was not known for patience. Gunner pulled on the rancid pants and slipped his feet into a pair of flip flops. He grabbed his pistol and stuck it in the back of his waistline and headed out the front door to face the music. The man stood in front of the Navigator, one hand holding the opposite wrist in front of his belt buckle, his facial expression as cold as a prison guard's. Gunner approached the towering man as if he were walking to a guillotine.

"Five thousand," the man said.

Gunner reached into a front pocket and pulled out a wad of bills. "Here's twelve hundred. It's all I got."

The man took the cash, counted it, stuck it in the pocket of his shirt and shook his head slowly.

Gunner raised his open palms at his sides. "Honest to God. It's all I got. I'll try to have the rest by this time next week."

"This time next week, huh?"

"Yeah."

The man pulled his cell phone from his pocket and made a call. "Yeah. He gave me twelve hundred. Says it's all he's got. Says he'll have the rest next Saturday."

Gunner watched as the man held the phone tight to one ear and listened. Gunner knew who the man was talking to. The man ended the call and returned his phone to his pocket. He looked down at Gunner like a hungry serpent at a mouse.

"Give me your right hand."

"Oh . . . yeah . . . sure. I'm more than happy to shake on it," Gunner said and extended his right hand. The man reached out and took Gunner's hand with his. In a flash, he ratcheted down his grip like a vice and twisted Gunner's wrist. Gunner dropped to his knees in agony. The man pulled a pair of wire cutting pliers from a back pocket. He held them up before Gunner's eyes. Beads of perspiration popped onto Gunner's forehead as the man lowered the tool to Gunner's throbbing hand. The man opened the jaws of the pliers and positioned Gunner's pinky finger between them.

"Come on, Man! I'll have the money! I promise! I'm telling you, I promise!"

The man squeezed the pliers. "Come on, Man! I'm begging you!" Gunner felt the sharp metal pinch against the flesh of his small finger. Gunner began to wail. The man opened the jaws of the pliers and moved them away. "Today was a service fee. I'll be back next Saturday. Same time. Five thousand in full or you'll need an emergency room. Got it?"

The man released Gunner's hand. Gunner collapsed to his all-fours. "I got it," he said without looking up.

The man shoved the pliers back into his pocket and walked to the driver's side of the car. He pulled the door open to get in, then paused. "Oh, and one other thing."

"Yeah," Gunner said, standing to his feet.

The man motioned to the house with an index finger. "If you're not here, I'll burn it down." He started to get into the vehicle but paused again and looked Gunner in the eyes. "And another thing. If I ever see you packing a gun again, I'll break both your legs." He jerked his chin upward and flared his nostrils. He lowered himself into the driver's seat, raised the passenger window and shifted the truck into drive. The hefty SUV lunged forward. Gunner jumped back. Dirt and gravel sprayed Gunner's legs and feet as the man U-turned. Gunner watched the Navigator barrel down the driveway and out onto the pavement. Five thousand by Saturday. A mountainous feat for sure. But Gunner HAD to get the money.

Gunner began rummaging through the house. Anything of pawn shop value he placed in the middle of the den floor. The kitchen yielded a KitchenAid mixer, a convection oven, a 40-quart stockpot, an eight-place setting of Royal Albert "Old Country Roses" bone china, and three cast iron skillets. From his bedroom he pulled two shotguns: a Belgium Browning "Sweet Sixteen" and a Winchester Model 12, both having once belonged to Lane's father. Then, he pilfered through Lane's bedroom and came up with Lane's Minelab metal detector, the Marlin 30-30 Lane had killed his first deer with, Lane's phonograph, and Lane's entire collection of sixty-eight country music vinyl albums. To this trove of stolen valuables, he added his Dewalt cordless drill, the Remington twelve gauge and his Snap-on 128-piece socket set. He changed into a clean pair of jeans, replaced the flip flops with his steel toed work boots and pulled on a Harley Davidson tee shirt. After several trips, his truck was loaded with the goods. He made one final tour through the house. As he reached for the knob of the front door it occurred to him that the house held one final item of value. The flat screen television. Hocking it would mean no entertainment. Gunner contemplated. It'd probably get him another hundred bucks. And that extra hundred bucks could prove to be critical in his plan. He unplugged the TV and hauled it to his truck.

The engine roared when he turned the key. Gunner dropped the shifter into the "R" position. Before he eased off the brake, he gazed at what he saw in the barn. Heck, somebody might buy it, he postulated. He shifted the truck back into park, turned off the engine, got out, and walked to the barn. With his phone he began snapping pictures of the Grasshopper zero turn. A new one would cost over ten grand. Surely, somebody would be willing to pay two for his even though it needed work. Well, for Lane's dad's actually. As he moved around to get a photo of the back of the big mower, he thought he heard a commotion coming from behind the barn. "Who's there?" he called out. Nothing. He shoved his phone into a front pocket and pulled his pistol from the back of his pants. With his gun raised, he walked out around to the back of the barn. An old feed bucket lay on its side near the water trough. Gunner scanned the scene. No one. *I'm just being paranoid. Who, in my situation, wouldn't be?*

He walked back to the truck. Before he drove away, he uploaded the pictures to one of his social media pages. Maybe, just maybe he'd get lucky, and someone would call him about the Grasshopper.

•   •   •

Gunner's objective was simple. Multiply his money three times over. In times past, he'd done it and more even. More times than not, however, he'd watched his money blow away before his very eyes like chalk dust in a March wind.

He took his seat at the table.

"You're here a lot earlier than normal. I don't usually see you till around seven," the lady said.

Gunner pulled the wad of cash from his pocket and handed it to her. "Yeah. I know. I woke up feeling lucky this morning, so here I am."

The lady smiled as she counted the money. She placed the stack of bills on the table and pushed them down. They disappeared out of sight. Gone for good. Gunner's well-being now hung in the balance. She peeled off eighteen hundred dollars worth of chips and slid them to him. "Well, Gunner, it's just me and you at this hour. I hope you ARE lucky today. You're long overdue."

The word overdue hit him in the chest like a punch from Mike Tyson. If she only knew how high the stakes were for him. Gunner declined to cut the deck and tossed a twenty-dollar chip on the table for the ante and a hundred-dollar chip for the bet. She discarded the first card then dealt each of them two cards, two face-up for Gunner, one down and one up for herself. Gunner showed a queen of hearts and a nine of spades. He signaled to stand. The dealer showed a five of diamonds. She turned over her down card. An ace of clubs. She dealt herself a hit. And, so it began. He hoped he'd eat lunch the following Saturday with all ten of his fingers.

$\bullet \qquad \bullet \qquad \bullet$

"Reckon where Gunner's at?" Desi said as Lane got out of the truck.

"I don't know. He's usually here at this time of day," Lane said, hoping his tone didn't reveal his utter delight that his loathsome stepfather wasn't home.

"Oh, well," Desi replied. "I'll let you know when I have some more work for you."

"Cool." Lane shut the door.

Desi drove away as Lane made his way to the house. Lane walked into his room, two fifty-dollar bills in his front pocket. Sticking to his strategy, he hid one in the Bible and laid the other on the nightstand. He'd enjoyed the day with Desi. They got the motor of the Cutlass pulled. The man at the Napa store said he thought the parts would be in by Wednesday. Lane looked forward to helping Desi get the classic car running or helping him with anything else for that matter. The Pritchards made Lane feel good about himself. Made him feel like a young man instead of a kid. Time flew when he was with them, almost as quickly as when he was with Abigail. He turned to put on an album on the phonograph. What? Where was it? And where were his albums? He looked around the room. His 30-30 was missing from the gun rack on the wall as well as his metal detector from its corner spot. Lane's blood boiled. "Uh!" he yelled, drawn out and full-throated. He slammed a fist on the top of the of the chest where the record player had been. "Gunner, I'm gonna kill you one day!"

The phone rang. The red Lane was seeing instantly began to cool at the notion that it could be Abigail calling. He quickly walked to the kitchen and picked up the receiver.

"Hello."

"Yes, my name's Denver Banks. I saw your ad about the Grasshopper zero turn mower. Is it still available?"

Still available? It was still broken down and in the barn. And what ad? Had Gunner put one of the last semblances of Lane's dad up for sale?

"Hello? Are you there?" Denver Banks said.

"Oh. Yeah. I'm here."

"Is this Gunner?"

"No. My name's Lane."

"I tried to call the other number and it went to voice mail. Is Gunner there?"

"No."

"Is he your dad?"

Lane gritted his teeth. He wanted to cuss out loud. "No. He's my stepdad." The words tasted like vinegar in his mouth.

"Okay, Lane. I'd like to come see the mower if it's still available. I'm not wasting your time. I have the cash."

Okay, so Gunner had the zero turn up for sale. Lane might as well agree to let this Denver Banks, whoever he was, come out and see the mower. If he didn't and Gunner found out, it'd be the strap for sure. And Gunner WOULD find out no doubt. There'd be a record of the man's attempted first call on Gunner's cell phone history. If Gunner was in a bind for money, and by every indication he was, he'd call Banks' number and Lane's failure to cooperate would be exposed. So, Lane played along, gave Denver Banks the address and agreed to show him the mower when he arrived.

In less than an hour, a late model GMC 4WD rolled up in the driveway, a landscape trailer in tow, the words "Banks Landscaping" decaled on the truck's front doors. Denver Banks was well over six feet tall, broad shoulders and a protruding stomach. He wore jeans, square toed boots, a khaki colored Carhartt short sleeve shirt, and a cap with a logo on it that matched that on the doors of the truck. Banks greeted Lane with a friendly smile and a thick, noticeably tanned outstretched hand. The man's calloused paw swallowed Lane's as they exchanged the shake. Lane motioned toward the barn. "It's over here."

Banks grabbed a satchel of tools from the back of his truck and followed Lane. When they reached the mower, the man began his inspection.

"What can you tell me about it?"

"It was running fine up until about two years ago. I'm the one that used it."

"Did you run over something that caused it to quit?"

Banks pulled a socket driver from the tool kit and began loosening the bolts of the battery housing.

"We replaced the battery, but it still wouldn't turn over. Just clicked a little when you turned the key. Gunner didn't want to go to the trouble of taking it to the shop. Said it'd cost a lot to fix it probably since it's a diesel."

"Uh huh. Diesels can be pricey to fix," Banks replied and continued checking various parts of the Grasshopper, his protocol revealing that he knew his way around such machines. "Would you be interested in a job?" he asked, lifting up the seat.

"Lately, I've been doing some work for a man. Not every day. He just calls me when he needs me. I'm supposed to work with him next Saturday, I think."

"What's his name?"

"Desi Pritchard."

Denver Banks smiled. "Desi's a good man. Works for the power company. When you're not working with him, I could use you, if you're interested. Pay you twenty bucks an hour."

Banks' words were like caffeine to Lane. "Sounds good. Only thing is I don't have a car."

"I'm sure we can work something out. Can you back a trailer?"

"Yessir."

Denver Banks lowered the seat. "What if I pick you up in the morning. Say, eight o'clock?"

Eight was good. Gunner would be gone by then.

"I'll be ready." Lane said.

"Good. I'll buy it," Banks said and began reattaching the battery housing.

•   •   •

Sitting on his bed, Lane heard the ratty truck backfire outside. Where had Gunner been? He'd be heading back out in a couple of hours Lane hoped. If he left sooner, even better.

"Headlight!" he hollered, coming in through the back door.

Lane closed his eyes, inhaled and exhaled through his nostrils as he shook his head and resumed reading the Gideon Bible.

Gunner pushed open Lane's bedroom door and charged in. "Headlight, didn't you hear me?"

Lane didn't look up from the pages.

Gunner threw up opened palms. "Oh, I guess that girl's done gone and made you get religion. Where's the money for the mower?"

Lane raised his eyes to Gunner. "It's on the coffee table in the den," he said, his words cool and dispassionate.

Gunner leered at Lane, his eyes fiery. He lunged toward him, one hand raised as if he would strike him. "You'll not talk to me in that disrespectful tone."

Lane closed the Bible and set it on the top of the nightstand. He stood to his feet and looked Gunner in the eyes. "I'm not afraid of you anymore. I feel nothing for you. I don't care what you say to me. I don't care what you do to me. I just don't care."

Gunner relaxed his expression and lowered his hand. Lane continued. "You've sold everything of value. Things that belonged to my dad, my mom and me. Things that were not yours. All that's left is this house and the land it sits on. And I know it's all mine when I turn nineteen. My mother told me so. Said it's written in her will. And three months from now when I turn nineteen, the first thing I'm gonna do is have my own will drawn up. And guess what, you won't get so much as a blade of grass. You'll be lucky if I let you live here and pay rent."

"Look, Headlight," Gunner said, groveling. "I know your mother's death was hard for you. It was hard for me too. I loved her. God knows I loved her. I've been under a lot of pressure—pressure you can't even imagine. I know I haven't been the kind of dad I need to be." Gunner made a crossing "no good" motion with his hands. "But, I promise."

Lane huffed.

"Trust me, Headlight. From now on—"

Lane cut him off. "You're a con man, Gunner. A LIAR."

Gunner's face turned venomous again. He lifted his hand and backhanded Lane across the face. The blow turned Lane's head to one side.

"Nobody calls me a liar," Gunner said.

Lane slowly turned his head back to look him.

"Nobody," Gunner repeated.

Lane, as cold as a stone, said. "I just did." He peered into Gunner's eyes. "Three months."

"You've lost your mind, Headlight. You can't survive without me. You don't even have a car."

Lane stood ramrod straight, his shoulders squared. "My name's not Headlight. It's Lane. And I'll be just fine without you."

Gunner shook his head and made a "forget it" gesture with his hands. He turned on his heels and exited Lane's bedroom. Thirty minutes later Lane heard the Gunner's truck fire up. Praise God he was gone . . . for now.

Lane called Abigail. She answered on the first ring. Lane hoped they could do something together. After all, it was Saturday night. Abigail informed him that she, Brodie, her mom, Tyler, and Tyler's mom were on the road headed to Abilene to visit her grandfather on her mother's side. He'd had a stroke shortly after breakfast. Abigail was unsure when she'd be back in Locust Fork. Her grandfather was in the hospital. Blood pressure was 180 over 94. Doctors were monitoring him closely. Lane told Abigail about his new job with Denver Banks. Abigail encouraged Lane to go to Soulshine's service on Sunday even though she wouldn't be there. "Dad will love seeing you in the congregation," she said. They said their goodbyes and ended the call.

What was Lane to do? He had no car. No television. No computer. No record player. And the biggest "no" of all—no Abigail. Lane walked to the bookcase and began perusing the titles. His mom and dad's library was one of the few things left that Gunner hadn't sold. The collection was eclectic, an assortment consisting of a variety of fiction genres and non-fiction topics. Lane ran an index finger across the spines as he scanned the titles. He paused at one. *The Art of War* by Sun Tzu. He pulled it from the shelf and began reading the concise, enumerated points of the first chapter entitled "Laying Plans." Number twenty captivated him. *Hold out baits to entice the enemy. Feign disorder, and crush him.* Number twenty-two added fuel to the flame of his intrigue. *If your opponent is of a choleric temper, seek to irritate him. Pretend to be weak that he may grow arrogant.* Lane fanned through the rest of the pages, noting the reader-friendly format of the text. The book was not very thick. Wouldn't be laborious to complete. He settled on it and walked to his bedroom.

CHAPTER TWELVE

Lane sat down in the same seat he'd sat in the Sunday before. The church bulletin outlined the protocol of the day's service. Different songs but the same number and arranged in the same order around announcements, prayer, the offering, a special song (whatever that was), and Dr. Weston's sermon. A paragraph encouraged the church members to pray for God's grace and healing power on behalf of Erica Weston's father. As the music minister led the congregation in song, Lane participated as best as one could expect, given the fact that he was not familiar with "church stuff." The time came for the special song. To Lane's amazement, Big Pop sang it—solo. Against the background music of a lone violin played by a lady wearing a navy dress, Big Pop's deep baritone voice filled the auditorium with words about what life would be like in heaven. Lane listened intently to the song's uplifting message. Lane had to admit that, if what Big Pop sang was true, life in heaven would be far better than anything life on earth had to offer. When Big Pop finished, the congregation applauded, the sound of their clapping seasoned with prominent "Amens" from various directions inside the worship center. The affirmations subsided and Dr. Weston stepped to the pulpit. He announced the sermon text. Revelation 21:1-4. Without having to consult the table of contents, Lane easily found the passage in the Gideon Bible. Even HE knew that Revelation was the last book of the Bible. The picture that Big Pop had sketched in his song was brought to life in vivid color by Will Weston's sermon. Lane felt that Dr. Weston painted with his words the way an artist does with a brush. By the time the sermon was over, Lane felt that he'd been shown a post card of the New Jerusalem the Bible passage spoke of. As he'd done the Sunday before, Dr. Weston stood at the front of the congregation and challenged them to respond as "the Spirit" prompted them. The music team members took their places and began playing. The song leader encouraged everyone to sing along by following the words on the overhead screen. They did and, once again, like the previous Sunday, several people from the audience left their seats, walked to the front, knelt near the platform and prayed silently. Just before the service ended, Dr. Weston introduced to the congregation five people who wished to join Soulshine from other churches in Locust Fork. Lane assumed it was because Dr. Weston preached better than the pastors of those churches. Dr. Weston prayed a final prayer and most of the people began leaving. Those that didn't hung around in small groups throughout the auditorium and talked. Some gathered at the front and waited to speak to Dr. Weston individually. As Lane filed out with the departing crowd, he felt a tap on one shoulder. He turned. Big Pop stood before him.

"Hello, Lane. Do you have plans for lunch?"

"No sir."

"Well, my wife and I and the preacher are going to The Hungry Fisherman. We'd love it if you joined us. My treat."

It was an offer that Lane could not refuse. "That'd be great. Thanks for inviting me."

Big Pop winked one eye and grinned. "You bet. The preacher will be just a few minutes. When he's finished talking to folks we'll get going."

The lady in the navy dress walked up.

"This is my wife, Brenda," Big Pop said.

Brenda offered a kind smile. "Nice to meet you, Lane. James has told me a lot about you. All good, of course."

"Nice to meet you too, Mrs. Babcock."

•   •   •

Lane had been to The Hungry Fisherman once when his mom and dad were alive. A Black Angus cattle auction was held at the farm arena of Northwest Community College. "Black Angus are the best beef on four hooves," Lane's dad used to say. To celebrate the purchase of a bull and eight heifers, Lane and his parents dined at the famous fish restaurant before trailering the livestock back home. Lane remembered two things about The Hungry Fisherman: the top hat-wearing catfish logo on the large mugs the iced tea was served in and the panoramic view of Sardis Lake.

Abigail was right. Dr. Weston was delighted that Lane attended the service even though Abigail was in Texas. The decision was made that the four of them would make the journey to The Hungry Fisherman in Will Weston's SUV. Big Pop insisted that Lane sit in the front seat next to Dr. Weston while he and Brenda sat in the backseat. In less than a half hour they were tooling through the parking lot of the popular eatery searching for a parking spot.

A line of people stretched out onto the long front porch of the log cabin structure. Lane determined by the way people were dressed that everyone at The Hungry Fisherman had been to church that morning. The line moved along and, in less time than it took them to drive over from the church, they were being seated next to the back of the restaurant overlooking the blue headwater of Franklin D. Roosevelt's Flood Control Act of 1936.

A waitress wearing jeans, a red and white plaid shirt and a red cap with a top hat-wearing catfish on it approached their table. She was a pretty girl, but not as pretty as Abigail. "Welcome to The Hungry Fisherman. My name is Caacie and I'll be your server today. Can I start you off with something to drink?" Lane, Dr. Weston and the Babcocks all ordered sweet iced tea. Caacie handed each of them a menu then whisked away to get their drinks. She returned in minutes with four large mugs filled with the deep south's beverage of choice, a top hat-wearing catfish on each one. Just as they'd ordered the same beverages, they also ordered the same meals: two-piece catfish fillet plates with baked potatoes, coleslaw and hush puppies. Caacie took their orders without the need to write them down and hustled away once again.

"Any update on Erica's father?" Big Pop asked.

Dr. Weston shook his head. "Same as yesterday. His blood pressure is still high. Doctor says he can't go home till it's in the normal range."

"We'll continue to pray," Brenda said.

"Thank you so much," Will Weston said, his face displaying his concern. "Jerry and I are close. Almost as close and me and my own father. He's a fine man. Loves the Lord."

"Amen," Big Pop said. "Seems like you and Lane here know each other a little."

Lane nodded. Will smiled. "Yeah, we do. He and Abigail have hit it off, it seems."

Lane loved the way that sounded. "Hit it off, it seems" sounded quite promising, especially coming from her father. "Lane's family's property connects to the church's," Will continued.

"As the high school's maintenance man, I get to know all the students. Lane is one of most respectful boys on campus."

Thanks for the plug, Big Pop.

James Babcock looked Lane in the eyes. "So, how do you like Soulshine so far?'

"I like it just fine. Hearing Dr. Weston preach has got me to reading my Bible."

"That's great. What are you reading currently?" Big Pop asked.

"The Gospel of John. Just finished reading about Jesus running the trade day guys out of the temple. Seems like Jesus doesn't take too kindly to the church being run like a business."

Big Pop turned his attention to Dr. Weston, his brow raised. "Well, Preacher, I'd say that sums it up pretty well. Don't you think so?"

Will Weston cocked his head and clicked his tongue. "I know people that've been church members for years and still haven't learned that." He nudged Lane with an elbow. "Attaboy, Lane. You keep on reading and let me know when you have questions."

Caacie returned with their meals. As they ate, they talked about a wide range of topics. Big Pop talked about his college days at Ole Miss and his history at Soulshine. Will discussed the two churches he'd pastored before moving to Locust Fork. That Texas had recently fired their head coach for failing to take the team to a bowl game for the past two seasons, and most importantly, for losing to their archrival, Oklahoma, for the past three years. Will voiced his hope that the Longhorns would hire the coach away from Georgia. Brenda Babcock talked about her retirement from FedEx and the five grandchildren that she and James adored. Lane told them about Desi and Becky Pritchard and the old Cutlass Desi was restoring and about the new job he'd start the next day with Denver Banks.

"I know Denver Banks," Big Pop said. "He graduated from Huntsville High School. Started a landscape business instead of going to college. Has done quite well for himself. Probably the best small engine mechanic in Locust Fork."

•   •   •

When Lane walked in the door, Gunner was watching NASCAR. He'd bought the television out of hock but let the pawn shop keep the other items. Lane kept his head down as he walked to his room. Gunner didn't acknowledge him. Hallelujah. Lane shut his bedroom door and locked it. Tomorrow couldn't come quick enough. Working with Denver Banks was going to be great, no doubt. Lane slipped off his shoes and sat on his bed, his back against the headboard. He picked up where he'd left off in *The Art of War*.

•   •   •

The sun was just making its introduction when the beams from the headlights of Denver Banks' truck painted the front of the house and speared around the edges of the curtains. Lane pulled on a cap and hustled out of the house. Denver Banks got out and walked around to the passenger side. "You're driving, Son."

"Yessir, Mr. Banks."

A landscape trailer was hooked to the back of truck. The trailer housed the Grasshopper, a push mower, a weed trimmer, some yard tools, and two large red gas cans. Lane sat down in the driver's seat and navigated a perfect back up and pull forward to begin their journey of the day's itinerary.

"I got two people out on vacation this week. So, I'm gonna have to throw you to the wolves right off the bat. You up to it?" Banks said.

"Sure. Yardwork's not complicated. By the way, I guess you got the Grasshopper running."

"Yeah. It needed a new carburetor and fuel line. I replaced the belts and the air filter. Changed the oil and greased it. Runs like a champ now. " Banks said.

Lane figured it'd be simple and inexpensive to get going. But Gunner had opted to just sell it off at a fraction of its value. What an idiot! A bonified jerk with rocks for brains.

"We're going to the hospital first."

"Got it," Lane said.

When they got there, Denver Banks pointed to the far end of the parking lot. "Park over there next to the grass."

Lane concurred. Banks got out and unhooked the trailer. He lowered its heavy tailgate, fired up the Grasshopper and drove it onto the grass. The big machine, indeed, ran like a Champ just like Lane remembered.

Banks got off the mower but left it idling. "Alright, Lane. It's all you this morning. I've got to go check on the other crew. You have any questions?"

"No, Sir. I can take it from here."

Denver Banks pulled a business card from his shirt pocket. "Call me if you need to. I'll be back about eleven."

Lane nodded. Banks walked to the truck, got in and drove away. Lane went to work. The Grasshopper was like an old friend to him. He used the push mower to cut around the hospital's courtyard, the weed trimmer for the finishing touches around the shrubbery beds and sidewalks. Denver Banks returned just after ten o'clock as Lane was loading the equipment back on the trailer. Banks got out of the truck and scanned the hospital property. "Is the back finished?' he asked.

"Yessir. Courtyard too."

Banks sighed and grinned. "Wow. Keith's my lead man. Been with me going on five years now." He looked at his watch. "This job would take him another twenty minutes. Good job, Lane."

"Want me to back the truck to the trailer or do you want to?" Lane asked.

Denver Banks didn't answer. He just continued gazing at the manicured hospital grounds.

"Mr. Banks?"

"Yeah, Son?"

"Shouldn't we hook the trailer back up and move on to the next job?"

"Oh, yeah . . . yeah. Of course," Banks said as if he'd been tapped on the shoulder by an invisible hand. "We need to cut the post office next."

Lane backed the truck to the trailer, Denver Banks directing. Once the connection was made and the light plug secured, they were on the way. Lane parked the rig on the street in front of the post office. Denver unloaded the zero turn and began mowing. Lane fired up the weed trimmer and started edging. As he edged the lawn where it met the pavement of the parking lot he recognized one of the vehicles. A maroon minivan, its windows lowered. In the back seat sat two children: Donnie Newhouse and his sister. Lane cut the power on the trimmer and walked over to the boy. "Donnie Newhouse, correct?"

The boy's face lit up as if he were handed a Christmas present. "Yessir."

"Well, let me hear one."

Donnie raised one side of his upper lip. "Well, it's one for the money. Two for the show. Three to get ready. Now go, cat, go but don't you . . . step on my blue suede shoes. Well, you can do anything but lay off of my blue suede shoes."

Lane raised an open hand to Donnie. "Gimme five, Donnie."

Donnie slapped Lane five.

"You keep it up, Donnie. I bet someone takes notice of you one day."

Donnie grinned.

"I've got to get back to work. See you later," Lane said.

"See you later, Alligator."

Lane fired up the weed trimmer up again and continued fine tuning the lawn of the post office. A few minutes before noon, he and Denver were pulling away, leaving behind a scene worthy of an advertisement photograph.

"Lunch?" Denver asked.

"Sure."

Denver covered the lunch bill. Burgers, fries and sodas from The Burger Depot, a family-owned local favorite that served up the biggest hand-patted burgers in Huntsville County.

Denver took a drink of his soda and set the cup down on the table. He pulled his cell phone from a pocket of his jeans. "What's your cell number?"

Lane began to chew his food slowly. "I . . . ah . . . don't have one." The words were painful in his throat. "Thought I'd get one when I get my first paycheck."

"You need a cell phone. We gotta be able to communicate. You got a bank account?"

"No, Sir."

"You got a hundred bucks?"

"Yessir."

"Good. Then, let's do this. Let's stop by the bank and open you a checking account. You gotta have one anyway for me to pay you every week. Then, we'll go by the phone store. You pick out the one you want. I'll pay for it. Then, I'll keep, say, a couple a hundred a month out of your paycheck until it's paid off. That way you don't have to pay for it all at one time. Sound like a plan?"

Denver's offer was like a shot of adrenaline. "That sounds great. And I promise you, Mr. Banks, I'll continue to work hard."

"I believe you. Let's get rolling. I've got a meeting with a potential new client at two."

By one forty-five Lane had a checking account in his name at Magnolia Bank and an iPhone in his pocket.

"Take me to the shop and drop me off," Denver said. "Then, go cut the grass at the driver's license place. When you're through there, go cut Carter and Collins Funeral Home. After that, do the Presbyterian Church on the square. After that, call me. Now, let's try the GPS out on your phone."

Lane swiped the screen of his new phone and entered his personal code. He found the GPS icon. "Banks Landscaping," he said.

The friendly lady inside the phone navigated them to Denver's shop. When they arrived, Denver exited the truck and Lane headed to the driver's license place. Lane loaded the Grasshopper on the trailer at a few minutes after five. The Presbyterian Church was done. He called Denver. His new boss's instructions made him feel ten feet tall. Lane was to drive the company truck home. He was to get started at 7 AM. Denver gave him eight properties he was to cut. He was to call Denver when the jobs were done. Lane felt respected, valued and independent; Lane felt like a MAN.

Gunner stood on the front porch, a "WHAT IN THE WORLD" look on his face. Lane got out of the truck and walked to the house, shoulders squared, his chin up in confidence.

"Well, well, well. What do we have here?" Gunner said.

"The man who bought the mower hired me. Today was my first day. Start again in the morning at seven."

"I was wondering where you were. Worried about you, Son."

You better be worried. Your days in this house are numbered.

"No need to worry. I'm okay. Just forget what I said the other day. I was having a bad day," Lane said as he passed by Gunner. He pulled open the screen door and looked back at Gunner before walking into the house. "By the way, I'm willing to try and get along if you are. After all, we do live in the same house."

Gunner nodded and raised an open palm, his face showing a hint of reconciliation. "I feel the same."

Lane entered the house and walked to his room. He shut his door but didn't lock it. He cracked a tight smile. His plan was underway. He'd be applying more of Sun Tzu's principles in the days to come.

Lane dropped down on his bed and sent his first text. To Abigail, of course.

Hey. Guess who?

Three dots pulsated. She was responding.

?

Lane smiled. *Hint: You've been in my treehouse.*

Lane!!!! Did you get a cell phone?

Yup. Can you talk?

Absolutely. Call me.

Abigail answered on the first ring. "Hey. Great to hear your voice."

If Abigail only knew how thrilling it was for Lane to hear her voice. She was occupying miles of real estate in his mind. He thought about her as soon as he woke up in the morning. He thought about her throughout the day. He thought about her when he laid in bed at night.

"Great to hear your voice too. How's your grandfather?"

"He's doing much better. The doctor may let him go home in a day or two."

Lane hoped so. Of course, he wanted Abigail's grandfather to be okay, but his motivation was saturated with his desire for Abigail to come back home. He wanted to see her. Be able to touch her. Smell her pleasant scent. He wanted to hear her laugh and feel the magnetism of her soul on his.

"That's good. I hope he gets to go home soon. When do you think you'll be back in town?"

"Mom says if he goes home tomorrow or Wednesday, we'll come back Thursday or Friday."

Lane screwed up his nerve. "If it works out, would you like to do something Friday night?"

"Let me check with Mom and Dad, but if they say it's okay, then yes, I'd really like that."

Lane felt his heart rate increase, a pleasant chill tingled in his chest. "Great."

"Okay, Mom," Abigail said. "Lane, I need to go. The nurse just came and told us we can go back and see Granddaddy. They've been running tests on him all day so he hasn't been in his room."

"Of course. Tell your mom and Brodie I said hello. Tell Tyler too."

"Will do."

They ended the call. Lane pushed back against the headboard and interlocked his fingers behind his head. It had been a great day. Lane looked forward to the next. He did it again—he smiled. He'd spend the remainder of the evening doing two things: reading the Gideon Bible and reading *The Art of War*.

CHAPTER THIRTEEN

Lane drove the truck and trailer through the opened gate of the chain linked fence. A large sign attached to the fence read Banks Landscaping. Gravel cracked under the mud grip tires of the pickup as Lane drove past the smaller of the two buildings and parked next to the larger one. The big building's raised roll-up door revealed a considerable array of mowers, trailers, yard tools, and other items essential to Denver Banks' thriving business. It was almost five o'clock. Friday. Lane had worked forty-six hours. Abigail had gotten back into Locust Fork late the night before. The plan was dinner and a boardgame at the Weston's. As Lane entered the door of the small building, Josie Banks greeted him with a smile. "Hey, Lane. I got your paycheck ready," she said and handed him an envelope over the top of her desk.

Lane took it. "Thanks, Mrs. Banks."

"You bet. We're glad to have you working with us."

The back door opened and in walked Denver Banks, his cell phone to one ear. He raised an index finger to Lane in a "Give me a minute" gesture. Lane nodded then turned back to Josie. "I'm glad too. I really enjoy it."

"Well, Denver says you're doing great."

"Okay, Victor," Denver said. "I'll come look the place over first thing Monday morning and give you an estimate. Maybe we can go grab a cup of coffee or something . . . Sure thing. See you then." He ended the call.

"Honey, that was Victor Bellamy at the Holly Springs Airport. Put me down for eight o'clock to give him an estimate."

Josie Banks made some notations on her desktop calendar. "Bill Overton from Overton and Associates called about an hour ago. He wants you to come by sometime Monday and give him one too."

"Make it for ten."

She wrote again on the calendar. "I'll tell him."

Denver looked at Lane and motioned toward the door with his head. "Come on, Lane. Let me show you where to unhook the trailer."

Lane followed Denver out the door and around to the shop. Denver raised one hand to a vacant space inside. "Back it in there."

With precision, Lane did as he'd been instructed and pulled the truck back out onto the gravel. "Where do you want me to park the truck?" he asked without getting out of the truck.

"Just keep it over the weekend. Drive it if you need to. Be here Monday morning at eight."

"Yessir. And thank you for letting me use it."

"No problem. Have a great weekend."

Lane drove straight to the bank, eager to endorse his first paycheck. He kept two hundred in cash and deposited the rest, a preventative measure to keep the majority of the hard-earned money from Gunner's thieving hands. On the way home he stopped at Sweet Tooth Bakery and bought a strawberry cake. It'd be a nice dessert at the Weston's later on. If there were people on earth who didn't like strawberry cake, Lane had never heard of them. When he got home, the hood of Gunner's truck was raised with Gunner leaned over the engine. Lane pulled around to the back of the barn where the faucet was. In case he and Abigail might end up going for a drive, he'd make sure it would be in a clean vehicle. As Lane walked to the house to get a bucket, some soap and a rag, Gunner stopped whatever it was he was doing, raise up and looked at Lane. "I guess your boss is providing you with a company vehicle."

Lane clicked his tongue and rolled one hand over. "I dunno."

"What are you doing tonight?"

"Having dinner with Abigail and her family."

"You gettin' mighty sweet with that preacher's daughter. Remember what we talked about, now."

Lane ignored Gunner's comments and kept walking.

"You forgetting something?"

Lane anticipated what Gunner was about to say. He stopped and turned to him. "What do you mean?"

Gunner wiped his sweaty forehead with the back of a greasy hand and continued laboring with the truck's motor. "You got a job now. So, you need to cover your fair share around here."

Lane raised one side of his mouth and shrugged his shoulders. "Okay. Sure." He pulled a hundred from his pocket, walked over to Gunner's truck and placed it on top of the battery. "Here you go. I'll be getting paid every week." Lane turned and continued toward the house.

Hold out baits to entice the enemy.

•   •   •

Lane arrived at the Weston's at six sharp. He rang the doorbell. Erica opened the door, a welcoming expression on her face. "Hello, Lane."

"Hello, Mrs. Weston. I'm glad your father is doing better."

"He is. Thank you. Please come in."

Lane extended the cake to her. "I thought this might be good for dessert. It's strawberry. I picked it up from the bakery."

Erica Weston cocked her head to one side and pressed her lips together. "Well, aren't you considerate." She took the cake from his hands. "It's heavy. I bet it'll be good."

Lane entered the house and shut the door. Erica walked through the den and into the kitchen. She opened the cake box. "It's beautiful. Like something out of a book. Abigail! Lane's here!"

"Okay. Be there in a minute!" Abigail replied.

Erica motioned to the bar chairs at the kitchen island. "Have a seat."

Lane pulled one out and sat down.

"I hear you started a new job this week."

"Yes ma'am. I'm working for a landscaping company. I really like it."

Erica slipped her hands into some kitchen mittens and pulled down the oven door. The aroma of something piping hot and savory began to saturate the room. She reached inside, retrieved a large casserole dish and set it on the stovetop. "I hope you like lasagna. It's Brodie's favorite. We let him decide tonight."

"Lasagna's great."

"What's up?" came Lane's favorite female voice from behind. Lane turned in his chair to look at her. What a knockout!

"Hey," he said.

Abigail gave him a friendly punch on one shoulder as she walked past him. Lane relished the contact. She pulled a chair away from the island and sat down. Will Weston entered the kitchen. "The press conference is at seven," he said and fist bumped Abigail. "Man, I hope and pray we get the guy from Georgia. If we do, Oklahoma better look out."

Erica began cutting the lasagna into squares with a spatula. "In case you didn't know, Lane, we are a Texas Longhorns family THROUGH AND THROUGH. They're announcing the new head coach tonight."

"I figured that much."

"Where's Brodie?" Will asked.

"Who knows with that boy?" Erica said.

Will turned his face toward the stairs. "Brodie! Come on, it's time to eat!"

Feet started down the steps, Brodie's body coming fuller into view as he descended. "I'm coming."

They took their seats at the dining table. As they ate, their conversation consisted of Lane's work experiences with Denver Banks thus far, Erica's father's scary stroke episode, and the much-anticipated coaching announcement that was soon to take place. The lasagna was more than just good, and the strawberry cake was a huge hit. They left their dishes on the table to be tended to later and retired to the den. Will pressed the TV remote and the big flat screen burst to life, the channel for the announcement already set. "Looks like we've got about six minutes," he said.

"Dr. Weston, sometime tonight I'd like to ask you a Bible question if you don't mind," Lane said.

"Sure. Go ahead and ask it now," Will said, his eyes still fixed on the television screen.

"What did Jesus mean in John chapter three when He told Nicodemus, 'Verily, verily, I say unto thee except a man be born again he cannot see the kingdom of God?'"

Will Weston muted the television and turned his attention to Lane. "Let's you and I go sit on the patio and talk."

"Oh, it can wait till later," Lane said. "The big news is about to come on."

Will stood to his feet, his warm eyes still fixed on Lane's. "Nothing's bigger than the question you just asked," he said. A kind smile stretched on his face. "I'd rather talk about it than watch football any day. Come on."

Lane stood from his place on the sofa and looked down at Abigail. "Ok, Abigail, I guess I'll be back in a bit."

She reached out a hand and took one of his. "You take all the time you need." She squeezed, then released.

Lane followed Will out the back door and onto the patio.

•   •   •

Gunner sat on the couch, fully clothed with his shoes on. He looked at the clock on the wall. The man would be arriving any moment, just like he'd said. Gunner had counted the money three times already. Each time he counted five thousand. He'd had several meetings before with the man about money, but he knew this one was the most serious by far. The man would stand by the threats he'd made. He'd cut off one of Gunner's fingers, or worse, if things didn't go according to the man's liking. Gunner heard the sound of a vehicle coming up the driveway. He got up and walked out the front door, the five grand clutched in one hand. The black SUV slowed to a stop. The intimidating man got out and walked around to the passenger's side. His white shirt fit tightly across his chest and around his biceps. The waistline of his black slacks lay flat against his lean abdomen. He reached for the handle of the back passenger door. He pulled the door open and held it. An Asian woman stepped out. Her black hair was pulled back tight on her head and secured in a bun by a broach with red blossoms. She wore a red, floral print cheongsam dress. Gunner had only heard of the woman. He'd never met her. To Gunner, and others like him, she was known simply as Miss Red. Gunner's palms grew clammy. The blood in his veins felt chilly all of the sudden.

Gunner held out the stack of money. "Here's five thousand."

The lady turned to the driver and nodded. The driver took the money from Gunner's hand and counted it. "Five thousand," he confirmed.

The lady peered at Gunner like a constrictor serpent at its prey. "This is good for you. Now, let me get to the reason for my being here today which is very uncommon."

"I know. I know," Gunner said.

The lady raised an index finger. "Don't interrupt. It's disrespectful."

Gunner nodded as if he had a gun to his head.

"People come to me when they need money. I never ask them what for. Investing. Purchasing. Or, as in your case, betting with it at a blackjack table. I don't care. Doesn't concern me. What does concern me is that you fulfill your obligation to pay it back in the agreed upon increments and on a timely basis. I'm saddened by the fact that you have fallen behind. It strains our relationship and makes things quite stressful for me. And, Mr. Gunner, I do not handle stress very well."

Gunner stood there. Frozen. Expecting at any moment to be shot or stabbed.

The lady continued.

"My records indicate that you have an outstanding balance of one hundred thirty-five thousand dollars. I have made the decision to void our agreement. You are no longer required to make monthly payments of five thousand. It is simply too stressful for me. As I said, I do not handle stress very well."

The fact that Miss Red was voiding their agreement and would no longer be requiring the hefty monthly payments gave Gunner a sense of relief. He inhaled and exhaled. "I really appreciate it," he said.

She raised her index finger again and pressed her lips. Gunner got the message. He'd interrupted her again.

Miss Red lowered her hand. She blinked her eyes twice and smiled. "I have decided on a new agreement." She motioned to the driver with one hand. "Mr. Blade here will come visit you again ninety days from today." She checked her watch. "At exactly 9:32 AM." She looked back into Gunner's eyes once again. "When he arrives, he will be expecting to collect the full amount due. One hundred thirty-five thousand. If for some reason you do not provide him with the full payment, he will make a phone call to me, and I will decide what —" Her words trailed off. She cleared her throat then resumed speaking. "I will decide at that time what necessary provision must be taken. Should you not be here when Mr. Blade arrives, it will cause a most unpleasant situation. I can assure you that there is nowhere you can hide where I will not be able to find you. Questions?"

Gunner's legs felt weak, his hands began to shake. "I really want to pay you every cent I owe you, but I have no idea how I can come up with a hundred and thirty-five g's in ninety days. I'm being honest with you."

Miss Red scanned the property. "Mr. Gunner, this is a very fine farm you have here. No doubt, for say, a hundred and fifty thousand it would sell quickly. I bet someone would snatch it right up."

"The place belongs to the kid. It's what the will says. I can't touch it unless he leaves. And he won't leave. I've tried everything to get him to. No matter how bad I treat him or how bad I beat him he just continues to stay."

"Mr. Gunner, surely there must be some clause in the will that could work to your favor."

"There's not I tell you. I've even talked to a lawyer. The only way would be for him to leave or deed it over to me and he won't do either."

"I see. Well, what if something were to happen to the kid?"

Gunner wrinkled his brow. "If something were to happen . . . like what?"

"Let's say, for instance, the kid was to die."

"Then the place would come to me. He's my stepson. I adopted him a few years ago."

"Sounds like a very effective solution to your problem."

Gunner peaked his brow, his mouth open in amazement. "You mean murder him?"

She shook her head. "No, Mr. Gunner. I never said, 'Murder.' But sometimes kids do have accidents. You know, they go hunting and a gun discharges unintentionally. They go swimming and the water is deeper than they thought. They go for a drive and the car has a malfunction. They feel sick and take too much medicine." She stepped closer to him and looked him dead in the eyes. "The possibilities are endless," she said as if she were indwelt by Satan himself.

She turned and got back into the SUV. Mr. Blade shut her door and turned to Gunner. "I see that you didn't pack your gun today. Wise. Very wise."

He walked around the truck and got in. Miss Red lowered her window. "Sounds like you have but two options, one really if the boy won't leave. Whatever measures you decide to take, Mr. Gunner, I do hope you have the money when Mr. Blade returns. One of his strongest points is his ability to follow detailed instructions. Should you fail to have the money, I'm afraid I will be forced to give him some."

She looked up into the sky. "My, what a beautiful Saturday. Not a cloud in the sky. A perfect day for fathers and sons to bond with one another." With narrowed eyelids she cut a look to Gunner. "Don't you think?" she said malignantly. She raised her tinted window and she and Mr. Blade drove away.

Gunner walked back in the house and into his bedroom. He pulled an Ariat boot box from under the bed and removed the box's top. Inside were various documents. A passport. The title to his truck. Lane's adoption papers. Gunner's high school diploma. The pawn shop receipt that detailed the items he'd hocked earlier in the week. And the two most pertinent documents to his current dilemma: Lane's mother's will and a five-hundred-thousand-dollar life insurance policy that Lane's mother and father had taken out on him several years prior. As he'd done countless times before, he read the will. He reminded himself of the fact that the attorney had affirmed the will's rigidness. "Iron clad" was the term he used. As long as Lane was living on the property when he turned nineteen, the farm was his. The house. The land. Everything. If Gunner ramped up his abuse, would it eventually drive Lane away? Gunner set the will aside and focused on the insurance policy. The premiums were paid up until Lane reached the age of 21. Lane's mother was the beneficiary which meant Gunner was the beneficiary now. Five hundred thousand dollars would fix all of Gunner's problems. Plus, the farm would belong to him too. All he had to do was . . . orchestrate Lane's death. Gunner's gambling addiction had caught up with him. The knife was at his throat. Ninety days would pass like the wink of an eye. Gunner placed the documents back in the box and slid it back under the bed. He walked to the kitchen, grabbed the last two beers from the fridge and headed out the back door. The truck coughed and backfired when he turned the key. He goosed the accelerator a few times to level off the struggling motor and popped open one of the beers. He took a long drink to cut the edge off his nerves and dropped the gear shifter into the "D" position. Gravel fanned from the rear of the truck and sprayed the side of the house as he U-turned and roared down the driveway. He felt he could strategize better sitting behind the wheel than he could sitting in his recliner.

•   •   •

It had been another great day with Desi. The motor was back in the Cutlass and she sounded like she did the day she rolled off the assembly line. Desi and Becky were thrilled at how Lane and Abigail's relationship seemed to be progressing and expressed their excitement to double-date with them sooner rather than later. Lane parked Denver Banks' truck next to Gunner's and texted Abigail.

Just got home from work.

She replied immediately. *Cool. I'm in the middle of something. I'll let you know when I'm free.*

Lane responded with a thumbs-up emoji.

When Lane walked in the back door, Gunner met him in the kitchen, his eyes void of affection. "How much did Desi pay you today?"

The question caught Lane by surprise. He hesitated.

Gunner clinched fists at his sides. "Answer me!"

"A hundred bucks," Lane said.

Gunner shot a hand forward. "Give it to me."

Lane pulled his wallet from his back pocket and unfolded it. He took out a C-note and handed it to Gunner.

"Is that all you got?"

Lane hesitated again. He didn't want to answer.

"Give me that!" Gunner yelled and snatched the wallet like a hungry predator snatching its prey. He took the remaining two tens from it. "I know you've been holding out on me. Leaving money on your nightstand. I'm not stupid. Where you keeping the rest of it?"

Lane wasn't about to tell him about the checking account or the twenty and the ten tucked inside the pages of the Gideon Bible. "I'm not telling you."

Fire filled Gunner's eyes. "You're not telling me, huh." He grabbed Lane by one arm and pulled him along as he made his way out of the kitchen and through the house. "You're gonna respect me or I'll beat you to death. What you said the other day about you wanting us to get along was a sack of bull crap. I'm your father and you're gonna treat me like it. And that little speech of yours about when you turn nineteen doesn't mean jack. I adopted you which means I can change the will." He paused from wrestling Lane along and looked him dead in the eyes. "And guess what, Headlight. That's exactly what I did. I changed it. Now, the only way this farm will ever be yours is if I give it to you. And guess what? I ain't never giving it to you. So, you can learn to like the way things run around here or you can leave. Move out and pay your own bills. I don't care. It's your choice."

Lane's eyes filled with tears. "You've taken everything else. But you can't take this farm. It's mine when I turn nineteen. Mom told me so."

"She lied to you, Headlight. This farm belongs to me."

Gunner jerked Lane into the back bedroom and pulled the strap from the closet door. The doorbell rang.

The rage subsided from Gunner's expression. "Who you expecting?"

"Nobody."

"Just a minute!" Gunner called out and returned the strap to the hook on the back of the door. He released Lane. "You mind yourself, now. You hear me."

In silence, Lane stood like a statue, his chin lowered to his chest.

Gunner shoved him on one shoulder. "I said, 'You hear me!'"

Lane nodded.

"Come on. Let's see who's here."

Lane wiped the wetness from his eyes as they walked to the front door. Gunner opened it. Abigail stood before them holding two small jars. "Surprise," she said and extended the jars to them.

"I made one for each of you. Pear preserves with peaches. They have your names on them."

Gunner took the one with his name on it, Lane the one with his.

"Well, that's mighty neighborly of you," Gunner said with the courteous demeanor of time share salesman. "Won't you come in?"

"Mom and Dad drove me over." She motioned toward her mom's Mercedes parked behind Gunner's truck. "They're in the car."

"Well, tell them to come in too."

Abigail threw up a hand toward the car and made a "Come on" motion. Will, Erica and Brodie got out and started up the driveway. Gunner stepped out on the porch. "Great to see y'all. Come on in. Me and Lane have been meaning to have y'all over for a visit."

Lane looked at Abigail and rolled his eyes. Once everyone was inside, Gunner encouraged them to have a seat and offered them something to drink. Each of the Westons assured Gunner that they were fine. Erica began scanning the house. "This is a beautiful home."

"Thank you," Gunner said.

Lane decided to apply one of the principles from *The Art of War*. "My dad built it with his own hands when he was still alive." *If your opponent of is choleric temper, seek to irritate him.*

Lane cut a look to Gunner in time to notice him tighten his jaw. Lane reveled inside at the blow he'd scored against Gunner. It was an opportune moment for another principle.

"By the way, I just got home from work. Greasy and sweaty from working on a car all day. Mind if I take a few minutes and get cleaned up?" *If we do not wish to fight, we can prevent the enemy from engaging us. All we need to do is to throw something odd and unaccountable in his way.*

Gunner adjusted himself in his chair. "Son, don't you think that'd be kinda rude. Our guests just got here."

Will Weston shooed with one hand and raised one side of his mouth. "Aw, we're perfectly fine." He looked at Lane. "Go ahead, Lane. It'll give us some time to get to know Gunner a little better."

Lane stood from his seat. "I'll only be a few minutes." He stepped to his bedroom to get some clean clothes. In less than ten minutes he was back in the den. Gunner was laying the manure on thick, talking about how he planned to monetize the farm again one day. Livestock. Crops. Fruit trees. Beehives. Lane recoiled on the inside.

"You clean up nice," Abigail said and smiled.

Her compliment was delicious to his soul. "Thanks."

"We thought we'd drive over to Oxford for some mini golf and go-carts. Lane, you wanna join us?"

Lane came alive. "Heck yeah. Sounds fun."

Will turned his attention to Gunner. "It's fine with you if Lane comes along. Right?"

"Absolutely. I wish I could join you all myself, but I have something I have to do this evening."

Will looked at his family and Lane and slapped his palms on the tops of his thighs. "Okay, then. Let's get going, gang."

CHAPTER FOURTEEN

Lane climbed the makeshift ladder and pulled himself up through the trap door. He reached down with his right hand. Abigail took it and Lane lifted her into the one structure on the property that stirred not a single bad memory in Lane's mind. Not only had Gunner never been to the treehouse, but he didn't even know it existed.

Abigail ran her fingers over the spines of the classic novels on the shelf. She slipped on the weathered baseball glove and pounded the inside a few times with a fist. She returned it to its place and straightened the picture of Lane standing in front of a wooden Indian.

"It was taken in the Smoky Mountains," Lane said.

"My favorite place," Abigail said in a tone just above a whisper.

"You never told me you'd been to the Smoky Mountains."

"Because I haven't."

"But you just said it's your favorite place."

"No, I didn't."

"Come on, Abigail. I just heard you say, 'It's my favorite place.'"

Abigail turned and looked him in the eyes. "No, Lane. You didn't hear me say 'IT'S my favorite place.' You heard me simply say, 'MY favorite place.'"

Lane drew down his brow. "Same thing."

Abigail shook her head. "No. Totally different." She raised her opened palms just above her waist. "I meant this place is my favorite place."

"This place, as in this treehouse?"

"Exactly." She sat down, leaned her back against the wall and wrapped her arms around her knees. "I love this old treehouse. I come here sometimes. It's a good place to think and pray and dream."

"I didn't know you'd been coming here."

"I know. I didn't think you'd mind."

Lane sat down against the opposite wall. "Not at all. Come here anytime you want."

She looked around and scanned the inside of the small room and studied the ceiling. "Good. Because I'd come even if you said it wasn't okay. You'd have to have me arrested for trespassing to keep me out." She turned her attention to Lane. "I want to ask you something."

"Sure. Shoot."

Her face displayed uncertainty. "I noticed when I was at your house that your record player and record collection were missing. Why's that?"

Lane curled his lip in disgust. "Gunner pawned them off somewhere. Said he needed the money. Didn't say for what. Just said it was, quote, necessary," Lane said, making quotation gestures with his fingers for emphasis. "He's taken just about everything from me. He'd even take the jar of marmalade you made me if you hadn't made him one too."

"I'll be making some more for the two of you. And for heaven's sake, don't ever eat any of his."

"Don't worry I won't. You saw what he did to my back. He'll take the strap to me again if I so much as look at him the wrong way. He was going to beat me with it yesterday, but you rang the doorbell just as he was about to start. Desi paid me a hundred dollars for helping him put the motor back in his car. When I came home, Gunner took it. He always takes my money. That's one of the reasons I opened a checking account—to keep him from taking it. I hate him. I wish he was dead."

"You do?"

"Yeah. I do."

"Then pray."

"Pray?"

"Yeah, ask God to change him or kill him. I'll be praying too." Abigail made a backhand motion. "Enough about him. Let's talk about something else. Tell me more about Desi and Becky. I'd like to meet them sometime."

Lane told her how the Pritchards lived in a cool cabin in the woods. About the signs posted on the trees and how Becky was not only cool but also was a great cook. That the yellow rose was her idea and that her truck was beautiful. That she and Desi didn't have children and how they treated him like he was their son. He also told her about Desi knowing his way around cars and how he'd given Lane some great advice about life and being a man. "And they're really interested in meeting you," Lane said.

Abigail smiled. "I'd like that. Let me know when."

"How's this Friday night?"

"Sounds good. Let me double check with mom and dad." Abigail stared into his eyes but said nothing.

Lane grinned. "What?"

"Come over here next to me."

Lane scooted across the floor on his backside until he was next to her.

"Look at me," she said.

Lane looked into her brown eyes.

Her expression was serious, inviting. "You can kiss me if you want."

"Really?"

Abigail nodded. "Really."

Lane leaned his face close to hers and gently pressed his lips to hers. She reached over with one hand and gripped the top of his leg just above his knee as they enjoyed each other's mouth. They slowly refrained and leaned their foreheads together.

Lane pulled back and combed one hand through her blonde hair. "Abigail, I don't mean to scare you, but I want to ask you something."

She held her eyes on his. "You're not gonna scare me."

Lane inhaled and exhaled through his nostrils. "Will you be my girl?"

Abigail reached up and touched the side of his face with her fingertips. Her eyes welled. A drop leaked over one eyelid and rolled down her cheek. "I've been your girl from the very beginning."

Lane grinned, his heart filled with affection for her. "Seriously?"

"Yup. When I looked at you through those binoculars that day, I knew."

"I'll always be good to you," Lane said. "Always."

"I don't doubt that for a minute. But there's one thing you have to do."

"Name it."

"You have to talk to my dad. You have to tell him how you feel about me and ask for his blessing. I promised him a long time ago that I'd trust him when this time came. My dad is a good man. The best, actually. And I can't break my word to him."

"I'll do it. When can I talk to him?"

"He's home right now."

"Let's go."

•   •   •

The door was open. Will Weston sat at his desk, reading one of the many books that lay stacked on top of it. Abigail rapped her knuckles on the door facing. Will looked up from the page. "Hey, Honey. What's up?"

"Lane needs to talk to you."

Will removed his reading glasses and set them on the desk. "Okay. Tell him to come in."

Lane stepped into the room.

"Hey, Lane," Will said.

"Hello, Dr. Weston."

Will motioned to the door. "Shut the door and come have a seat."

Two stationary chairs sat across from the office desk. Lane eased the door shut and sat down in one of them, Dr. Weston the other.

"Okay. What's on your mind?

Lane cleared his throat. "Well, Sir. It's about Abigail." Lane paused and searched for words.

"I see. Go on," Dr. Weston said.

"She's some kind of girl. I mean she's really special."

Will smiled. "She really is."

"Well, the fact is, Sir. I care very deeply for her. I think about her all the time. To be honest, she's the only girl I think about. She cares for me too. I asked her to be my girl and she said she would be, but that I had to come get your blessing. And that's what I'm here for, to ask for your blessing. I promise you I'll always be good to her."

"I believe you, Lane. And I'll give my blessing for the two of you to spend time together and see where things go. But I do have some things that I expect from you."

"Anything, Sir. Anything at all."

"First of all, in light of our conversation on the patio the other day, I want you to seriously pray about doing what we talked about."

Lane nodded. "I will."

"The next thing is, I want you and I to establish a time to meet once a week for about an hour or so until I say otherwise. Our conversations will be man to man about the Bible and about you and Abigail."

"I'd really like that."

Dr. Weston narrowed his eyes and peered into Lane's. Lane felt his heart begin to pound. He adjusted in his chair. "Now, for the third thing. Lane, there are boundaries that you and Abigail are not to cross. And I'm expecting you to be the leader and set the tone when it comes to those boundaries." Dr. Weston raised his brow and nodded deliberately.

"Yessir."

"Abigail being your girl is not the same as Abigail being your wife. Do I need to go into detail?"

Lane shook his head. "No, Sir. I understand exactly what you are saying."

Dr. Weston interlocked his fingers in front of his stomach. "Good. Here's the rule I want you to follow. If it's not something you'd do in the presence of her mother and me then you don't do it. Got it?"

"Got it."

"Now, I realize that you and Abigail are human. And that you are attracted to each other. You have my permission to hold her hand and you have my permission to kiss her. Beyond that, remember, she's your girl. She's not your wife. When you bring her home from whatever it is the two of you might go out and do, I expect her to be just like she was when you picked her up. Do you get my drift?"

"Totally."

Dr. Weston relaxed the intensity in his face and smiled. "Okay, then. Go get Abigail and bring her in here. I want to speak to the two of you together."

"Yessir."

Lane stood to his feet and exited the room. In less than a minute, he and Abigail were seated in the stationary chairs, Will Weston in the chair behind his desk.

"Abigail, I have given my blessing to Lane. I believe he is a young man of character who genuinely cares for you and will strive to defend your honor."

Dr. Weston's words made Lane feel like he had the Superman logo on his chest and a cape hanging down his back. The preacher slid open a drawer of his desk and pulled out a gold chain necklace. At the end of it dangled the arrowhead Lane had given Abigail.

"I think you recognize this. Don't you, Lane."

Lane grinned. "I sure do."

Dr. Weston handed the necklace to Abigail. "Abigail, I think you have something you'd like to say to Lane."

Abigail held the necklace up before Lane. "Because it came from you, this arrowhead is one of my most treasured possessions. In anticipation of this day, I went and had it made into this necklace. I want you to put it on me. I'll wear it to let everyone know that I'm your girl."

Lane's chin began to quiver. He pinched the tears from his eyes.

"Would you put it around my neck?" she asked.

"I'd love to," Lane replied.

They both stood and Lane placed the necklace around her neck. He embraced her, then looked at Dr. Weston. "May I?" he asked.

The preacher smiled. "Yes, you may."

Lane kissed her and embraced her again. They sat back down. Dr. Weston reached into the drawer again and pulled out a large silver coin and handed it to Lane. Lane studied the coin. It had the image of a crowned woman on the front and was dated 1921. On the back it had the image of an eagle.

"It's a silver dollar. Pure silver," Dr. Weston said. "I'd like for you to look at it often and, when you do, think about this day and the character commitment you've made to look after my daughter and your girl."

Lane clutched the big coin and looked Abigail's father in the eyes. "I give you my word."

CHAPTER FIFTEEN

Lane opened the brown paper bag Abigail had sent him home with and took out one of the jars of jelly. It had his name on it, so he placed it in the cabinet where he kept HIS food items. Gainful employment had unshackled him from Gunner's dietary bondage. Gone were the days of the cardboard cereal and the meager rations allocated to him by the nemesis he had to live with. Lane now had his own cabinet, and he filled it with plenty of the foods he loved. He took out the second jar. It had Gunner's name on it. Lane left it on the counter in plain sight for Gunner to see and pulled open the refrigerator. He took a can of soda pop from a shelf inside the fridge and retired to the back porch. The sun was half on the horizon, but it was still pushing ninety degrees. Lane chugged down a trio of swallows of the soda and set the can next to one leg of his chair. He pulled out his recently acquired most prized earthly possession from his pocket, a silver dollar minted during a time when Warren Harding was the US president. The vintage coin was valuable monetarily, no doubt. Probably a hundred dollars or more. But to Lane it was worth a fortune, more even. As he studied it, he dreamed of the future, Abigail at his side, not just as his girl (she'd always be his girl) but as his wife. He'd revive the farm, make it alive and robust like it used to be when his dad was alive. Abigail could help if she wanted, or she could get her degree from Ole Miss and work teaching kids. Whatever she wanted to do was fine with Lane. He just wanted her to be happy and he'd do everything in his power to make her happiness a reality. They'd have children. Go on vacations. Have amazing Christmases. Grow old together.

"What do you have there?" came the voice that made Lane's blood curdle.

How come Lane didn't hear Gunner drive up? Was he so much in a zone that he was oblivious even to the obnoxious sound of Gunner's ratty truck? In a flash Lane fisted the big coin and cut a look to the back door of the house. Gunner stood in the threshold with the door open. "Surprised you, huh? A guy in the shop at work welded the exhaust on my truck so it doesn't run loud no more."

Lane said nothing.

Gunner shot him a devilish grin and raised his chin. "So, what'ya got?"

Lane turned his attention toward the horizon and held his silence.

"Come on, Headlight," he said and stepped onto the porch. "I know you're hiding something." He walked around in front of Lane and extended an open hand. "Let me see it."

Lane squeezed the dollar tight and looked at Gunner defiantly. "No. It's got nothing to do with you."

Gunner narrowed hateful eyes. "Oh, but it does. Everything about you has something to do with me, so let me see it." He punched Lane on the shoulder then shot his hand back in front of Lane's face.

"No!" Lane said defiantly.

Gunner stepped back, lifted a foot and kicked the arm of Lane's chair toppling it over on one side. The impact slammed Lane hard against the floor. As he struggled to get to his feet, Gunner shoved him down on his back. Gunner grabbed the hand with the dollar in it and pressed it to the floor and placed his boot on Lane's wrist. He transferred his weight to the leg that pinned Lane's arm. Lane winced in pain.

"Open it or I'll break it."

Lane slowly opened his hand. Gunner took the silver dollar and backed up a few steps, studying the coin.

"Well. Well. Well. Lookie here. Probably worth something."

Lane stood to his feet, rubbing his throbbing wrist. "That's mine! You can't have it!"

"This must be real special to you. Where'd you get it?"

"None of your business."

Gunner leered at Lane then shot his eyes open wide, his brow raised, an evil grin on his face. "Oh, I see. That little whore gave it to you, didn't she?"

A volcano of rage erupted in Lane.

Therefore the good fighter will be terrible in his onset, and prompt in his decision. Sun Tzu.

Lane rushed forward and tackled Gunner at the waist. The impact thrust Gunner hard against the wooden planks. Lane drew up on his knees and straddled Gunner's torso. He started pummeling him in the face with his fists. Blood flowed from Gunner's nose. A cut opened up over one of his eyebrows. Gunner released the silver dollar. It fell on the porch surface with a thud. Lane stopped punching and grabbed Gunner at the throat. He reached for the coin and held it close to Gunner's face. "You listen to me. If you EVER touch this again, I'll kill you." He clinched the coin into a fist. "If you EVER call her that again, I'll kill you. You got it?" he said, applying pressure to Gunner's throat.

Gunner looked at Lane as if Lane held a gun to his head. "Yeah . . . yeah, I got it."

"And another thing. In a couple of months, I'll be nineteen. Start looking for another place to live."

Gunner nodded as best he could. "Okay . . . okay."

Lane gnashed his teeth, one side of his upper lip curled. He flinched his fist close to Gunner's nose. "Hmph!"

Lane let go of Gunner's throat and climbed off of him. Gunner got up. Lane cold-stared him in the eyes. Slowly, Gunner backed away a few steps then turned and scurried down the steps and onto the yard. Lane stood and watched as Gunner trotted to his truck, one hand cupped over his nose. He fired up the bag of bolts and drove away. Lane opened his hand and gazed at the shiny antique dollar. He'd defended Abigail's honor. Not just because he'd told Will Weston he would, but for a reason that resided deep in the core of his soul. He loved Abigail.

•   •   •

Word around Locust Fork was that Michael Birelli was the richest man in town. Exactly what it was he did for a living, no one seemed to know for certain. Some said he owned a shipping company that transported containers from China to the United States. Others swore he spent most of his days in his pajamas sitting in his bed and, with nothing more than his laptop, raked in millions each year playing the stock market. To hear others tell it, he owned a New York City real estate empire. Whatever the man did, one thing was certain—he lived in the biggest house in town. Birelli Villa looked like a cover of *Architectural Digest*. The Sicilian mansion set on a posh five acres secured by a nine-foot wrought iron fence, greystone posts with finial caps every ten feet. A row of shaped evergreen shrubs lined each side of the cobblestone drive that led from the public road to the front courtyard. Halfway between the house and the road, water cascaded into a marble pool from the mouths of four bronze male lions. Each stood on its hind legs and faced outward. Lane drove the Grasshopper off the trailer and began transforming the ankle-high grass into a carpet, Johnny Cash playing in his ear buds. As he trimmed around the stately water fountain, two vehicles rolling up the drive caught his attention. The first was a Banks' Landscaping pickup truck, the other a Locust Fork patrol car. They came to a stop when they reached the house. Two police officers got out of the squad car; Denver Banks emerged from the truck. Banks threw up an arm and motioned for Lane to come to him. Lane concurred. He stopped the zero turn a few feet from where the men stood, shut down the engine and removed his earbuds. Denver Banks' expression displayed concern.

"Are you Lane Hubbard?" one of the officers said.

"Yessir."

"Would you please get off the machine and put your hands behind your back?"

Lane looked at the officer and then at Denver. "What's going on?"

Denver shook his head and shrugged as if to say, "I don't know."

"Mr. Hubbard, get off the machine and place your hands behind your back."

Lane obeyed. The second officer began cuffing Lane.

The first officer continued. "You have the right to remain silent. If you do say anything, what you say can be used against you in a court of law. You have the right to consult with a lawyer and have that lawyer present during any questioning. If you cannot afford a lawyer, one will be appointed for you, if you desire. Do you understand these rights?"

"Yessir."

The officers escorted Lane to the squad car and sat him in the back seat.

"I'll see you at the police station," Denver said.

As the policemen drove Lane away, Lane looked back and watched another of Denver Banks' employees get out of the truck and climb onto the Grasshopper.

Lane had never been inside the Locust Fork police station. The activity inside set his nerves on edge. A lady sat against one wall, a cool, couldn't care less expression on her face. A man wearing a blue sport coat and paisley tie sat next to her. "Rochelle, I'll do my best, but I'm not sure I can get you out of this. It's the third time in two months."

On the other side of the room a teenage boy that Lane didn't recognize sat next to a lady. She wore a brown skirt, a matching jacket and beige pumps.

"I'm telling you. He told me it was his car. If I'd known it was stolen I woulda never agreed to drive it," the boy said, his eyes red and moist. He shot his hands to the sides of his head. The lady patted him on one knee. "I'll do my best to have you out of here first thing in the morning."

"This way," one of the officers said to Lane and tugged him by one arm.

Denver walked into the station, Becky Pritchard with him. Lane cut her a look. She shot him a wink. Lane felt a little comforted by it and raised his chin toward her.

A door buzzed. The first officer opened it and held it as the second officer walked Lane into whatever was on the other side. A female officer sat behind a plexiglass partition. The officer uncuffed Lane.

The lady officer slid a metal bowl through the opening of the plexiglass. "Empty everything from your pockets."

Lane placed his cell phones, ear buds, wallet, and the silver dollar in it.

"You'll see him next," she said and motioned to an officer at a counter opposite her.

Lane stepped to the counter. "Give me your right hand and spread your fingers," the officer said.

Lane abided by his command. One by one the officer rolled Lane's fingers on an ink pad and then rolled them on a piece of paper. Lane was being booked. When finished, the officer took three pictures of Lane. A frontal face shot and a profile of both his right and his left sides. Lane was then escorted to another room, told to strip, given an orange jump suit and a pair of rubber slides for his feet. On the front just under Lane's left shoulder was the number 56732. On the back the words *Locust Fork City Jail*. Lane was then taken into a long room further in the complex. An aisle extended down the middle of the room. Iron bars formed cells along each wall.

"All the way down to the end and to the left," an officer said.

Lane lumbered down the aisle. He'd heard horror stories about what men did to each other in prisons. Did they do that kind of stuff in the Locust Fork jail? He prayed not and hoped he'd have a cell all to himself.

His hopes proved futile. A rotund white man with fiery orange hair sat on one of the benches inside the cell, a short, lean Hispanic man sat on the other. Lane eased into the cell. The door clanged shut behind him. The white man looked up at Lane. His goatee stretched as he smiled. "Welcome home, Kid."

Lane stood in the middle of the cell, speechless.

"I'm Leroy," he said and motioned with his head. "Might as well come have a seat. It'll be an all-nighter at minimum."

"I'm fine. I think I'll just stand."

"First time?" the Hispanic man said, his mouth populated with a handful of gold teeth.

He reached out a hand. "I'm Emilio. But people call me Mill."

With trepidation Lane shook Mill's hand.

"Don't worry. We know how you feel. But, trust us, you'll be fine," Leroy said. "You won't sleep at all, but you'll be fine. Now, have a seat and tell us who you are."

Lane sat down and introduced himself as Lane, just Lane.

"What're you here for?" Mill asked.

"I'm really not sure."

Leroy stroked his beard. "We know how that is too."

"Si," Mill added.

"I'm guessing," Lane said. "It has something to do with a confrontation I had with my stepdad yesterday. We got into it and I just snapped."

"Why'd you snap?"

Lane told them about the silver dollar and the story behind it and about Gunner calling Abigail a whore.

Mill pointed to the heart tattooed on his forearm, the name Rosa written in cursive underneath it. "I'd snap too if someone called my Rosa a puta. She's my world and the mother of my two kids."

"What went down after that?" Leroy asked.

"I just lost it. I turned into something I've never been before. I tackled him and started punching him in the face. His nose was pouring blood and he had a big cut over one eye."

Leroy grinned and offered Lane a fist bump. "My man."

Lane touched a fist to Leroy's.

"How old are you, Amigo?"

"Eighteen. About to be nineteen."

Mill made a shooing motion with one hand. "You'll be fine. It's your first time. The judge will probably just throw it out."

Leroy nodded. "Yeah. First offense. It'll be nothing."

The door at the end of the aisle buzzed. The sound of footsteps got louder as whoever it was came closer. Lane, Leroy and Mill paused their conversation and waited. A tall black man stopped in front of their cell. His narrow hips and broad shoulders bore witness that he was no stranger to a gym. He wore a hunter green three button jacket and matching pants, cream-colored vest, a white shirt, a necktie the same color as the vest, and a pair of brown and white wing tips. In one hand he held a brown briefcase. He shot Lane a movie star smile. "You must be Lane."

"Yessir."

"I'm Drexel Reece and I'm your lawyer."

Drexel Reece looked back toward the cell block entry door. "Warden, I need to speak privately with my client."

The warden stepped to the cell, unlocked it with a key and pulled open the door.

Lane didn't move.

Drexel motioned to Lane. "Well, come on. Let's go."

Lane jumped to his feet. "You mean I can leave."

"Not just yet. You'll have to appear before the judge. We'll meet in a conference room here. Hopefully, you'll be able to appear before the judge first thing in the morning and we'll go from there."

Lane followed Drexel down the gangway. The warden opened a door and Drexel and Lane passed through. An officer cuffed Lane and led them to a small room. It had two chairs and a stainless-steel table.

"Let's sit down and get started," Drexel said and sat down in one of the chairs.

Lane sat down in the other. Drexel unzipped his briefcase and pulled out a file. He took a document from the file. "Do you know a Gunner Hubbard?"

"Yessir. He's my stepdad."

"Well, it seems your stepdad has filed charges against you for assault and battery. Have you ever been in jail before?"

"No, Sir. And I can explain what happened."

"We'll get to that in a minute. How old are you?"

"Eighteen."

"Do you and Mr. Hubbard live in the same house?"

"Yessir." Lane leaned forward. "He's a bad man. Been abusing me ever since my mother died."

"This police report says you attacked him. Did you?"

"He took something from me and called my girlfriend a whore!" Lane exclaimed, his words jacked with passion.

Drexel set the police report on top of the file and looked Lane straight in the eyes. "Look, Lane, I'm on your side. I promise. We can talk in detail about your homelife later, but for right now I need you to get control of yourself and simply answer my questions. Trust me, I know what I'm doing."

Lane inhaled and exhaled and tried to wrestle his anxiety into submission. He nodded. "Yessir. I beat him up pretty good."

"Did you use anything?"

"Like for a weapon or something?"

"Yes."

"No. I just tackled him and punched him in the face with my fists some."

"Did you tell him you were going to kill him?"

"I told him I would if he ever touched the silver dollar he was trying to steal from me or if he ever called my girlfriend a whore again."

Drexel studied the report. As he did, he drew down his brow and pushed up his top lip with his bottom. "Mm. Says here that Mr. Hubbard came out on the porch where you were and told you to come in the house and clean the kitchen and wash the dishes. He stated that you swore at him then tackled him and proceeded to beat him up yelling, 'I'm gonna kill you. I'm gonna kill you.' Mr. Hubbard stated that, though injured, he managed to free himself and run from the scene. He then drove himself to the emergency room where he was given medical attention."

"That's not how it happened. Like I said I did beat him up, but not because I didn't want to clean the kitchen and wash dishes."

"I see. I've heard all I need to know for now. I'll be back tomorrow. Should anyone pay you a visit, don't tell them anything. Let me do all your talking for you. Got it?"

"Yessir."

Drexel slid the file back into his briefcase. He zipped the briefcase closed and stood from his chair. "Remember," he said, using an index finger for emphasis. "Don't speak to anyone."

Lane acknowledged the command and stood from his chair. They exited the room. An exit door buzzed, and Drexel left. The officer escorted Lane back to the warden and uncuffed him. The warden returned him to the cell. Leroy and Mill started quizzing him about his meeting with Drexel.

•   •   •

Drexel returned the next day at 8:30 AM. He wore a navy three-piece suit with noticeable pinstripes, a white shirt, a red and white striped necktie, and black wingtips. A white handkerchief plumed from the chest pocket of his coat and, in one hand, he carried the brown briefcase. "Good news, Lane. You're appearing before the judge in thirty minutes. Let's go."

Lane hadn't slept the night before. Who could in a room with no bed shared with two strangers. Nice strangers, but strangers, nonetheless. Lane stood to his feet. Mill and Leroy wished him good luck. The warden opened the cell door and Lane followed Drexel out of the cellblock. An officer cuffed Lane once again and escorted Lane and Drexel out of the facility. The Huntsville County Courthouse was the focal point of the Locust Fork town square and located directly across the street from the jail. When they reached the courthouse, the officer motioned toward a side door. "Lane you and I are going through that door." He looked at Drexel, "Counselor, you'll have to go through the front." Before they parted ways, Drexel assured Lane of the fact that he'd see him in the courtroom.

Lane was taken to a holding room inside the courthouse. Several people, both men and women, were already seated in the room when Lane arrived. All wore orange jumpsuits. Lane had no more than just sat down when a well-dressed woman appeared. "When I call your name, please come forward."

Lane's name was the first name she called. In less than five minutes he found himself standing in front of the judge's bench, Drexel at his side and what looked like more than one hundred onlookers seated behind him in the courtroom. Lane guessed the judged to be about the same age as Will Weston. The knot of his gray necktie barely could be seen just above the zipper of his black robe. His black hair was combed straight back on his head and held in place by styling gel. The gel made his hair shine a bit. Black rimmed glasses set low on the bridge of his nose. He focused his attention on Lane. "Are you Lane Hubbard?"

Lane answered in the manner Drexel had instructed him. "Yes, Your Honor."

The judge looked at Drexel. "And I'm assuming you are Mr. Hubbard's counsel."

"I am, Your Honor."

"This is the first time I've seen you in my courtroom. Would you please identify yourself?"

"Drexel Reece, Your Honor."

"Mr. Reece, are you new to this area?"

"No, Your Honor. I'm out of the Jackson office of Stein, Reinhold and Fitzpatrick."

The judge looked at Drexel over the top of his eyeglasses. "You hunt with some mighty big dogs, Mr. Reece. I hope our small-town court is not below you."

"Not at all, Your Honor."

"Mr. Reece, your client is charged with assault and battery. How does he plead?"

"Not guilty, Your Honor."

"Well, Mr. Reece, it's going to be interesting hearing you defend Mr. Hubbard. I looked at the police photos of the victim. You're gonna have your work cut out for you when it comes to convincing a jury that the wounds incurred by the victim were somehow either not criminal or Mr. Hubbard had nothing whatsoever to do with them. Trial is set for November 3rd."

"Your Honor, might I speak freely?"

"Yes, Counselor. You may."

"My client has never had as much as a speeding ticket. We'd like to request that the charges be dismissed."

The judge pushed his eyeglasses up on the bridge of his nose. "Mr. Reece, if the matter at hand involved a traffic violation or a petty theft even, I'd be glad to honor your request. But we're talking sixteen stitches and possible reconstructive surgery. Your client may be a teenager, but what the victim suffered is major. We're not talking about a situation where your client may have made a foolish youthful misstep. It looks like he may have possibly caused permanent damage to the victim. And on top of that, the report says your client told the victim during the supposed altercation, and I quote, 'I'm gonna kill you. I'm gonna kill you.' The wheels of justice need to turn in this situation. Therefore, your request is denied. Bond is set for fifty thousand dollars. I'll see both of you here on November 3rd." The judge rapped his gavel. "Bailiff, bring in the next one."

CHAPTER SIXTEEN

The warden unlocked the cell door. "Lane Hubbard, you're free to go."

Lane stood to his feet. Leroy shook his hand. "Take care of yourself, Little Brother. It'll all work out."

Mill patted Lane on the shoulder with a cupped hand and pulled him in for a hug. He positioned his mouth close to Lane's ear. "We're family now, Amigo," he said in a tone just above a whisper. "When I get out, my boys and I are available should you ever need us. If your stepdad gives you any problems, just let me know. Remember, Miguel's Cantina on Fifth Street. Ask for Berto. He knows how to hit me up twenty-four seven."

"Thanks, Mill."

Mill clapped Lane on the back a few times. "Be safe."

Lane walked out of the cell and put his hands behind his back, anticipating the cuffs.

"No cuffs," the warden said. "Somebody posted your bail."

Lane followed the warden to the door. The door buzzed and Lane stepped into the next room. Three officers sat on chairs at the table where Lane had been booked. Lane's clothes and belongings were returned to him. When he had changed back into his clothes, one of the officers motioned to a door where a lady officer stood. "Through there."

The door buzzed. The lady pulled the door open, and Lane exited. The large main room of the police station was alive with numerous conversations.

A female voice prevailed over all the others. "Lane!"

Lane looked cut a look in the direction of the voice. Becky Pritchard stood, her raised hand motioning in order to get his attention. They left the police station. Becky's truck was parked across the street. The truck chirped when she pressed the key fob. They got in and drove away.

"So, what's going on?" Becky asked.

"I beat Gunner up yesterday and he filed charges against me."

"What did he do to start a fight with you?"

At last! Not 'Why did YOU beat HIM up,' but 'What did HE do to start a fight with YOU?'

Lane told her the whole story as well as much of his and Gunner's history together. Becky's body language and the comments she interjected from time to time revealed her shock and anger at what had transpired in Lane's life since the death of his mother.

"I'm taking you to our house tonight. You're staying with us for at least the next few nights. This is all insane. Desi'll be talking to Gunner. I can promise you that."

"Okay. But I need to talk to Abigail and Dr. Weston about all of this."

"We'll swing by your house so you can grab some clothes. You can take me home and then use my truck to go to their house."

"Thanks, Becky. I need to explain everything to Denver too."

"He probably knows already. The lawyer told him, I'm sure."

"Why would he be talking to the lawyer?

"As soon as the cops came looking for you, Denver called Desi and then Michael Birelli. Birelli referred him to the law firm he uses down in Jackson. They sent Drexel up here. I'm sure Drexel's good."

"Who posted my bail?"

"Denver."

•   •   •

Lane called Will Weston and asked to meet with him, Erica and Abigail. Lane suggested that Brodie occupy himself in his room or busy himself with something outside. "What I want to talk to you about is of a mature nature," Lane said.

When he arrived at the Weston's, Abigail met him on the sidewalk. Hand in hand they walked into the house. Dr. Weston and Erica were waiting in the den. Lane and Abigail sat down next to each other on the sofa and Lane filled them in on what had happened. As he'd done with Becky, he also told them of his burdensome history with Gunner, matters that Abigail was aware of, but which were new revelations for Will and Erica. Abigail squeezed Lane's hand and leaned her head on his shoulder during the parts of the story that caused Lane to get emotional. When he finished, he asked Will, "So, Dr. Weston, was I wrong to beat up Gunner?"

"I would have done the same thing if I were you."

Lane perked up. "Really?"

"Really. Being a Christian doesn't mean being weak and passive. As a matter of fact, the Bible says in the book of Ecclesiastes that there is a time for war. When Gunner took the coin from you and said what he said about Abigail, he was declaring war in a sense. What you did was honorable and manly and, as Abigail's father, I want you to know that I appreciate it and that I'm proud of you. I thought a lot of you before and I think even more of you now."

Once again, Lane felt like he was wearing Superman's cape. "Thank you, Dr. Weston. I was afraid you'd be disappointed in me."

"Well, I'm anything BUT. And I'll do all I can to help you. Tell your attorney I'll be glad to be a character witness for you when the trial comes."

•   •   •

Gunner pushed the mute button on the remote when he heard the doorbell ring. Could it be that Miss Red's henchman had come to pay a threatening visit? He still had six weeks to come up with the money. Had she changed her mind and wanted the money now? If such was the case, Gunner's life was over. At best, he'd be maimed for life. At worst, he'd be tortured slowly and then killed. "Just a minute!" he called out. He took a long swig of his beer and went to his bedroom. When he reached for knob of the front door, the semi-automatic handgun was tucked in the top of his jeans and covered by his shirt tail. He opened to the door. Will Weston stood before him.

"Oh . . . uh, hey preacher. Wasn't expecting you. You uh . . . you wanna come inside?"

Will Weston looked Gunner in the eyes. "No, Gunner. I'll say what I've come to say from where I stand."

Gunner swallowed a hard lump.

"I had a conversation with Lane just a while ago."

Gunner felt his blood cool in his veins. "That boy's dangerous and he's lying to you."

"No, he's not and I believe every word he told me. And I've come to tell you that if you ever lay a hand on him again or take anything of his or say anything about my daughter ever again, you'll have to deal with me." Will looked at the pathetic excuse of a man as if he would run through him. "Trust me, that's something you don't want to happen. I have no problem spending the rest of my life in prison should I have to. Feel free to read whatever you want to into what I'm saying."

"Preacher, are you threatening me?"

Will shook his head. "Nope. I'm simply telling you the truth."

Will reached into a front pocket of his trousers and pulled out his cell phone. He held it up before Gunner. "By the way, I just recorded this conversation in case you're considering running back down to the police station and filing another false report. Now, if you ever have a change of heart and want your life to turn around, I'm glad to help you. You know where to find me."

Will turned and walked away. Gunner shut the door and locked it.

•   •   •

Two ladies jogged on the track together. A man and woman pushed two toddler boys on the swing set of the playground area. Four college-age boys played doubles on the tennis court. The six tables under the picnic pavilion were vacant. Gunner arrived five minutes earlier than the time they'd agreed on, a McDonald's bag and large soda in hand. He sat down at one of the tables and took the Big Mac and large order of fries from the bag. He unwrapped the burger and emptied the half-dozen packets of ketchup on a vacant space of the wrapper. A familiar truck pulled into the lot and parked next to his truck. Desi got out, no lunchbox or fast food. He walked onto the pavilion and sat down across from Gunner.

"Where's your lunch?" Gunner asked.

Desi leaned forward and folded his arms on the top to the table. "I'm not really hungry. Besides, I came here to talk, not eat."

Gunner stopped chewing. "What's on your mind?" he said, trying to play ignorant.

"Cut the crap, Gunner. You know exactly what's up. You had your stepson thrown in jail. He's eighteen and you're a grown man. What were you thinking?"

"I asked him to clean the kitchen and do the dishes and he just went ballistic on me."

"He's telling a different story."

"He's lying. You can't trust him."

"A man who won't steal from you won't lie to you. You know why?"

Gunner sat there as silent as a stone.

"Because you can't separate a man from his character," Desi continued. "He is what he is no matter where he is. He'll do right no matter how easy it might be to do wrong. When the tree fell on the back of my shop, I hired Lane to come over and clean it out before the contractor came to rebuild it. While he was doing it, he found two hundred dollars in a coffee can. When I got home from work, Lane basically handed me the money as soon as I got out of my truck. That's character. Lane's is good. I've witnessed it firsthand. I say all that to say this: I believe Lane."

Gunner sighed. "Well, that's just fine, Desi! Believe a kid you barely know over me! Someone you've known for years!"

Desi shook his head and rolled his eyes. "Let me ask you a question, Gunner. Let's say I would've hired you to clean out my shop and you found the two hundred dollars would you have handed it over to me or would you have kept it?"

"Heck, Desi, you know I would've handed over to you."

"The fact is, Gunner, I don't know that you would have because you've been stealing from Lane. Haven't you?"

Gunner squirmed on the picnic table bench. "I wouldn't say stealing. Just asking him to pay his fair share is all."

"Oh, so you ASK him for his money. You don't just take it from him."

"Yeah. Pretty much."

"The first time I ever paid Lane was when the two of you helped me saw up the tree that fell on the shop. I paid each of you a hundred dollars. Did you take his?"

Gunner looked down and began fidgeting with some of his fries.

Desi hammered a fist on the top of the picnic table. "Answer me! DID YOU TAKE HIS?"

Gunner looked up slowly. "Yeah. I did."

Desi turned his head away. "Pathetic," he said, shaking his head, his top lip curled in contempt. He turned back and fixed his eyes on Gunner's again. "Here's how it's going to be. He misses being close to Abigail. So, you're going to drop the charges and he's going to come back home."

Gunner pointed an index finger to himself. "Look at what he did to me, Desi. He said he was going to kill me."

"You deserved every bit of it. Too bad he wasn't able to stand up to you sooner. I've heard all about the way you talk to him. How you were rationing his food before he had his own money. I know about the strap too." Desi leaned in close, his nostril flared, his eyelids narrowed. "You hurt him again and I'll make you disappear. They'll find Jimmy Hoffa's body before they'll find yours. If you don't believe me, try me and find out."

Gunner's face turned pale. "I believe you."

"Lunch hour is almost up." Desi stood up from the table. "And one other thing."

"Yeah," Gunner said.

"I'll give you a week to get back all the stuff of his that you hocked. If you don't, I'll tell everyone we work with about you and about that bogus police report you filed. I bet management won't take kindly to it all. You'll be ruined in this town. Nobody'll hire you."

Desi walked back to his truck. Gunner stuffed the food back in the bag and tossed it into a garbage can.

•   •   •

Gunner parked his truck near the front door of the establishment. Didn't look to be too busy. Only a few cars and a half dozen Harleys. He'd driven past Crawdaddy's Keg many times over the years but had never stopped in. At home, he had a few beers in the fridge, but he needed something with a sharper point. He sat down on a stool at the bar. Numerous fluorescent signs throughout the room illuminated the names of the "big" brews. Heineken, Corona. Budweiser. O'Doul's. Michelob. Dos Equis. Pink Floyd's *Have a Cigar* played through the speakers mounted in the corners of the ceiling. The television behind the bar provided a muted rerun of Ole Miss versus Mississippi State football game, because, in the South, anytime of year is a good time for college football. The bartender stepped over to Gunner. Her heavy makeup was doing its job effectively, making her face look smooth in comparison to the wrinkled flesh of her neck and upper chest. "What'll you have, Cowboy?" she asked, her voice raspy from years of more than one pack a day.

"A double shot of George Dickel number twelve."

"You got it."

Gunner surveyed the other patrons. He guessed the four men seated at the table furthest in the back to be riding companions of the two who were shooting billiards. All six had an abundance of tattoos and wore black boots and black leather vests. The insignia on the back of one of the pool shooters caught Gunner's eye. A sunglass-wearing skull with a gold tooth and steampunk top hat, the words *Hell Hogs* inscribed below the skull's chin. At a booth along one wall, a man and woman sat across from each other. They exchanged laughs as they engaged in robust conversation. A man dressed in a two-piece navy suit sat at one end of the bar. He gazed into his drink, a look of hopelessness on his face. Gunner could relate.

"Here you go, Cowboy. That'll be eight bucks." the bartender said.

Gunner pulled a thin wad of cash from a front pocket and peeled off a ten. He slid it toward her. "Keep the change."

She smiled and shot him a wink. "Thanks."

Gunner took a swig of his whiskey and contemplated his options. He knew Desi meant business so cracking down harder on Lane in hopes of motivating him to run away was out of the question. Besides, the preacher seemed just as serious as Desi though his was a bit more diplomatic. If gossip around town was true, he'd played football professionally and that meant he could handle himself, no doubt. Even more frightening was Miss Red. Her reputation for heartless brutality was legendary. Word on the street was that a man from Birmingham once had tried to weasel his way out of paying her twenty grand. She paid him a visit and threatened to alter his life if he didn't pay up. The man took to life on the run, hoping she'd never find him. Last time he was seen was in Knoxville, his finger counting ability reduced from ten to six. Gunner threw back the rest of the whiskey and plopped the glass back down on the bar. "I'll have another."

The bartender strolled back over. "Okay, Cowboy. But be careful. Don't get yourself snake bit and then try to drive home."

The words "snake bit" struck a chord in Gunner's thinking. He pondered for a few seconds. "You're right. On second thought I'd better not." He pulled his cell phone from his pocket and began searching the net. Bingo. New Orleans was not that far away. He could make the trip down and back in a day. He stood to his feet.

"Come back sometime, Cowboy. I'm Freda." She smiled and shot him another wink. "I'm here Thursday through Saturday. Off Sunday through Wednesday."

Normally Gunner would've taken her up on her flirting and hung around to see where their conversation might've led. But time was against him. He felt as if a knife were at his neck. He walked away without saying goodbye. Sunlight jumped into the dark den when he pulled the door open. An early model Ford sedan was parked next to his truck. Mexican flag plate on the front. Chrome wheels. Body lowered. High gloss custom paint. Windows down. Mariachi music playing. Two men sat in the front seat, two in the back.

"Hola," the front passenger said as Gunner side-stepped between his truck and the lowrider.

Gunner made eye contact and raised his chin. "How's it going?"

"Fantastico, Amigo."

Gunner eased his truck door open, careful not to let it make contact with the beautiful Ford. He slipped inside, put the key into the ignition and turned it. Nothing. He tried again. Nothing. He pulled the hood release, eased the door open and slid back out. Everything under the hood seemed to be in order. The plug wires were secure, the battery cables tight.

"Perhaps it's the main solenoid, Amigo," a voice said.

Gunner turned to see one of the Mexicans leaning against the side of his truck gazing at the motor.

"You think so?"

"Could be," he said and began removing the plastic cover of the solenoid bank. "Si, falta."

"What?" Gunner asked.

"The main solenoid is the problem, Amigo. It's missing."

"Here, I have one," said another voice.

Gunner looked up to see the other three men standing over the engine. What was going on? How was it that the man JUST HAPPENED to have the solenoid needed. The one who spoke handed the solenoid to the first man. The first man plugged it into the vacant spot of the electronic bank. The other men gathered in close to Gunner. He scanned their faces, their eyes piercing into his.

"Your name is Gunner. Correcto?"

Gunner's pulse felt icy. His tongue felt thick in his mouth. "Ah . . . yeah. How'd you know?"

A devilish grin stretched on the man's face. "How I know is no matter to you, Gringo. What should matter to you is that we are watching you. Should you do anything that makes Lane feel even a LITTLE uncomfortable, we will make you feel VERY uncomfortable. Entiendes?"

Gunner drew down his brow.

One of the men nudged Gunner with an elbow. "My brother is asking you if you understand."

"Yes. I understand."

"Okay. Adios for now."

The four men got back into the tricked out vintage car. The driver backed the car at a ninety then pulled forward a few feet. The man in the front passenger seat threw up a gang sign. "I'd sleep with one eye open if I were you, Amigo." They all laughed as if suddenly demonized and drove away. Gunner wished he'd never borrowed the first dime from Miss Red.

CHAPTER SEVENTEEN

The internet advertisement said New Orleans. In actuality, the man lived in Simons Slough, a bayou community with a population of less than a hundred some thirty miles south of the Big Easy and well off the beaten path. It wasn't listed on any map, at least none that Gunner had consulted. He'd stopped and asked directions at a transmission shop in Pointe a la Hache. When he mentioned Simons Slough to the only mechanic in the place, the grease monkey rolled out from under a late 90's Chevrolet Malibu and asked, "Why, for the love of God, are you going down there?" Gunner shot him a line of bull about catching up with a distant cousin from childhood. The mechanic scratched him out a map on a blue shop towel and then encouraged him to have one in the chamber when he turned off the paved road. Gunner thanked the man and offered him five bucks for the knowledge he'd relayed. The man refused the money. "You might need it to get out of Simons Slough once your catching up is done," the mechanic said.

The dirt road to Simons Slough was little more than a hunting camp road. Dogs barked and *Deliverance*-like kids with dirty faces stood and gazed at Gunner as he drove along, jostling and jerking inside the cab of his rust bucket truck. He was looking for a double-wide trailer on poles. Gunner had never heard of such, much less seen such, but he felt the description was clear enough that when he came to such an abode, he'd recognize it. The kink in his search was that most every dwelling he saw on either side of the dirt road was some kind of modular dwelling on poles. The only hope he had of pulling into the right driveway without risking his life was to be on the lookout for the numbers 303 and the name Toussiant.

The mailbox was a repurposed tool chest mounted on the top of an I-beam that stuck four feet out of the ground. It had a putty knife screwed to one side of it. Gunner guessed that when there was mail going out, the putty knife was perpendicular, horizontal when there was none. The tool chest had 303 painted on the side along with a large letter "T." Perhaps Toussiant didn't want to take the time to spell his name out or maybe he was the only person on the road whose name started with the letter. Either way, Gunner felt certain he'd arrived at the right house . . . or trailer . . . or whatever the things were called. He turned in and was immediately greeted by a brindle pit bull. The dog looked like it'd been fed plenty of protein and an abundance of steroids. The greeting was not one that declared, "We've been expecting you. Get out, come in and have a beer." Instead, the beefy mongrel was telling Gunner, "You get out of that truck, and I'll eat you clean through from your mouth to your anus." Gunner stopped the truck in front of the steps that led up to the door of the trailer. A man stepped out onto the planked porch, an AR-15 firmly gripped in his hands, the business end pointed in Gunner's direction. Gunner lowered his window which seemed to tell the dog it was time to attack. The beast jumped to his hinds and planted his front paws against the driver door. Not only did Gunner get the opportunity to hear how ferocious the dog could sound, but he also got a firsthand, up-close look at the dog's jaws, canines and cavernous throat.

"Atilla, heel!" the man shouted.

As if a switch had been flipped inside his brain, the dog ceased barking, dropped back down on all four feet, trotted up the steps, and took his place at the man's side as if he were an usher. The dog fixed his eyes on Gunner and panted, his jaws widened, drool falling from his gray tongue.

Gunner stuck his head out of the window. "I assume he'll bite me if I get out."

The man spit tobacco juice to the ground beneath and repositioned the chaw in his mouth. "He'll rip your throat out if I tell him to. Where're you from?"

"Mississippi."

"Wasn't sure you'd show. Most don't. I do business on a discreet basis. I don't want to know anything about you. I ain't telling you anything about me. I have what you want. You pay for it and leave. It's like we never met. Is this agreeable?"

"Absolutely."

The man lowered the barrel of the gun and looked down at the dog. "Atilla, friend!"

Atilla hustled down the steps and resumed his position on Gunner's truck, his tail slapping back and forth. The monstrous dog's demeanor now transformed into that of a puppy. It whined as it labored to lick Gunner on whatever part of his body it could make contact with.

"You can get out and pet him now," the man said.

Gunner opened the door and wrestled the suddenly affectionate dog back so he could exit the truck. Atilla sniffed and licked Gunner's hands, demanding to be petted. Gunner obliged the big dog's wishes.

"Come on up and I'll show you what I got," the man said.

Gunner ascended the steps, Atilla at his side.

"Atilla, lay down," the man said.

The dog flopped down on the porch near the steps, stretched out and gently closed its eyes as if he'd take a nap. The man pulled open the door and held it for Gunner. "All the way through the house and to the back room."

Gunner walked in. The man followed. The den furnishings inside the house were symmetrically placed. Floors clean. The books on the shelves were aligned according to height. On an end table set a police scanner, its small red lights blinked as it chirped and belched. "Suspect is in custody and we're enroute to headquarters," an officer said. Gunner continued into the kitchen. Two chairs were pushed snugly under a small dining table. A ceramic bowl filled with apples set in the table's center. The countertops were clean. No dishes in the sink. No pots or pans on the stove. A flame danced on top of a candle inside a glass jar filling the house with the aroma of baked apples.

When they reached the back room of the house, the man pulled a ring of keys from his pocket. He found the key he wanted and used it to unlock the deadbolt of the back door. The door opened into a large room. Three stories of glass terrariums lined the walls of the room. In its center was a long stainless-steel table with storage drawers underneath.

"Are you wanting the death to be slow and messy or quicker and cleaner?" the man asked.

"Quicker and cleaner."

"Alright, so we're talking neurotoxic venom as opposed to hemotoxic."

"Yeah. I guess. What's the difference?"

"Well, with a hemotoxic envenomator, like a rattlesnake, you're gonna have a lot of blood and disfiguration. With a neurotoxic envenomator like a cobra or a krait, it'll attack the nervous system. Shut down the lungs and such."

"Then neurotoxic is what I'm wanting."

"Are you looking for an exotic snake or one native to the US?"

"US. Definitely. I'm wanting to facilitate an accident."

"So, you'll want it to be common to the southeast. That narrows it down to one."

"And which one would that be?"

The man walked over to one of the terrariums and tapped on the glass. "This girl right here. She's an eastern coral snake. Most potent venom of any snake in the country."

"How much?"

"Five hundred."

"I'll take her. Anything I should know."

"She's reclusive and non-aggressive but I'd still use leather gloves when I handled her. She's not easily provoked like a rattlesnake or a copperhead. She'll need to come into direct contact with the victim and feel threatened in order for her to strike. Physical contact would be best."

"Any suggestions?"

"That'll cost you another hundred."

"I'll pay it."

"A man from Arkansas had a wife that started getting extracurricular with her boss. The man found out about it. He and his wife had a falling out as you would expect. He started sleeping on the couch. Thing was his wife's daddy was loaded. I'm talking big money so he had to play it smart. Didn't want to get cut out of the pie by causing a nasty divorce. So, he came to see me. Bought an eastern coral. Slipped it in her bed one night when she was asleep. Next morning, he goes to check on her and she's cold as a wedge." The man shrugged his shoulders. "Death was ruled an accident." The man tapped on the glass. The snake jerked its head back in defense. "Poor snake was just looking for a place to rest, they determined. Last I heard, the man was living big in Key West with a girl half his age."

Gunner gazed through the glass at the deadly serpent. "Sounds like a plan."

CHAPTER EIGHTEEN

Abigail rested her head on Lane's shoulder as they sat on the patio of the parsonage, both of them looking toward the tree line.

Lane gently squeezed her hand in his. "Is it just me or doesn't it feel like we've known each other for a long time?"

"I feel like I knew you before we ever met."

Lane pulled away a bit and turned to look at her. "What?"

"When my family and I were praying about moving here I believe the Lord impressed it on my heart that I would meet the man He had for me."

"So, I'm your man, huh?"

"Absolutely."

"You sure? School's starting back soon. Guys'll be breaking their necks trying to get you to go out with them."

Abigail straightened up in her chair and looked at Lane. She pulled the chain from under the collar of her tee shirt and held the arrowhead up. "I'm unavailable." She leaned in and gave him a quick kiss. "How do you think it's gonna go between you and Gunner?"

"Desi said he talked to him and everything should be fine. Told me if I had any problems to let him know and he'd take care of it."

"Desi's a good friend to you, isn't he?"

"Yeah. So is Becky. Denver too. He's the one who bailed me out of jail. He even gave me keys to the gate and the shop yesterday."

"He knows he can trust you."

"Feels good to be trusted. Trust is a powerful thing, you know."

"Mom says trust is one of the pillars of her and dad's marriage."

"They do seem to have something special." Lane checked his watch. "Well, I wish I could stay longer but I guess I need to get going. Got an early day tomorrow."

They stood from their seats and ambled to Lane's company truck. They embraced and shared a parting kiss. Abigail stood in the driveway and watched Lane back out. Before he pulled away, Abigail gave him an affectionate wave with one hand. With the other she held the arrowhead, part of the chain between her lips.

•   •   •

Gunner slept with his cell phone in one hand. He'd set the alarm tone to go off at 2 AM. When it did, he rose from his bed and utilized the phone's flashlight. He'd left two things on his nightstand. A pair of leather welder's gloves to protect him from lethal fangs and a pair of thick socks to give him more stealth. First, he slipped on the socks, then the gloves. He reached under the bed and pulled out the box that contained the snake. He crept from his bedroom to the kitchen and turned on the fluorescent light above the sink. He placed his phone face down on the kitchen counter and walked on the balls of his feet to Lane's bedroom door. With the calculated prowess of a cat burglar, he twisted the knob and eased the door open halfway. As he'd intended, the light of the kitchen stole some of the darkness from Lane's room. In the dimness Lane lay in his bed, sleeping soundly, oblivious to the fact that his murder was in the making. Like a ghost, Gunner entered the room. He turned back the covers at the foot of the bed. Lane continued to rest, motionless. Gunner could hear his own pulse as he set the box on the bed near Lane's feet. He turned it up on one edge and removed the lid. The deadly creature slithered out of the box and coiled as if it would strike. Gunner lifted the ends of the covers and lowered them over the alert and agitated snake. He backed up a few steps, then turned and walked out of the room. As he was pulling the door closed, he paused for a moment. He looked down at the scene he'd created. By the work of his hands, an innocent, orphaned boy, completely unaware, would soon be dead. It was unfair, but necessary. It was dastardly, but unavoidable. A boy would die. A man would go on living. Gunner shut the door the rest of the way.

•　　　•　　　•

As the big tractor plowed along it left a wake of soft, black soil. Once hidden from sight, diamonds, emeralds, rubies, and gold coins now sparkled in the newly turned earth. Lane and Abigail followed the mighty machine, gathering the treasures it unearthed.

"Isn't this wonderful," Abigail said. "All this wealth just ours for the taking."

Lane plucked an emerald the size of a golf ball from the loose dirt and added it to the collection in the wagon they pulled together. "Where are we going to put these? The loft of the barn is full already," he said.

The man driving the tractor turned and looked back. "Put them in the treehouse!"

"Who's that man?" Abigail asked.

"That's my dad," Lane said.

A lady nudged Abigail on one shoulder. "And I'm Lane's mom. I'm so excited to finally meet you. Lane's told us all about you."

Lane's father stopped the tractor and turned off the engine. He jumped down to the ground and began walking toward them. When he reached them, he embraced Lane's mother and gave her a kiss. Then, he reached into the bib of his overalls and pulled out a gold pocket watch. He checked the watch and said to Lane and Abigail. "We need to head on over to the church. By the time we get there Dr. Weston will be ready to marry you two." The four of them joined hands and began running across the field.

A sudden, sharp pain stabbed into Lane's ankle arousing him from his sleep. He switched on the lamp that set on the nightstand and inspected his stinging foot. Blood trickled from two small puncture wounds. In horror, Lane threw back the covers. The snake coiled in defense. It retracted its raised head as if it'd strike again. Lane grabbed his phone and called 9-1-1.

"I've been snake bit!" he declared to the operator. "It's red, yellow and black! It's a coral snake! I'm sure of it! Please send an ambulance A-S-A-P! Hurry please! Please hurry!"

Gunner opened Lane's bedroom door as Lane was finishing up giving the dispatcher the address.

"What on earth are you doing up at this hour?"

Lane tossed his cell phone on the nightstand. "There's a snake in my bed. A coral snake. And it bit me."

Gunner shot his hands to his temples. "My God, Headlight. How in the world did it get in the house?"

Lane stood on one foot, favoring the one the snake had bitten. "It must've come in through the duct work or a window or something."

"I'll get something and kill it."

•   •   •

A team of Memphis Regional doctors and nurses looked on, gurney in hand, their scrubs plastered to their bodies from the wind of the spinning blades. The medical chopper eased down on the tarmac, and they rushed to it. The emergency ensemble transported Lane from the helicopter to the gurney and brisked him away into the hospital. Inside the operating room reinforcements stood ready at their stations along with state-of-the-art machines and a herpetologist from the Memphis Zoo. The reception team rolled the gurney into the room and the army of skilled lifesavers went to work as if the room was on fire. One doctor and the herpetologist began examining Lane's ankle while a nurse began checking his vitals.

"Count to thirty in one breath," said another doctor as he evaluated Lane's pelvic lymph nodes.

Lane took a breath and counted all the way to thirty without problem.

"There's no blistering around the bite area," said the doctor at Lane's ankle.

"Possible dry bite," said the herpetologist. "Eastern corals have a forty-percent dry bite rate when it comes to humans."

"No sign of respiratory failure," said one of the nurses.

"Blood pressure is 158 over 87," said another. "But he is under emotional distress."

The doctor moved up from Lane's pelvis to his neck. "Let's get a culture of the bite area to see if there's venom in the tissue," he said as he applied fingertip pressure around Lane's spinal cord.

"Microscope," said the doctor at Lane's feet.

A microscope sat on a wheeled table against one wall of the room. A nurse rolled it over to the doctor. He placed a small piece of Lane's flesh on a glass slide and covered it with a smaller piece of glass. The doctor placed the slide on the platform of the microscope. He positioned one of his eyes over the eyepiece lens and began adjusting the magnification. "There are no signs of venom."

He looked up from the microscope at the herpetologist. "Would you verify?"

The herpetologist looked at the specimen. "Confirm that. No traces of venom."

The doctor at Lane's head pulled down his mask and smiled. "Looks like you're a very lucky young man,"

"Blood pressure is 131 over 82," said a nurse.

The doctor patted Lane on the shoulder. "Good. Let's observe him for a few hours. If his vitals are good and his breathing is normal, he can go home."

• • •

The double glass doors of the hospital entrance slid open. A nurse pushed Lane in a wheelchair out under the hospital awning. Will and Erica Weston sat in the front seats of the SUV, engine running as Abigail held the back passenger door open for Lane. The nurse pushed the wheelchair close to the truck. Lane stood from the chair and thanked the nurse. He and Abigail embraced and shared a kiss. Lane got into the backseat. Abigail walked around the vehicle and got in on the other side.

Dr. Weston looked back at Lane. "I hear the ribs at Rendezvous are great. What do you think, Lane?"

"Yeah. They are. I used to go there with mom and dad."

"Sounds great to me," Erica said. "I'm starving."

Dr. Weston pulled the shifter down into drive. "Alright. Let's hit it."

Abigail reached over and placed her hand in Lane's as they drove away.

•   •   •

The sight of two items in Lane's bedroom surprised him. The Marlin 30-30 and the metal detector. The place where the record player had been was still vacant. Gunner walked into Lane's room. "How you feeling?" he asked, his hands on his hips.

"I'm fine. The bite was dry."

Gunner lifted his hands in a praising gesture. "Thank God."

Gunner praising God? Right. He was probably wishing Lane was dead.

Gunner piped up. "I got your gun and metal detector back."

You're such a loser. A fake.

Lane nodded. "Yeah. I noticed."

"Couldn't get the player and the records. The clerk said somebody bought them yesterday. Don't worry though. I get paid next Friday and I'll buy you a new one. The thrift store in town sells old records. We can swing by and see if they have any like the ones you had."

"Why are you trying to be nice to me all of the sudden? You haven't been nice to me ever since mom died."

"Lately, I've been examining myself and I realize I need to change and treat you differently. You ARE my stepson after all. The snake bite situation made me realize how sad I'd be if something happened to you. I'd really like to make things right with you."

Who was this guy? And what made him think he could make things right after all he'd done?

"Don't worry about it. Wouldn't be the same. The records and the player were my dad's. That's why they were special to me."

The ringing of the landline rescued Lane from the awkward moment.

"I'll get it," Gunner said and walked out of the room.

Lane texted Abigail. *Gunner is acting really weird. He's trying to be all nice to me.*

She responded. *Don't fall for it.*

Lane replied with an OKAY gif.

Gunner walked back into the room. "Lane, there's been a bad wreck on Highway 7. Poles snapped. Lines down. Lots of people are without power. I've been called out. I don't know what time I'll be back home. Let's pick this conversation back up later. Be thinking of something you'd like to do or someplace you'd like to go. Maybe we could pull a road trip or something."

He turned and walked away.

As if things were not weird enough already. Was Gunner taking drugs or something? The man was insane if he thought for a minute Lane would hang out or do anything with him.

Gunner appeared in Lane's doorway again. "By the way, Lane, I tossed the strap in the trash. I promise I'll never whip you with it again."

Okay. The dude was definitely on something. Lane stood there, astonished that Gunner had actually called him by his name instead of Headlight. The back door slammed shut and Gunner's truck cranked. Lane texted Abigail again. *Just told me he threw the strap away. Can you believe it?????*

He's evil, she shot back.

•   •   •

Gunner parked his truck in the same spot he'd parked before. It was early in the afternoon. Crawdaddy's Keg was open, but only one car was in the lot. A white Honda Accord. Fifteen years old at least. Streams of rust highlighted the crimps in the damaged front passenger fender testifying to the fact the owner hadn't bothered or been able to get the car fixed. Gunner got out and walked inside. Freda sat on a barstool watching a courtroom show on the television. The squeak of the door caused her to turn and look. She grinned. "Hey, Cowboy. I see you're back."

"Came back because of the nice scenery."

She stood to her feet and walked around behind the bar. Gunner checked her out and took a seat at the drinking counter.

"What'll you have?"

"George Dickel. Straight."

"Same as the other day," she said. "You're consistent. I like that in a man."

She set a small glass in front of him and poured a shot of the redeye in it. He threw it back and set the glass down with purpose. "Is it just you and me, or is someone else here?"

She leaned forward on her elbows and gave him a provocative smile. "Just you and me, Cowboy."

"I've got a problem. A matter of life and death. Do you know anyone who solves problems? You know, someone who doesn't have a conscience that gets in the way."

"Hm. Someone willing to meander over to the dark side, huh? How intriguing."

"You know someone like that?"

She pulled the liquor bottle from under the counter and twisted off the cap. "You're serious, aren't you?"

"As serious as a blow torch in a room full of dynamite."

She poured him another shot. "This one's on the house." She returned the bottle to its place below.

"You a cop?"

Gunner sighed. "I'm not even a crossing guard."

She chuckled. "A sense of humor too. Alright. Alright. You're getting more interesting by the minute."

Gunner pulled a twenty-dollar bill from his pocket and placed it on the counter. "Give me a name."

She took the money and stuffed it in a back pocket. "Rayburn."

"Rayburn who?"

She gave him a witchy grin and tapped an index finger on the bar. Gunner pulled another twenty from his pocket and placed it where he'd placed the first one. She took it and added to the one in her pocket. "Slide."

"Rayburn Slide. He's the man I need to speak to, huh?"

She nodded, her eyes locked on his. "Yeah. He's a real vampire I tell you."

"Fifty more if you arrange the meeting."

"A hundred and you've got a deal."

"Done."

"Give me a minute," she said and walked away.

Gunner watched her pull her cell phone. He threw back the complimentary shot of liquor and watched her have a private conversation. She ended the call and walked back over to him. "He'll be here in thirty minutes." She tapped on the bar again, demanding the money.

"When he gets here," Gunner said.

In thirty exactly minutes the door opened. In walked a bald man. Just shy of six feet tall. Clean shaven. He wore faded jeans and black combat boots. His chest and biceps caused strain on his plain, black knit shirt. A skull buckle secured the leather belt that lay tight against his lean midsection.

"Your date has arrived," Freda said and walked away.

Gunner made eye contact. The man raised his chin in acknowledgment, walked over and sat down on the barstool next to Gunner.

"You Rayburn Slide?"

"In the flesh."

"Can I buy you a drink?"

"I don't drink. Stuff'll kill you."

"It will indeed. I have a problem that I need fixed."

Slide raised his eyebrows. "I'm a real handyman."

"Do you do extermination?"

Slide shrugged his shoulders. "Extermination. Elimination. Incineration. You name it."

"I need someone to have an accident . . . a fatal accident."

"Accidents are the best way to avoid looking guilty, but they're a gamble. It's impossible to guarantee a fatality. An injury, yes. One hundred percent. But not a fatality."

"How much would it cost me to gamble?"

"Car accidents are the easiest and the cheapest. One will run you two grand. Half up front. The other half after the crash, even if the driver lives because, as I said, it's impossible to guarantee a fatality."

"Sounds good."

"I'll need some information. Name. Age. Address. Phone number. Workplace. Work schedule. Any regular routines like trips to a gym, trips to and from school, etc."

"Sure. Do you need to write these things down?"

Slide shook his head. "Writing things down on paper is dangerous. Can land a man in prison. A man in my business has to use his brain." He touched an index finger to one of his temples. "I write things down up here."

"Okay. The kid's name is Lane Hubbard. He's eighteen."

Slide drew back his head, his open palms raised in protest. "Woe. Wait a minute. I didn't know you were talking about a kid. I thought it was an ex-wife or a brother-in-law or something."

"He's my stepson and he's about to turn nineteen."

Slide wasn't buying. "There's a big difference in being nineteen and almost being nineteen," he said.

"Tell me about it. Believe me, I understand. I mean I really understand. You willing to do the job or not? Time is critical for me. It's got to be done before he turns nineteen which will be in less than two months."

Slide made a hammer fist and bumped the bar counter a few times as he thought about it. He inhaled a belly full of air then exhaled. He pinched the corners of his eyes at the bridge of his nose then turned and looked at Gunner. "I'll do it for three grand."

"Deal. I'll meet you here with the first fifteen hundred this Friday, 5:30."

Slide nodded and stood to his feet. "I'll need a picture too."

"I'll have one."

Rayburn Slide walked out of the bar. When the door squeaked again, Freda returned from the back room. She walked over to Gunner. "So, how was your meeting?"

"Promising. When I get my business squared away, I'll have a little fun money in my pocket. What do you think about you and me doing a little traveling? Maybe go to Vegas and see if we're lucky together."

She reached down and put a hand on top of one of his. "Sure. I could use a vacation."

"It's a date, then. I'll be in touch . . . soon."

Gunner pulled a hundred from his shirt pocket and laid it on the counter.

"I'll start packing," Freda said and stuffed the money in pocket of her shirt.

Gunner walked away.

CHAPTER NINETEEN

Lane packed the dirt around the final post. The next Saturday he and Desi would begin running the barbed wire. When the job was finally complete, Becky's cuties would be able to graze and frolic on five fenced-in acres of pastureland. Her "cuties," as she referred to them, were a pair of miniature Scottish Highland cows. For more than ten years it had been Becky's dream to get into the mini cow business. As soon as Pritchard Farm was livestock ready, Becky and Desi would drive to the breeder in Clanton, Alabama and pick up Popcorn and Petunia along with their protectors, two donkeys named Banjo and Hub Cap.

Lane said his goodbyes to Desi and Becky and started the drive back to Locust Fork, a hundred dollars wealthier than when he arrived at their place earlier that morning. The roads were still wet from the twenty-minute drizzle that had fallen a few hours before quitting time. Lane stopped at a convenience store on the way home. He refueled Denver's company truck and bought a grape soda and a bag of barbeque pork skins to tide him over till dinner. It was all-you-can-eat catfish night at The Hungry Fisherman. Lane and Abigail's plans were to drive down to Sardis Lake and do their part to put away some of the southern delicacy.

As Lane pulled back onto the blacktop from the convenience store's parking lot he noticed a black Chevy 4X4 take to the road behind him. The truck had been lifted, its big mud grips almost as tall as the tailgate of the company truck. Across the front of the truck stretched a custom-welded heavy duty iron bumper. The driver of the intimidating truck seemed to be void of highway consideration, maintaining only about a two car-length distance from Lane. As they crossed over the Huntsville County line the countryside turned hillier, the road curvier. When Lane sped up, the black truck sped up. When Lane slowed down, the black truck slowed down.

What the heck was the driver thinking? The road wasn't heavy with traffic. In fact, there were no other vehicles even on the road. So, why the tailgating? As Lane topped a hill and headed downward toward the Yallaboosa River bridge, the truck drew up closer. "Come on, Buddy. What's your problem? You're gonna cause a wreck," he said out loud as he eyed the black truck in the rear-view mirror. The bridge was no less than a hundred yards away. Lane placed his hands on the steering wheel in the 10-2 position and eased on the brake a bit. The black truck roared as the driver accelerated. The iron bumper slammed against the back of Denver's truck. The impact thrusted the smaller truck forward and jerked Lane's head back. Lane white knuckled the steering wheel as the black truck surged again sending the passenger side of Denver's truck onto the soft shoulder of the road. It began to fishtail. Lane turned the wheel to the right to avoid head-on contact with the bridge's concrete railing. The truck hooked to the right and left the wet pavement. As the front of Denver's truck shot to the right of the bridge, the back of the truck spun to the left and made contact with the railing. The impact flipped the truck and sent it wheels upward into the muddy waters below.

•   •   •

If all the facts had come out during his trial, Rayburn Slide would've done thirty years minimum at the maximum-security prison known throughout the Magnolia State as Parchman Farm. But shoddy due diligence measures by investigators with bumpkin IQs tied Slide only to the drugs and totally missed his connection to the murder. So, instead of justice being served, Slide slid by with a meager ten-year stretch at the Marshall County Correctional Facility, a medium-security level prison. While there, he took advantage of a special good-behavior-based college education extension cooperative. During this time, Slide gained a proficiency level that bordered scholarly in computer technologies, advanced mathematics, biology, and chemistry. His computer skills enabled him to hack and track. His mathematic skills turned his brain into a calculator. His knowledge of biology extrapolated into how to both repair the human body, as well as how to exterminate it. And his chemistry prowess gave him the ability to alter compounds. One such compound of special interest to Slide was automotive paints. He came to be known among his fellow inmates as "The Automobile Picasso."

Slide parked the truck close to the water spicket next to the shop behind his house. He removed the wig from his head and tossed it into the trash barrel. He connected the hose, turned on the water, and cranked the pressure washer. He engaged the machine's wand and began fanning the powerful pressurized water back and forth on the truck's body. The specially compounded paint washed off like makeup. In fifteen minutes the once black truck was back to its original blue pearl and the chrome bumper was gleaming.

•   •   •

The man was under the bridge and getting a bite when the upturned truck crashed into the water. He threw down his spinning reel rig and rushed over to the scene. The surface of the river bubbled and gurgled as the cab of the truck took on water. The man jumped in and swam to the truck. He reached the driver's side door just before the tires disappeared. He dove down and jerked the truck's door handle. The door popped open. He breaststroked inside, found the seatbelt buckle and released it. He took hold of the collar of Lane's shirt and pulled him out of the truck. When he reached the surface, he towed Lane to the river's edge and pulled him up on the bank. He reached into a pocket and pulled out a cell phone. It was still functioning and showing a strong signal. Thank God. He dialed 9-1-1 and informed the dispatcher of the situation and the location. The dispatcher assured him that an ambulance was on the way. The man ended the call and started administering CPR.

•   •   •

Abigail's face came into focus. Lane felt her hand in his. With one hand she combed the crown of his head with her fingers.

A tender smile stretched on her face. "Hey."

"Where am I?"

"The hospital. The doctor says you have a concussion, but other than that, you're all fine. You've got some company. You want to sit up so you can see them?"

"Yeah."

Abigail pressed a button on the remote of the hospital bed and it began raising Lane up into a reclining position. Standing around the room were Dr. Weston, Erica, Brodie, Desi, Becky, Denver, and Gunner. All were smiling at him. Lane had his doubts about Gunner's sincerity. Lane focused on Denver. "Sorry about the truck."

"Don't worry about it, Son. The main thing is that you're okay."

Lane blinked his eyes a few times as he gathered himself.

"What happened?" Desi asked.

"I stopped at a store at the county line for gas and bottle of soda. There was this black truck parked off to one side. It had a heavy push bar on the front. When I pulled out on the road, it started following me. I was coming down the hill on Highway 7 and the truck was on my tail. Right before I got to the Yallaboosa River bridge it rammed me from behind and forced me off the road. Denver's truck fishtailed and the back quarter panel clipped the rail of the bridge. The truck flipped upside down and crashed into the water. Next thing I know I'm on the bank and a guy's telling me the ambulance is on the way. I blacked out again. I don't remember anything after that."

A police officer pulled back the privacy curtain of the small emergency room. "Lane Hubbard?"

"Yeah. He is. He's my son," Gunner answered.

The officer stepped inside. "I was wondering if you could tell me what happened."

Lane recapped his story to the officer. The officer scribbled notes on a pad as Lane talked.

"We pulled the truck from the river. The damage on the tail gate would indicate possible contact with another vehicle. A man named Todd Doulos called 9-1-1. Said he was fishing under the bridge when the wreck occurred. When we arrived on the scene, you were laying on the riverbank, unconscious, but Doulos was nowhere to be found. We're still trying to locate him."

"Let me know when you do. He must have pulled me from the truck. He saved my life. I'd sure like to thank him personally."

"We've searched Huntsville County and the surrounding counties. Can't find anyone with the last name Doulos. But we'll let you know if we turn up something. That's all for now. You folks have a nice day."

The policeman exited. Abigail looked at her parents. "What do you think about all that?"

"Hebrews 13:2," Erica said.

"That's exactly what I'm thinking," Abigail replied.

Lane drew down his brow. "What does Hebrews 13:2 say?"

"Do not forget to entertain strangers, for by so doing some have unwittingly entertained angels," Dr. Weston said.

"What?" Lane said. "Don't angels have wings."

Dr. Weston chuckled. "A lot of people think so, but that's not what the Bible says."

The emergency room doctor pulled the curtain back and walked in.

"I'm Doctor Atworth."

He focused on Lane. "How are you feeling, Young Man."

"I feel fine. Got a little bit of a headache is all."

"We'll prescribe you something for that. We've checked you out. You have a minor concussion, but other than that, you're all good."

"Can I go home?"

"I don't see why not. Take it easy for the next day or two. You don't have to stay in bed, but don't lift anything over ten pounds and no strenuous labor." Dr. Atworth motioned to the others in the room. "Let them wait on you and take care of you." He scanned their faces. "Who are the parents?"

"I'm his dad," Gunner said.

Lane wanted to protest and spit, but he held his composure and said nothing.

"If his headache hasn't gone away by the end of the weekend, contact your family physician first thing Monday morning. By the way, who is your family physician."

Gunner's body language suggested that the doctor might as well have asked him the name of the capital of Burkina Faso or some other small African country. He rubbed the stubble on his face with a nervous hand. "Well . . . ah. Doctor, it's ah . . . it's been a while since either of us have been to a doctor. We're both pretty healthy. Is there one you'd recommend?"

"Melvin King is a fine doctor. We interned together."

"Oh, yeah. I've heard some real good things about him," Gunner said.

Lane guessed that it was the first time Gunner had ever even heard Melvin King's name, let alone that he was a fine doctor. Gunner's response was probably bull crap, just a dishonest attempt to look like a responsible parent.

Dr. Atworth made a few notes on the clip board he held. "I guess that'll about do it,' he said. "You're a very lucky young man, Lane. A nurse will be in shortly. You can go ahead and get dressed if you have some dry clothes."

Gunner reached down and picked up the brown paper bag that was near his feet. "Right here, Doctor."

"Very good. It was nice meeting you folks. Have a great rest of your day."

•   •   •

Using only his lips and teeth, Blondie adjusted the cigar in his mouth and said to Tuco in a cool, condescending, breathy tone, "You see there are two kinds of people in this world, my friend. Those with loaded guns," he paused and pulled the trigger on the empty revolver and then continued. "And those who dig. You dig."

Lane grinned. It was one of his favorite scenes in his favorite western movie, *The Good, The Bad and The Ugly*. He'd lost count of how many times he'd watched it. It was his dad's favorite as well, and the two of them had spent many quality father/son hours watching the classic spaghetti cowboy flick back when Lane's father was still alive.

The doorbell chimed. Lane paused the movie and answered the door.

"Hey," Abigail said. "Thought I'd come check on you. Good day to hang out in the treehouse. Feel like you can climb?"

"Of course. Let me put on some shoes and we'll go."

Abigail walked in, two jars of preserves in her hands. "Mom and I made some new flavors. These are green apple and apricot. I'll just put them in the refrigerator." She walked through the den to the kitchen. "They have names on them as usual. I know Gunner's been acting nice the past few days, but I didn't want to take any chances."

Lane walked into the kitchen, sneakers now on his feet. "Yeah. He's been acting really odd lately. Yesterday he told me he wanted to take me hiking over in Alabama. It's like he took some nice pills or something."

"He came over the other day and met with dad. Told dad he was sorry for saying what he said about me. Said he thought I was good for you."

"Maybe he is changing."

"I'd still be leery if I were you. It could all be an act to avoid being homeless."

•   •   •

When they reached the treehouse ladder, Abigail demanded to climb first.

Lane objected. "But I always climb first so I can help you up through the floor."

Abigail grabbed a board on the tree and began her ascent. Lane stood on the ground and watched her for a few moments then started up himself. He shot his eyes open in delight as he drew up into the treehouse. A checkered tablecloth was spread out on the floor. Place settings for two. A covered dish of fried chicken. A small basket of baked rolls. A bowl of grapes. A bag of mini powdered donuts.

Abigail spread her hands apart. "Ta Da! Welcome to The Treehouse Café."

"This is great. What's the occasion?" Lane asked.

"I just wanted to have a special lunch in our special place."

"Well, you did great!"

Abigail filled their glasses with lemonade from a thermos. "And there's one more thing."

"What's that?"

She pressed a button on a portable cassette player. The unmistakable voice of Johnny Cash. The song: *Tennessee Stud.*

•   •   •

Gunner was twenty feet in the air working on a transformer when the first pain hit him. He slumped over on the rim of the bucket.

"Gunner, what's going on," said his coworker, Dwight Ballard, from the ground below.

"Ugh. I don't know but I feel like I have a screwdriver stuck in my side."

The second pain collapsed Gunner to his knees inside the bucket.

"Gunner! Gunner! You alright, Man?"

Gunner wailed in agony, unable to get back to his feet.

Dwight hurried to the toggle panel near the cab of the truck. He manipulated the bucket back down to the truck's bed. He helped Gunner out and down to the ground. In an attempt to cope with the excruciating pain, Gunner drew his body into a fetal position and folded his arms tight against his midsection. Dwight Ballard called for an ambulance as Gunner writhed.

Three hours later Gunner lay in an emergency room bed at Baptist Memorial Oxford, his blood pressure punching 190/128. Six hours later he was slurring his words; he complained of a splitting headache and was breathing like he'd just run a ninety-nine-yard touchdown.

Another three hours later, the electrocardiogram monitor next to his bed flatlined. Gunner Hubbard was dead.

•   •   •

Lane laced his boots. He was to be at Desi and Becky's in thirty minutes. The cuties along with Banjo and Hubcap were to make their Mississippi debut the next day so the barbed wire had to be run, stretched and nailed. Lane pulled on the Texas Longhorns cap Abigail had given him up in the treehouse the day before. Gunner was gone. Great! Lane wasn't grieving. Not in the least. He was about to walk out the door when the doorbell rang. Who could it be? It was Saturday for crying out loud. Lane walked to the front door and looked through the peep hole. What? The cops. They had questions about Gunner, no doubt. Who knew how long they'd hold him up? Lane texted Desi. *Cops just arrived. I may be a few minutes late.*

Lane opened the door.

The officer standing in front gripped his belt with both hands in front of his stomach. "Hello, Sir. I'm Officer Polk." He twisted in his boots toward the officer that stood behind him. "And this is Officer Varden. We'd like to talk to you about Gunner Hubbard."

Lane grimaced. "I've got to be at work in a half hour."

"Sorry for any inconvenience it may cause, but this is a very important matter. Might we come in?"

Lane dropped his chin and exhaled. "Yeah, I guess so."

He pulled the door open wider and held it. The two officers walked in. Lane shut the door behind them and motioned to the furniture in the den. "Feel free to have a seat."

The two officers sat down on the couch. Lane took the recliner.

"What's your name, Sir?" Polk said.

"Lane. Lane Hubbard."

Varden wrote on a pad.

"Well, Mr. Hubbard, an autopsy of Gunner Hubbard's body revealed ethylene glycol."

Lane gave the officer a look of confusion. "What's that?"

"It's an alcohol component of antifreeze."

"Antifreeze? The emergency room doctor said something about a heart attack and kidney stones."

"Initially that was thought to be the case. But forensics indicate otherwise."

"Otherwise?"

"We're not sure. Do you mind if we look around?"

"Not at all. Help yourself."

The officers stood up. "Where did Mr. Hubbard sleep?"

"I'll show you," Lane said.

"I'll look around outside while you check things out in here," Varden said to Polk.

"Sure thing," Polk replied.

Lane led Polk back to the master bedroom. The policeman looked around the room, pulled open some drawers and rummaged through the contents. He checked out the closet. Then, he strolled to the master bathroom. He looked at the items in the mirror cabinet over the sink. "I think I've seen what I need to see in here. Take me to the kitchen."

On his way, Polk paused at the door of Lane's bedroom. He stepped into Lane's private space and looked it over. "Were those your parents?" he asked, gazing at a framed photo. "Yessir."

Polk walked to the gun rack on the wall. "Marlin 30-30. Good gun. Killed any deer with it?"

"Just one. Haven't hunted in a while."

Polk turned and walked out of the room, Lane following. When they reached the kitchen Polk pulled open the refrigerator door. "Is this sweet tea?"

"Yessir."

Polk reached into one of his front pockets and pulled out a pair of latex gloves. He snapped them on and took out the glass tea pitcher. "Did you make it or did Mr. Hubbard?" He said as he sniffed the top of the container.

"He did. About two days ago."

"Have you drank any of it?"

"No, Sir. I make my own and use a different pitcher. Gunner wouldn't allow me to drink from his."

"Mind if I take this?"

"Not at all."

Polk set the pitcher on the counter and began browsing through the cabinets. Varden re-entered the house through the back door. "I checked the barn and the trucks in the driveway. Nothing."

"Alight," Polk said and shut a cabinet door. He leaned down and opened one of the doors under the sink. "I think I just found something."

He pulled out a jug of antifreeze and set it on the counter next to the pitcher of tea. "You recognize this?"

"Yeah. It was out in the barn. I don't know how it got under the sink."

"We'll need to have the lab examine it as well."

"No problem," Lane said.

Polk began fishing the cups and drinking glasses from the collection of dirty dishes in the sink. "We'll need to take these as well."

Lane said nothing. Polk was going take them whether he agreed or not anyway. Lane started to mention the words lawyer and search warrant, but what was the use?

"I'll get a bag from the squad car," Varden said and headed out the door. He was back in less than a minute, two large, clear plastic bags in one hand. The first one popped when he slung it open. Polk began placing the jug of antifreeze and cups inside it. Varden slung open the second one and Polk eased the pitcher of tea into it. "I'll hold it while we're in the car," Varden said.

Polk nodded. "Anything else outside we need to check?"

"Naw, we're good." Varden replied.

Polk turned back to Lane. "Well, that'll do it for now. If we have any other questions, we'll be in touch." He pulled a business card from one of his shirt pockets. "In the meantime, if you think of anything that might be helpful, I'd appreciate it if you'd give me a call."

"Will do," Lane said.

The officers left. Lane texted Desi. *Cops just left. I'm headed your way.*

•   •   •

The sparse gathering sat at the front of the room. Lane, the Pritchards, Denver Banks, Abigail and her family, and Big Pop. A spray made of carnations draped over the casket. The small card attached to the flower arrangement simply read, *North Mississippi Electric Cooperative*. Organ music piped softly through the audio system. To one side of the casket, Dr. Weston sat in a chair near a podium, his legs crossed at the knees, a small New Testament in one hand. His solemn facial expression transformed suddenly to one of surprise as he looked toward the back of the room. Lane and the others turned to see. The man's presence hit the attendees like hammers. Lane's heart pumped ice water through his veins. The man stepped to the open casket and gazed down at the corpse. After a few moments he turned and walked over to Lane. How could this be? Was this reality or was Lane having a nightmare? How could Gunner be standing before him if he was dead and laying in the coffin.

The man reached out a hand for a shake. "I'm Garner Hubbard. Gunner was my twin brother. You must be Lane."

●   ●   ●

It was rewards night at the movie theater which meant tickets were five dollars cheaper than they were regularly. Lane and Abigail were double-dating with Desi and Becky. The plan was to make the six o'clock showing of the dystopian thriller that was dominating the box office then hit the Mexican restaurant that had just opened in town. The eatery was getting rave reviews. Its fried ice cream was said to be "the bomb." Lane heard a vehicle pull up in the driveway. He grabbed his wallet and cell phone and headed out the door. The blue Raptor was parked near the house, engine running, Desi and Becky inside. Lane locked the front door of the house. As he walked to the truck, a Huntsville County Sheriff's car rolled up the driveway. The cops would just have to come back another time. Lane wasn't altering his date plans in order to give the same answers to the same questions—again. The squad car stopped close to the Raptor. Two officers got out, hats tilted forward in intimidating fashion, Glock 45's at the sides, their belts loaded up with whatever it was cops carry in those leather compartments.

Desi and Becky opened their doors and got out. They stood next to the truck, curious as to what the reason might be for the officers' visit.

"Are you Lane Hubbard?" one of the officers said.

"Yessir."

"Mr. Hubbard, you are under arrest for the murder of Gunner Hubbard. You have the right to remain silent. If you do say anything, what you say can be used against you in a court of law. You have the right to consult with a lawyer and have that lawyer present during any questioning. If you cannot afford a lawyer, one will be appointed for you if you desire. Do you understand these rights?"

The other officer began patting Lane down. He took Lane's cell phone and pocketknife, then cuffed him.

"We'll be right behind you, Lane," Desi said.

Lane looked back at Desi and Becky as he was being put into the back seat of the patrol car. "Make sure Abigail knows!"

At the station, they processed Lane in as they had before. He was taken into the cell block and placed in a cell by himself. It would have been nice if Mill and Leroy were with him, but he was glad for them that they weren't. Three hours later, he heard the cell block door buzz and open and the sound of footsteps on the concrete floor. Lane stood to his feet, hoping it was the warden saying he was free to go. The warden did come, but his purpose was simply to usher someone else. The warden unlocked the cell door and in walked Drexel Reece, once again, dressed like a fashion model.

"So, we meet again."

"Can you believe this? They are trying to say I murdered Gunner."

Drexel brought an index finger to his lips. Lane got the message: silent. Drexel turned back to the warden. "Give us a few minutes, if you don't mind."

The warden shrugged his shoulders and pushed up his upper lip with his bottom lip. "You got less than five minutes. Don't push my patience."

The warden turned and headed toward the cell block entrance. Drexel gave him enough time to get out of earshot and then he began. He lifted an open palm to Lane. "Don't speak here. No questions. No statements.

Nothing. Things said in a jail cell have been known to wind up in a courtroom."

Lane gave an affirming nod and leaned in close to Drexel. "I didn't kill him," he whispered.

"I believe you."

"I want out of here."

"The judge set the bond at two hundred thousand. It's being posted now. You should be walking out of here within the hour. We'll talk then."

"Counselor, your time is up!" the warden said.

CHAPTER TWENTY

The court date was right around the corner but, for the moment, the future ordeal and what it might involve were set aside. It was time to celebrate. It was Lane's day. He was the big one nine and, with the signing of a few documents, he'd be the legal owner of the farm that had been in his family for nearly a hundred years. The party attendees feasted on Will Weston's burgers along with Erica's potato salad and special recipe baked beans. Abigail set the cake in the center of the dining table. She'd made it from scratch. Yellow cake with milk chocolate icing. The celebratory crew gathered around. Abigail lit the nineteen candles. Lane made a wish and blew them out with a single breath. His wish was certain to come true. On Abigail's cue, everyone in unison, sang *Happy Birthday*.

When everyone had their fill of the tasty treat, Abigail announced that it was time for gifts.

"We'll go first," Becky said and handed Lane an envelope. Inside were two tickets to the Professional Bull Riding World Finals in Arlington, TX.

"We bought two for ourselves, as well. So, we'll have to make it a double date weekend next spring," Desi said.

Next spring? That was more than six months away. Would Lane be able to go? Or would he be in prison?

"My turn," said Big Pop and handed Lane a package. Lane opened it. A special collector's edition of *Pilgrim's Progress*. "Other than the Bible, it's my favorite book," Big Pop added.

Denver Banks and his wife gave Lane a crisp one-hundred-dollar bill. The Westons gave him a laptop computer.

Drexel Reece reached for his briefcase. "Just a minute, now. I didn't come empty handed." He unzipped it, took out a document and placed it on the table in front of Lane. He pointed to a line. "Sign and date right here and your name will no longer be William Lane Hubbard. Instead, your name will once again be the name you were born with, William Lane Masterson."

Drexel pulled a pen from the briefcase and handed it to Lane.

When Lane finished signing the document, Big Pop notarized it and Drexel returned it to his case.

Will Weston looked at Abigail. "Okay, Abigail, your turn."

"I'll help you carry them," Brodie said.

The two of them slipped away to Abigail's room and returned, each carrying a large, giftwrapped box. They placed the boxes on the dining table.

"These must be opened at the same time," Abigail said. "So, Lane, close your eyes tear the paper off each one. I'll tell you when you can open your eyes."

Lane closed his eyes and ripped off the wrapping paper.

"Okay, now open the boxes."

Lane used his fingers to find the strip of tape on the first box. He pulled it off and popped open the box's top. He did the same with the second one. When the contents of both boxes were exposed, Abigail told him to open his eyes. When he did, his chin began to quiver and his eyes welled with tears.

"Wow. I don't believe it," Lane said, his voice quaking as he spoke.

Inside one box was his record player. Inside the other was his entire collection of albums.

Abigail drew in close to him. He embraced her and gave her a kiss. He released her and looked down into her eyes. "How on earth—"

Abigail spoke up before he could complete the question. "Let's just say I'm good at finding things."

Erica's cell phone rang. She checked it and raised an index finger. "It's mom. I need to take this."

She stepped into the kitchen. The others continued celebrating.

"Oh, no! No!" Erica wailed.

The party went silent as if a switch was flipped. Will rushed to the kitchen.

"Abigal! Brodie! Come in here!" he called out.

The two of them hustled to the kitchen. Lane and his party attendees listened in sadness as they heard the Weston family's loud sobbing. Will returned to the dining room. "Erica's father just passed. Heart attack."

"I'll spread the word to the church," Big Pop said.

Will Weston nodded and walked back to the kitchen.

Denver looked around at the faces of the others. "I think we should all leave them. They need their time."

Becky stepped closer to Lane and placed a hand on his shoulders. "Let us know if we can help in any way," Becky said.

Everyone but Lane left. He stayed with Abigail and the Westons.

•   •   •

Lane wanted to attend the funeral. Denver was willing to give him the time off and Becky was willing to travel with Lane to Texas. The judge, however, balked at the notion. Drexel Reece argued on Lane's behalf, but to no avail. Lane couldn't leave the state of Mississippi. The grandfather of a girlfriend did not qualify as family, the judge had declared. So, since Lane couldn't be at Abigail's side during her time of grief, he'd devised a way to cheer her up when she returned home.

•   •   •

A half mile from his house, Lane pulled over on the shoulder of the road and opened the glove box of the truck. He pulled out a piece of cloth two feet long and two inches wide.

"Turn around. I need to blindfold you."

"What for?" Abigail asked.

"Just trust me and turn around."

She adjusted herself in the passenger seat and turned her back to him. Lane positioned the cloth over Abigail's eyes and tied the ends behind her head. "Can you see anything?"

"Nothing."

"Okay," he said. "You can turn back around now."

When they got to the farm Lane parked close to the barn and helped her out of the truck. He led her into the barn and stopped her in the breezeway. "Stand right here. And remember, no peeking."

Abigail giggled. "Okay, but hurry up. The suspense is killing me."

"Okay, you can take the blindfold off now."

Abigail pushed off the blindfold. Lane stood before her, a chestnut quarter horse reigned at his side. Abigail shot her eyes open, her mouth rounded.

"His name's Sundown," Lane said. "You like him?"

Abigail walked up to the horse and rubbed him between the eyes. He knickered and she moved her hand down to his mouth. Sundown nuzzled her palm with his upper lip. "Lane, he's beautiful. Can we ride him?"

"Of course." Lane stepped to the barn crib and came back with a saddle. "Here you go," he said.

Abigail shot him a look and grinned. "So, you're gonna make me saddle him? Is that the way this works?"

"Why not? He's your horse."

Abigail shot her hands to the sides of her head. "What! You're joking. Right?"

"Nope. I got him for you."

"Oh, Lane!" Abigail threw her arms around Lane's neck and hugged him. "We had a horse back in Texas but had to sell him when we moved here." She kissed him on the cheek. "Thank you." She took the saddle and swung it up on Sundown's back. In five minutes, she had Sundown at a canter.

"He's smooth," she said. "Let's ride him to my house so I can show my parents.

She rode Sundown up close to Lane, removed her left foot from the stirrup and reached out a hand, her face beaming. Lane took her hand, stepped up into the empty stirrup with his left foot, threw his right leg over Sundown's back and settled in behind her on the horse's rump.

"Hold on," she said.

Lane wrapped his arms around the waist of his favorite person in the world. Abigail clicked her tongue and nudged Sundown with her heels. The great steed responded meekly. Lane's heart filled with satisfaction, knowing he'd accomplished his objective: he'd made her happy. He'd strive to do it as often as he could. It was now his great aim in life. He thought about Becky Pritchard's optimistic words, that one day the sun would shine again. Lane was not oblivious to the great cloud that hovered over his life. Whether it would bring a storm or simply blow over, he was unsure. For the time being, however, rays were piercing through it. He'd enjoy them and concern himself with the trial later. The two of them moved in complimentary unison atop the beautiful horse as it carried them. Lane and "his girl."

CHAPTER TWENTY-ONE

Lane walked in wearing a navy pin striped suit and a light blue necktie. It was the first time in his life he'd donned formal attire. Abigail picked it out. Drexel Reece stood behind a table and waited for Lane to join him. The two of them sat down. Lane looked around the room. "Who are all these people?"

"Most of them are just nosey and starved for entertainment."

"You'd think it was advertised on TV."

"A murder trial in a small town is a big event. Forget about them. Focus on what we've talked about."

The bailiff entered through a door near the witness stand. "All rise for the honorable Judge James Redford!"

The crowd stood to its feet. James Redford entered through the same door as the bailiff and made his way to the bench. "Please be seated," he said.

The people in the courtroom sat down as if they were all one person.

The judge interlocked his fingers in front of himself on top of the bench and leaned forward. "We will now begin proceedings in case number three eight six one one, the State of Mississippi versus William Lane Masterson." Redford looked at the man and woman seated behind the table in front of him to his left. "Is the state ready?"

The man pushed his chair back and stood up. "The state is ready, Your Honor," he said and sat back down.

The judge turned to Drexel and Lane. "Is the defense ready?"

Drexel stood to his feet. "The defense is ready, Your Honor," he said and sat back down.

"Very well. We'll begin with opening arguments. Mr. Buckman, the state will go first."

"Yes, Your Honor." Marvin Buckman rose from his seat again and stepped from behind his table. He gave the lapels of his black suit a tug and adjusted the knot of his red necktie. His suit was in order and his tie didn't need adjusting. Both actions were simply Buckman's M.O. in the courtroom. Drexel Reece had seen Buckman in action on more than a few occasions and had even done battle with him on three cases. Drexel was one-for-three against Buckman. Buckman squared his shoulders and approached the jury box. "Ladies and gentlemen of the jury, the State of Mississippi will provide damning and compelling evidence to show that Lane Masterson planned and carried out the murder of Gunner Hubbard. You will see documents and hear testimony that make it clear to any rational mind that Lane Masterson is guilty. Don't let Mr. Masterson's youthfulness and humble demeanor fool you or affect your judgment. The state will prove that, by the means of ethylene glycol poisoning, Mr. Masterson murdered Gunner Hubbard in cold blood, a man who was there as a father figure in Mr. Masterson's life and even adopted him because he loved him as his very on natural son. He fed Mr. Masterson. Clothed Mr. Masterson. Sheltered Mr. Masterson. Taught Mr. Masterson certain life skills that have led to Mr. Masterson's current gainful employment." Marvin Buckman turned away from the jurors and began pacing back and forth before them. "And yet, Mr. Masterson, in vile depravity, plotted and orchestrated Gunner Hubbard's death." He hammer-fisted his open palm when he said the words plotted and orchestrated. He stopped and faced the jurors again. He put one hand on his hip and raised an index finger as if he were a college professor giving a lecture on philosophy. "When all is said and done, you will be able to render a guilty verdict and do so with a clear conscience and strong sense of justice." He cut a high-minded look at Drexel and began walking back to his seat.

Lane leaned over to Drexel. "That's all a load of bull crap."

"I know," Drexel said. "Now, it's my turn."

Drexel rose from his chair and strolled to the jury box. "Ladies and gentlemen of the jury, before I begin, let me just acknowledge something." He turned to Marvin Buckman. "Nice suit. Bet it cost you a grand or more."

The crowd chuckled. Buckman smirked. The judge rapped the gavel. "Mr. Reece, this is a courtroom, not a cocktail party. Please keep that in mind."

Drexel Reece nodded to Buckman. "Of course, Your Honor." He turned back to the jury. "My client, Mr. Masterson, is accused, let me emphasize, ACCUSED of murdering Gunner Hubbard. We will be calling witnesses and presenting evidence to prove, let me emphasize, PROVE that Mr. Masterson is innocent of the charge brought against him. You'll be hearing testimony and evidence from the state. It will be speculative and circumstantial. What the state will present will only show that Mr. Masterson merely LOOKS guilty, APPEARS guilty. But the purpose of our system of justice is not to convict a person because the person looks or appears guilty. I would remind you that our moon looks and appears to be a source of light when, in actuality, it is not. The moon simply reflects the light of the sun. The sun is responsible for the light of the moon and not the moon itself. The purpose of our justice system is to convict people who are, in fact, guilty not those who simply look or appear guilty."

Drexel walked back to his seat and sat down. "Good work," Lane whispered.

"We've still got a long way to go," Drexel replied.

Buckman rose to his feet. "Your Honor, the state would like to call its first witness."

"Go ahead, Counselor."

"The state calls Garner Hubbard."

Garner Hubbard stood from his seat in the back of the room and walked to the witness stand. He raised his hand and vowed to tell the truth, the whole truth and nothing but the truth.

"Mr. Hubbard, would you tell the court what your relationship is . . . uh, excuse me. What your relationship WAS with Gunner Hubbard?"

"He was my twin brother."

"And did you and your twin brother ever discuss his homelife?"

"We did. Often."

"And would you tell us how your brother characterized his life with Lane Masterson who, up until recently, was known as Lane Hubbard?"

"Let me stop you right there, Mr. Buckman. I need to make a point of clarification," Judge Redford said. He looked to the jury. "Ladies and gentlemen of the jury, please be advised that the defendant recently changed his legal name from William Lane Hubbard to William Lane Masterson."

"Thank you for clarifying that, Your Honor. The defendant's motivation to change his name was ill will and spite, no doubt," Buckman interjected.

"Objection, Your Honor," Drexel Reece proclaimed. "The defendant changed his name back to his birth name, the name given to him by his beloved, natural parents. Something entirely legal and well within his right to do. We ask that Mr. Buckman's judgmental opinion as to the defendant's motivation be stricken from the record."

"Sustained," the judge said. He looked at Buckman. "Mr. Buckman, spare us of your psychiatric analysis of the defendant and get back to the business of this court."

"Of course, Your Honor," Buckman said and turned his attention back to Garner Hubbard. "Mr. Hubbard how did your brother characterize his life with Mr. Masterson?"

"He told me that his stepson, Mr. Masterson, was hard to live with. That he often threw tantrums. Swore at him and never accepted him as his stepdad. He told me he loved Mr. Masterson but that his love was not reciprocated."

"Uh huh. When was the last time you talked with him?"

"About two weeks before he was murdered."

Drexel stood to his feet. "Objection, Your Honor. It has not been determined that Gunner Hubbard was murdered."

"Sustained. The witness will need to rephrase the statement."

"About two weeks before he died," Garner Hubbard said.

"And did he express any sort of concern or trepidation?" Buckman asked.

"He said that Mr. Masterson had threatened to kill him and that he had beaten him up."

Marvin Buckman turned and started toward his table. The lady that accompanied him opened a file and pulled out a document. "Your Honor, for the record, the state would like to present this police report as evidence item A."

"You may."

"Your Honor, this is a copy of the report that was filed immediately following the confrontation Mr. Hubbard just spoke of. The report states that the confrontation occurred on the back porch of the house where Mr. Hubbard and Mr. Masterson lived. It also states that Mr. Masterson slammed Gunner Hubbard down on the porch, beat him profusely about the face and told him he'd kill him."

Buckman handed the document to the judge. "Your Honor, the state has another item of evidence it would like to enter, if it pleases the court."

The judge started reviewing the police report. "You may."

Buckman's partner pulled another document from the file. Buckman walked over and took it. "Your Honor, I have in my hands, item B, which is a hospital report. It states that on the day of the assault on the porch . . ."

Drexel Reece stood to his feet again. "Your Honor, my client has not been found guilty of assault."

"Sustained. Mr. Buckman, you'll need to reword your statement."

Buckman nodded. "Of course, Your Honor. The hospital reports that on the day of the alleged assault—"

Reece rose again and cut Buckman off before he could complete his sentence. "Objection, Your Honor. As I stated, my client was never found guilty of an assault."

"Because he murdered my brother before the case could go to court," Garner Hubbard lashed out.

The courtroom erupted. The judge pounded the gavel. "Order! Order!" The crowd quieted. The judge turned to Garner Hubbard. "Another outburst like that and I'll fine you."

"Yes, Your Honor."

The judge looked to the stenographer. "Strike Mr. Hubbard's comment from the record. And now back to Mr. Reece's objection."

Marvin Buckman turned over an open palm and displayed a look of confusion. "Your Honor, it is not inaccurate to say that there was an alleged assault. Afterall, Gunner Hubbard did file a police report that a crime had been committed against him."

"Overruled."

Drexel sat back down.

Buckman continued. "Your Honor, the hospital report states that Gunner Hubbard was treated for a broken nose and received sixteen stitches because of the beating Mr. Masterson inflicted upon him."

Buckman handed the hospital report to the judge and walked back over to Garner Hubbard. "Mr. Hubbard, did your brother tell you anything else?"

"He told me he was having panic attacks and trouble sleeping because he feared that Mr. Masterson would kill him sooner or later."

"Thank you, Mr. Hubbard. That's all."

Garner Hubbard proceeded to stand up.

"The defense would like to question the witness, Your Honor," Drexel said.

"Go ahead."

Garner sat back down again and Drexel approached him. "Mr. Hubbard, where do you live?"

"Chicago."

"And, exactly what do you do for a living?"

"Objection, Your Honor! Irrelevant!"

Drexel interjected. "I assure you, Your Honor, what Mr. Hubbard does to acquire money and where he lives are relevant."

Judge Redford drew down his brow and pondered, his eyes fixed on Drexel. "I'll allow it, Counselor. But you better get somewhere fast. Overruled!"

"I do various things. Odd jobs and what not."

"The odd jobs and what not that you do, really amounts to simply living off money you inherited from your three previous wives who are now all now deceased. Don't they?"

The court erupted again.

"Objection, Your Honor!" Buckman yelled.

Drexel was not deterred. "That's the way you and your brother rolled, wasn't it. Marry women with resources so you can collect when they die. And they always die questionable deaths. Don't they?"

Redford pounded his gavel as if he were driving nails. "Order! Order!"

The crowded quieted.

"Counselors, both of you approach the bench."

Reece and Buckman walked to the judge.

"Mr. Reece, what on earth are you trying to pull?"

"Your Honor, a trend can be clearly seen in the Hubbard brothers. They have a history of inheriting money from deceased wives. Mr. Hubbard is not a credible witness. The supposed conversations he had with his brother could be nothing more than pre-planned made-up stories to make my client look violent."

"Your Honor, the witness's marital status and financial wherewithal have nothing to do with Mr. Masterson's actions," Buckman protested.

Judge Redford looked at Drexel. "I'll not have any more of this kind of shenanigan in my court. You hear?"

"Yes, Your Honor."

Redford turned to Buckman. "And you, you know good and well that your witness's credibility would be questioned. You should have done your homework better on Mr. Hubbard. Any lawyer worth his salt is going to go after a witness's character, especially one that hints at being an interloping gold digger. I'm not saying your witness is, but I am saying he's an easy target to shoot at."

"Yes, Your Honor."

"Now, let's get on with it."

Buckman returned to his seat, Drexel Reece to the front of the witness stand.

"Objection sustained. Strike Mr. Reece's remarks from the record."

Reece launched his next assault. "Mr. Hubbard, Chicago is a long way from Locust Fork, Mississippi. You say you and your brother communicated on a regular basis. Is that correct?"

"Yes."

"How many times would you say you communicated with your brother, say, during the six-week period leading up to his death?"

"Four or five, I'd say."

"And exactly how did you communicate?"

"By phone."

"Cell phone?"

"Yes."

Reece walked to his table and took some papers from a stack. He walked back to Garner Hubbard. "I have here Gunner Hubbard's cell phone history for the six weeks leading up to his death." Reece pointed to an entry on the record. "Is this your number right here?"

Garner Hubbard looked at it. "Yes."

Reece pulled the document back and peered into Garner's eyes. "That number appears only once in the six weeks prior to his death. That's not a regular basis. You're lying. Aren't you, Mr. Hubbard?"

"No, I'm not. Most times he used his landline."

Drexel Reece turned to the judge. "No more questions, Your Honor."

"Would the state like to call another witness?"

"The state would like to call Freda Blassengame."

Reece got to his feet quickly. "Objection, Your Honor, the defense wasn't informed of the witness."

"Your Honor," Buckman said. "We made contact with the witness in the last twenty-four hours. She had personal encounters with Gunner Hubbard before his death."

"I'll allow the witness. Overruled."

Freda rose from her seat and approached the witness stand. She took the oath and sat down.

"Miss Blassengame, you knew Gunner Hubbard personally, didn't you?"

"I did. He came to the bar where I work as a bartender."

"And how would you describe your relationship with Mr. Hubbard?"

"He was friendly. Easy to talk to."

"Were the two of you involved?"

"We planned to be. We talked about it. But then he—" Freda's voice quaked. "He passed away."

"Do you have any reason to believe his passing was due to foul play?"

"Yes. One time when he came in he had a bandage over his eye and his nose looked a little swollen. I asked him about it, and he said he'd been jumped and beaten up."

"Did he say who did it?"

"No, just said it was someone he knew and trusted. Said it made him really sad."

"Did he tell you anything else?"

"He told me he was in a tight situation and that his life was in jeopardy."

"Thank you, Miss Blassengame. No further questions."

"Would the defense like to question the witness?" Redford asked.

Drexel Reece shook his head and made a shooing motion with one hand.

The judge looked at Buckman. "Carry on."

"The state calls Roger Polk."

Lane recognized Roger Polk. He was one of the two county officers who'd come to the farm.

"Mr. Polk, would you tell the court what you do?"

"I'm a deputy sheriff for Huntsville County."

"I understand that you and your partner paid Mr. Masterson a visit shortly after Mr. Hubbard's death. Did you not?"

"We did."

"Tell us why and what you found?"

"We went to Mr. Masterson's house because the autopsy revealed ethylene glycol in Mr. Hubbard's body. We always check things out when that's the case."

"And why is that, Officer Polk?"

"Because ethylene glycol in the body means the victim died of antifreeze poisoning."

"When you went to Mr. Masterson's house did you find any antifreeze?"

"Yes. We found a partial container of it in the kitchen under the sink."

Buckman walked to his assistant. She handed him a plastic one-gallon container sealed in a large clear plastic bag. Buckman took it and approached Officer Polk. "Is this the bottle you recovered?"

"It is."

"Your Honor, the state would like to enter this as item C into evidence, if it please the court."

Buckman turned his attention back to Polk. "Did you check the container for prints?"

"The lab did."

"And whose prints did they find on the container?"

"They found three sets. Mr. Hubbard's, Mr. Masterson's and those belonging to a stock clerk at the local AutoZone."

"Did you find anything else in the home?"

"Yes. We found a pitcher of sweet tea. There were some dirty dishes in the sink. We took the cups and glasses for the lab to check."

Buckman retrieved a drinking glass from his assistant. It was enclosed in a plastic bag as well. "Is this one of those glasses, Officer Polk?"

"Yes."

"Your Honor, the state would like to submit item D into evidence." Buckman set the glass on display next to the plastic jug. "Was there anything unusual about this glass?" he asked Polk.

"The lab found antifreeze residue in it."

The collective sound of voices began to rise in the courtroom.

Judge Redford rapped his gavel. "Order!"

Buckman continued with Polk. "Officer Polk, did the lab find Mr. Masterson's fingerprints on the glass?"

"Yes."

"And you say you also found a pitcher of sweet tea in the refrigerator. Correct?"

"That is correct."

Buckman walked to his table. His assistant handed him a clear plastic bag, a glass tea pitcher inside. He walked back over to Polk and held it up before him. "Is this the tea pitcher you speak of, Officer Polk?"

"It is."

"Your Honor, the state would like to submit this pitcher into evidence as item E."

Buckman set the pitcher next to the glass and jug of antifreeze. "Did the lab examine it?"

"Yes."

"And what did they find?"

"The tea inside contained antifreeze."

The court room rose to a chatter.

Redford pounded his gavel. "Order! Order!"

The crowd quieted.

Buckman picked back up with Polk. "Did the lab check it for prints?"

"They did. It had two sets. One set belonging to Hubbard and one set belonging to Mr. Masterson."

"Did Mr. Masterson say anything to you about the tea pitcher?"

"Yes. He told me that he never drank from it. He said he always made his own tea and used a different container."

"And Officer Polk, was there another tea pitcher in the refrigerator besides Mr. Hubbard's?"

"No."

Buckman turned to the jury. "Ladies and gentlemen of the jury, please note what Mr. Masterson told Officer Polk. He said he always made his own tea and used a different container than Mr. Hubbard's. Now, let me ask you, if he always used a different pitcher for the tea he made for himself, why are his prints on Mr. Hubbard's? I'll tell you why."

Buckman picked up the bag that contained the drinking glass. With one hand he held it up before the jury and with the other he held up the bag containing the pitcher. "Because he mixed antifreeze in Mr. Hubbard's tea pitcher so that this glass could become a weapon, a weapon that poisoned Mr. Hubbard!"

"Objection, Your Honor!" Reece shouted. "Speculation!"

Buckman cut in. "Your Honor, it is a fact confirmed by a scientific lab that antifreeze was in the pitcher and that antifreeze residue was found in the glass."

"Overruled."

"Thank you, Your Honor," Buckman said and turned back to Officer Polk. "Did you find anything else at the farm?"

"The house didn't have much in it. A few pieces of furniture in the den. A bed and a nightstand in the master. A bookshelf with books in the hallway. A bed in Mr. Masterson's bedroom. A nightstand. A chest of drawers. That was about it."

"And did you notice anything else in Mr. Masterson's bedroom? Say, next to his bed?"

"There was a book."

"And did you notice the title that book?

"The title was *The Art of War*."

Buckman's assistant pulled a book from her briefcase. Buckman held it up to Polk. "Is this the book, Officer Polk?"

"Looks like it."

"Objection, Your Honor," Drexel Reece said. "The book is a popular classic. It's in all major bookstores and libraries. Just because it LOOKS like the book Officer Polk saw next to Mr. Masterson's bed doesn't mean it WAS the book he saw next to his bed."

"Sustained!"

"Let me rephrase the question. Officer Polk. Was the title of the book you saw next to Mr. Masterson's bed the same as the title I'm holding?"

"Yes."

Buckman turned to the jury and opened the book. "Ladies and gentlemen this book is indeed a popular work of classic literature just as the defense pointed out. It is a book written by Sun Tzu, a Chinese general and war philosopher who lived between 544 BC and 496 BC. In it he gives advice on how to wage war, how to KILL. Listen to one entry. *'Now, in order to kill the enemy, our men must be roused to anger, that there may be advantage from defeating the enemy, they must have their rewards.'* Chapter two. Number 16." Buckman clapped the book shut with force. The sound echoed throughout the courtroom. "Ladies and gentlemen of the jury, don't you find it odd that Mr. Masterson was reading this book?" Buckman began pacing. "Why not read Dickens or Melville or Tolkien or Hemmingway?"

He held the book up to the jurors. "Why read a copy of this book?" He paused a moment. "I'll tell you why. Because he needed to psyche himself up to kill someone and that someone was Gunner Hubbard." Buckman raised his voice. "Gunner Hubbard went to work that morning with the intent of putting in an honest day's work and then returning home to care for his stepson, Lane Masterson. But unbeknownst to Mr. Hubbard, Lane Masterson had laced his sweet tea with antifreeze hoping Mr. Hubbard would drink it and die. Mr. Hubbard did drink it that very day and he DIED just as Mr. Masterson hoped he would." The flamboyant attorney pointed an index finger at Lane. "That man, Lane Masterson MURDERED him." Marvin Buckman paused and scanned the crowd, an angry, judgmental look on his face. He gave the jury a dose of the same non-verbal medicine. "No further questions, Your Honor," he said and walked back to his chair as cocksure as a professional boxer.

"Would the defense like to question the witness?" Redford asked.

"Yes, Your Honor."

Reece approached Officer Polk. "Officer Polk, you say that anytime an autopsy reveals antifreeze poisoning, an investigation is conducted. Correct?"

"That is correct."

"And why do an investigation? If someone is poisoned it means they were murdered. Doesn't it?"

"Not necessarily."

"Oh, so it could be something other than murder. Correct?"

"Yes. It could be an accident. Antifreeze is sweet and should be stored safely away from children. And it has also been used to commit suicide."

A sigh rose in the courtroom.

"Thank you, Officer Polk," Reece said. "No further questions, Your Honor."

"Mr. Buckman, does the state have another witness it'd like to call?"

Buckman stood up and retweaked his necktie. He swelled his chest and rolled his hand over toward the judge. "Of course, it does, Your Honor," he said with a display of arrogance.

"Mr. Buckman, curb the drama. This is a courtroom, not a theater. A simple yes or no is sufficient."

The crowd laughed.

Buckman smiled. "Yes, Your Honor. The state calls Dwight Ballard to the stand."

Ballard took the oath and sat down.

"Mr. Ballard, would you tell the court how you knew Gunner Hubbard?"

"We worked together at North Mississippi Electric."

"Were you with Mr. Hubbard when he fell ill?'

"Yes, we were replacing a transformer out on Highway 178."

"Were you with him the entire day?"

"Yes."

"Did Mr. Hubbard complain of not feeling well or having a headache or anything?"

"When we first got started that morning, he said he had a little bit of a stomachache but that was about it. When he was up in the crane bucket is when it seemed to hit him all at once."

"And what time would you say this occurred?"

"It was early. About 8:30 I'd say."

"No further questions, Your Honor."

Judge Redford looked at Reece. "Your witness, Counselor."

Drexel stood and addressed Ballard from his table. "Mr. Ballard, was there ever a time that day when you were not with Gunner Hubbard?"

"Well, I wasn't with him before he came to work."

"But when he got to work, the two of you were always together?"

"Yes."

"Thank you, Mr. Ballard. No further questions."

Judge Redford looked at Buckman. "Does the state have another witness it'd like to call?"

Buckman stood up. "No, Your Honor. But the state would like to request a recess."

Judge Redford looked at his watch. "We'll take a lunch recess and reassemble at 1:30 PM." He looked at Drexel Reece. "When we do, Mr.

Reece, it'll be your turn at bat." Redford rapped his gavel. "Court is now in recess."

People began filing out of the courtroom. Marvin Buckman stepped over to Drexel Reece. "You're about to be one-for-four, Reece."

CHAPTER TWENTY-TWO

The crowd gathered back into the courtroom, their hunger for food quenched by the lunch they'd just had, their hunger for courtroom drama, however, every bit as ferocious as it was when the day began.

"All rise," the bailiff commanded.

Everyone in the room stood. A robed James Redford walked in and retook his place as the courtroom boss. "Be seated." He gave the people a few seconds to settle in and then hammered the gavel once. "Court is now in session." He looked down at Drexel. "The defense may call its first witness."

Drexel stood to his feet. "The defense calls Amelia Rutherford."

A middle-aged woman dressed in a brown business suit approached the witness stand. She was sworn in and took her seat in the box. Drexel walked up to her. "Mrs. Rutherford, can you tell the court what you do for a living?"

"I'm the chancery clerk for Huntsville County."

"And as the chancery clerk for Huntsville County you are the person who is in charge of all real estate deeds. Correct?"

"That is correct."

"If a parcel of real estate, say a farm with a house and a barn, were to change legal owners, would you and your staff be the people responsible to see that such a change is done properly?"

"Yes."

"Mrs. Rutherford, in the recent months, have you had to make any changes to the deed for the property where Mr. Lane Masterson lives?"

"I have."

"Can you tell us about it?"

"The ownership of the property was transferred over to Mr. Masterson."

"And why was it necessary to do that?"

"Because Mr. Masterson turned nineteen. It was in his parents' will that in the event they were both deceased, the farm they owned was to be transferred over to him when he turned nineteen."

"And on what date did you transfer the ownership to Mr. Masterson?"

"October sixth of this year, Mr. Masterson's birthday."

"Now, Mrs. Rutherford, as the legal owner of the property, Mr. Masterson has every right to do with it as he sees fit. Is this correct?"

"He can, as long as it's legal."

Drexel nodded, his upper lip pushed up with his bottom lip. "Okay. So, he could do things like till the ground, cut the timber, tear down the barn, add on to the house, etc.?"

"That is correct."

"He could also rent out the property if he wanted. Could he not?"

"He could."

"Objection, Your Honor! What Mr. Masterson might do with the property now that he owns it has nothing to do with the death of Gunner Hubbard."

Drexel countered. "Your Honor, I promise you that establishing the fact that Mr. Masterson now is the legal owner of his family farm is very relevant to the charges he's facing."

"Overruled, but do hurry, Mr. Reece."

"Yes, Your Honor." Drexel turned his attention back to Mrs. Rutherford. "Mrs. Rutherford, let's say someone happened to be living on the property before it was legally Mr. Masterson's. Once it became his, could he make the person move?"

"I suppose he could."

Drexel turned to the jury. "Ladies and gentlemen of the jury, Mrs. Rutherford, the chancery clerk of Huntsville County, has just informed us that the farm was deeded over to Mr. Masterson on October sixth. Gunner Hubbard died on September the fourteenth, a mere three weeks before Mr. Masterson's birthday. What did Mr. Masterson stand to gain by murdering Gunner Hubbard when all he had to do, if he wanted him gone, was wait three weeks and then make him move out?"

"Objection, Your Honor! Gaining something is not necessarily a motivation for committing murder. Throughout history evil people have committed murder for no other reason than to end life."

Drexel Reece grinned. "Your Honor, the state produced a book as evidence. Mr. Buckman read a portion in the hearing of the court. I have the quote right here in my pocket." Drexel pulled out a piece of paper. "Mr. Buckman read, and I quote, *'Now, in order to kill the enemy, our men must be roused to anger, that there may be advantage from defeating the enemy, they must have their rewards.'* Mr. Buckman stated that Mr. Masterson was reading this book to, as he put it, 'psyche himself up to murder Gunner Hubbard.' Well, the book clearly states that to kill the enemy, a reward must be had. Mr. Buckman characterized Gunner Hubbard as Mr. Masterson's enemy. If Mr. Masterson gained nothing by murdering Gunner Hubbard, then, according to the book Mr. Masterson was reading, he had no motivation to murder Gunner Hubbard. Mr. Masterson was simply reading a classic work of literature as one might read Shakespeare or Agatha Christie. Therefore, the book should not be considered as credible evidence."

The crowd began to murmur. Judge Redford used his gavel to get their attention. "Order!"

"Overruled, Mr. Buckman! Mr. Reece does have a good point."

Buckman inhaled a belly full of air then exhaled. He closed his eyes and shook his head, his lips pressed tightly. Drexel Reece had landed a blow.

"No more questions, Your Honor," Reece said.

The judge looked at Buckman. "Your witness."

"No questions, Your Honor."

"The defense may call it's next witness."

"We call Desi Pritchard, Your Honor."

Desi rose from his seat and walked to the witness stand. He promised to tell the truth and took the seat.

"Mr. Pritchard, in what capacity do you know the defendant?"

"He works for me on a regular basis and he's a friend."

"Do you consider Mr. Masterson to be an honest man, a man of good character?"

"Yes."

"Can you tell the court something that Lane Masterson has or has not done that has caused you to think so well of him?"

"Some months ago, a storm blew a tree down on my shop. I had to have about half the shop rebuilt. I hired Lane to clean out the shop before the contractor came. It was cheaper to have Lane clean it out and it would enable the contractor to finish the job quicker. Before Lane started cleaning out the shop, I put two hundred dollars in a coffee can and placed the can in the shop. It was a test. I wanted to see if Lane would steal the money or give it to me."

"And what did he do when he found it?"

"He gave it to me."

"So you have found him to be an honest man?"

Desi looked at Lane and then at Drexel. "He's one of the finest young men I know."

"Do you think Lane Masterson is the kind of person who would commit murder?"

Desi shook his head. "Absolutely not."

"No further questions, Your Honor."

"Would the state like to question the witness?" the judge asked Buckman.

Buckman's assistant whispered something to him. "Yes, Your Honor," Buckman said.

He stood to his feet and walked a few feet from his table. "Mr. Pritchard, how long have you known Mr. Masterson?"

"About eight months, I'd say."

"Are you married, Mr. Pritchard?"

"Yes."

"Could you point her out to us today?"

Drexel stood up. "Objection, Your Honor! Irrelevant!"

Buckman touched a hand to his chest and gave a comical expression. "Your Honor, I figure if the defense is allowed to bring up a witness's three previous wives, the state can bring up a witness's current wife."

The crowd laughed.

The judge gave them the gavel and called the court back to order.

"Mr. Buckman, I'll give you a little rope, but not much. Objection overruled. The witness' wife will please stand if she's present."

Becky stood up. Buckman threw up a hand. "Nice to meet you, Mrs. Pritchard."

Becky didn't acknowledge the greeting. She just sat back down.

"Mr. Pritchard, how long did you know her before you asked her to marry you?" Buckman asked.

"Fourteen months."

Marvin Buckman began to pace in front of the jury. He stopped and looked at them. "Mr. Pritchard, do you really expect this jury to believe that in eight months you could accurately evaluate Mr. Masterson's character while it took you fourteen months to evaluate your wife's?"

The courtroom filled with laughter.

"Objection, Your Honor! Irrelevant!" Drexel Reece proclaimed.

Judge Redford pounded his gavel. "Order! Order!"

The crowd gathered itself. Redford looked at Buckman. "Mr. Buckman, this is the second time I've warned you. If I have to warn you again, I'll fine you. You're a professional and I expect you to act like one in my courtroom."

Marvin Buckman raised open palms. "Sorry, Your Honor. No further questions."

"Mr. Reece, you may call your next witness."

"The defense calls Dr. Will Weston, Your Honor."

Will Weston came forward and took the oath.

"Dr. Weston, can you tell us what you do?"

"I'm the senior pastor of Soulshine Church."

"And how many years, in total, have you been a minister?"

"I've been a senior pastor for over thirteen years now."

"That's a considerable amount of experience. How do you know the defendant?"

"I'm Lane's pastor."

"Is Mr. Masterson a faithful member of your church?"

"Very."

"Dr. Weston, how large is your congregation?"

"We average between four fifty and five hundred on Sunday mornings."

"Wow! That's a large church for a town the size of Locust Fork. A large church for any town for that matter. I'm sure you're very busy. Would it be safe to say that it's difficult to give personal time to each member of your congregation?"

"It can be. But we have deacons and teachers who assist me greatly in ministry."

"Dr. Weston, how well do you know Lane Masterson?"

"I know him better than any other member of the church, besides my own family."

"And why is that?"

"Because Lane and I meet with each other one-on-one for an hour or more each week."

"I think it's called discipleship, isn't it?"

"Yes."

"So, you are knowledgeable of his character?"

"Yes, very knowledgeable."

"As an experienced pastor, do you think he would commit murder?"

"I can say, unequivocally, 'No.'"

"Thank you, Dr. Weston. No more questions, Your Honor."

When asked if the state had any questions for Dr. Weston, Buckman answered in the affirmative. He stood to his feet and strolled up to Will Weston. "Dr. Weston, you said something that intrigued me. You said that you know Mr. Masterson better than any of your other church members. Correct?"

"That is correct, with the exception of my own family."

"Mm. I see. Is Mr. Masterson the only church member you meet with weekly on a one-on-one basis?"

"I meet with a couple of groups of men, but Lane is the only one I'm currently meeting with on an individual basis."

Marvin Buckman rubbed his chin. "And what kind of things do you and Mr. Masterson talk about?"

"We talk about the Bible, of course. We talk about him personally, as well."

"By personally, do you mean things like Mr. Masterson's behavior, his habits, his hobbies and what not?"

"Yes."

"In the police report Gunner Hubbard filed when Mr. Masterson 'allegedly', as the defense puts it, attacked him, Mr. Hubbard stated that the defendant told him, 'I hate you and I'll kill you.' Did Mr. Masterson ever tell you that he hated and wanted to kill Gunner Hubbard?"

The question sucked the air out of the room. Lane felt he was pinned to a wall.

Will Weston relaxed his shoulders and exhaled. "He told me he hated him and that there were times when he wanted to kill him."

Unified sighs filled the courtroom.

"I'll take that as a yes." Buckman said.

Will attempted to expand. "But—"

"No buts, Reverend. He told you he hated him and wanted to kill him." Buckman turned to Judge Redford. "No further questions, Your Honor."

Dexter Reece jumped to his feet. "Your Honor, I suggest we adjourn for the day."

James Redford checked his watch. "It's not even four o'clock, Counselor, but it has been an a rather eventful day. Court adjourned until tomorrow morning at 9 AM." He hammered his gavel once and the crowd began exiting the courtroom.

●　　　●　　　●

Since Drexel Reece's office was almost two hundred miles away in Jackson, he stayed at a motel when he came to Locust Fork. The Weston's house served as the "war room" for the battle in which Lane found himself. Drexel arrived at the parsonage at 8 PM, two hours later than planned. Lane, the Westons, the Pritchards, the Banks, and Big Pop sat around the den, eager to hear the counselor's strategy for ensuring that he'd improve his record to two-for-four against Marvin Buckman. Drexel sat down on the couch and placed his briefcase on the coffee table. He leaned forward. "I'm sorry to be so late but I've been in a remote meeting with a team of six other lawyers from my firm since four thirty. We've hashed and rehashed every detail of the case. The fact that Lane slept in the house the night before and the fact that he doesn't have an alibi. The fact that he had opportunity to lace the tea with antifreeze. The fact that the antifreeze found under the sink matches the antifreeze that was found in the pitcher and that Lane's prints are on both of them. The fact that a drinking glass in the sink had antifreeze residue in it and Lane's fingerprints on it. The fact that he and Gunner didn't get along."

"That's an understatement," Lane said.

Reece continued, his eyes fixed on Lane. "The fact that the two of you had an altercation and a police report is on file. That you beat him up and threatened to kill him." Reece looked at Will Weston. "And your testimony that Lane told you he hated Gunner and wanted to kill him sometimes." Reece returned his attention to Lane. "It all looks bad, Lane."

"What does Lane have in his favor?" Big Pop asked.

"Not much. We're treading water big time."

"Which way do you think the jury is leaning?" Will asked.

"It's hard to read a jury, but if I was betting, I'd say they're with Buckman."

"So, what about tomorrow? What's the plan?"

"Well, I and the other six lawyers are in full agreement in recommending something that is extremely rare and seldom advised."

"Which is?" Erica said.

"Putting Lane on the witness stand."

Lane jumped in. "I'm good with that. I'm innocent. The jury needs to hear my side anyway."

"Yes, Lane, you ARE innocent," Drexel said. "But Buckman will come at you hard when he cross-examines you. His objective won't be for the jury to hear your side. He'll be on a mission to destroy you. He'll try to paint you into corners. Use your words against you. Press you when he wants you to say more. Cut you off when he wants to keep you from expanding and explaining yourself, just like he did with Dr. Weston."

Drexel looked at Will. "Don't take that the wrong way, Reverend. You told the truth, but Buckman clipped you, then shut you down. He's a savvy prosecutor. A predator."

"No offense taken," Will said.

Drexel turned his attention back to Lane. "Lane, I can prep you, but not for everything that Buckman might throw at you. I'm sure he'll hit you about sleeping in the house the night before, about the antifreeze being under the sink, and about the pitcher of tea and the glass. I know he'll hammer the fact that you beat Gunner up and said you wanted to kill him. But Buckman will come at you in other ways too. And there's no way to know them all ahead of time. You'll be up there all alone and you'll be taking it as it comes."

Denver Banks raised an open palm. "So, why put him up there then?"

"Because it's the only play we have."

Big Pop touched his chest with the fingertips of one hand. "But I thought you were going to put me on the stand tomorrow to vouch for Lane's character?"

"We think Buckman will pulverize your credibility by painting you to be a naïve school janitor who sees only the good in kids much like an uncle or grandfather,"

Will Weston shook his head. "Umph. And what if putting Lane on the stand doesn't work? What if Buckman does what you say he's capable of?"

"If Lane's convicted, he'll get thirty years to life, possibly the death penalty," Drexel Reece replied.

The room fell silent. Tears began to well in Erica and Becky's eyes.

"Then put me on the stand," Abigail said.

CHAPTER TWENTY-THREE

At 9:25 AM Judge Redford, Marvin Buckman, Drexel Reece, Lane, and Abigail walked into the courtroom. The trial was delayed in starting because of the twenty-minute sidebar in the judge's chamber. Reece had exhorted the judge to allow Abigail to take the stand. Buckman had protested vehemently. Ever the pursuer of justice, James Redford set aside the passion of the two attorneys and made his determination. He sat down on the bench and declared court to be in session.

"The defense may call its witness."

Drexel Reece stood to his feet. "Your Honor, we call Abigail Weston."

After being sworn in, Abigail took her seat in the box.

"Miss Weston, one Saturday morning you witnessed something. Would you tell the court what that was?"

"I was in the loft of Lane Masterson's barn and heard some men talking. When I looked, I saw a black SUV parked in the driveway next to Lane's house. Gunner Hubbard was talking to a big man. And I saw Gunner give the man some money."

Drexel raised an index finger. "Let me stop you right there, Miss Weston. You say you saw Gunner Hubbard give the man some money. Do you know how much money?"

"Twelve hundred dollars."

"How do you know it was twelve hundred?"

"Because Gunner said, 'Here's twelve hundred. It's all I got.'"

"Okay. Go on."

"When I saw him hand the man the money, I pulled out my cell phone and snapped a picture."

"Let me stop you again, Miss Weston."

Drexel pulled a small remote from his pocket and aimed it toward the large projection screen positioned at the front of the courtroom. He pressed the remote and a picture appeared. A tall muscular man stood next to a black late model Lincoln Navigator and Gunner was handing him money.

"Miss Weston, is this the picture you are referring to?"

"Yes."

"Your Honor, the defense would like to enter this photograph into evidence as item A."

James Redford nodded, a solemn expression on his face. "So noted."

"Miss Weston, did you see anything else?"

"Yes. After the man took the money, they talked some more."

"Did you happened to hear what they said?"

"Gunner told the man he'd have the rest the following week. The man called someone on his cell phone and told whoever he was talking to that Gunner had given him twelve hundred and that Gunner said he'd have the rest the following Saturday. The man ended the call and told Gunner to give him his right hand. Gunner was nervous, real nervous. He thought the man was going to shake his hand. Instead, the man twisted Gunner's hand and forced him down on his knees. The man then took a pair of pliers from his pocket and acted like he would cut Gunner's little finger off. I took another picture."

"Once again, Miss Weston let me stop you a moment."

Drexel pushed the remote again and a different picture appeared on the screen. The big man with a pair of pliers. Gunner on his knees, the little finger of one hand in the jaws of the pliers. A look of horror on his face.

"Is this the picture?"

"Yes."

"Your Honor, the defense would like to enter this photograph into evidence as item B."

"Agreed," Redford affirmed.

"Please continue, Miss Weston," Drexel Reece encouraged.

"The man said the twelve hundred was interest and that he'd be back at the same time the following Saturday to get five thousand. The man told Gunner if he didn't have the five thousand when he came back the following Saturday he'd burn the house down. As the man was getting back into the SUV he told Gunner if he ever saw him packing a gun again he'd break both of his legs."

"Miss Weston, did Gunner Hubbard have a gun?"

"Yes. It was sticking in the back of his pants."

"What happened next?"

"The man got into the SUV and drove away. I thought I'd better leave so I started down the barn steps. When I got to the bottom step I stumbled and fell. I guess Gunner heard me because he started walking toward the barn. I scrunched down in a back stall. I saw Gunner through the cracks of the boards, but he didn't see me. He looked around behind the barn. He had his gun drawn. Then went back to the house. When he went inside I ran back home."

"Did you go back to Lane's house again?"

"Yes. I went back the following Saturday. I was curious to see if the man would come back. I climbed back up into the loft and waited. The man came back at the exact time just like he said."

"And what happened when he arrived?"

"Gunner came out of the house. The man got out of the SUV. He walked around to the other side and opened the back passenger door. A lady got out. She was an Asian lady. I'd say Japanese by the way she was dressed. She started talking to Gunner."

"Could you hear what they were saying?"

"Yes."

"Did you take pictures this time?"

"No, I took a video."

Drexel lifted an open hand to her. "Once again, let me stop you right there, Miss Weston."

He pressed the remote again and a video of Miss Red's visit with Gunner started playing on the screen. The court attendees watched with fixed attention as Miss Red dealt with Gunner in an elitist, condescending manner. *"You know the guidelines of our agreement,"* she said to him. *"People come to me when they need money. I never ask them what for. Investing. Purchasing. Or, as in your case, betting with it at a blackjack table. I don't care. Doesn't concern me. What does concern me is that you fulfill your obligation to pay it back in the agreed upon increments and on a timely basis. I'm saddened by the fact that you have fallen behind. It strains our relationship and makes things quite stressful for me. And, Mr. Gunner, I do not handle stress very well."*

Drexel paused the video. "Ladies and gentlemen of the jury, notice the expression on Gunner Hubbard's face. The man looks terrified. He fears her and what she might do to him."

Drexel pressed the remote and the drama continued to play out. *"My records indicate that you have an outstanding balance of one hundred thirty-five thousand dollars."*

Drexel paused it again. "Did you hear that? Gunner Hubbard owed this woman the astronomical sum of one hundred thirty-five thousand dollars. Mr. Hubbard worked as a lineman for North Mississippi Electric Cooperative. His salary was fifty-three thousand dollars a year. So, he owed her more than twice his annual salary. Let's continue watching."

"I have made the decision to void our agreement. You are no longer required to make monthly payments of five thousand. It is simply too stressful for me. As I said, I do not handle stress very well."

"I really appreciate it," Gunner said.

Drexel addressed the court. "Notice how relieved Gunner Hubbard looks now. He's thinking he's just been forgiven his debt. But he's about to be in for a rude awakening. Let's continue watching and see what happens."

"I have decided on a new agreement. Mr. Blade, here, will come visit you again ninety days from now at exactly 9:32 AM."

"Notice how calculating and specific she is," Dexter said. "She checks her watch and then gives Mr. Hubbard the exact time of nine thirty-two, not nine-thirty but nine thirty-two. And she spoke the name of her enforcer,

Mr. Blade. He's a cold-blooded monster, no doubt. Remember the pliers? Let's keep watching."

"When he arrives, he will be expecting to collect the full amount due. One hundred thirty-five thousand."

"Okay, ladies and gentlemen, now we learn the details of the new agreement the woman has for Mr. Hubbard. She expected him to pay the full amount in ninety days. One hundred thirty-five thousand. We can only imagine the stress this caused Mr. Hubbard."

"If for some reason you do not provide him with the full payment, he will make a phone call to me and I will decide what . . . I will decide at that time what necessary provision must be taken. Should you not be here when Mr. Blade arrives, it will cause a most unpleasant situation. I can assure you that there is nowhere you can hide where I will not find you. Questions?"

"That was a threat. Mr. Hubbard knew he'd be killed if he didn't pay the one hundred thirty-five thousand in a mere three months. Can you imagine what Mr. Hubbard's mindset became when he heard her words? He became an emotional wreck. There was no way he could come up with such a large sum of money in such a short time based on the salary he was making. He even tells her that. Watch."

"I really want to pay you every cent I owe you, but I have no idea how I can come up with a hundred and thirty-five g's in ninety days. I'm being honest with you."

"Mr. Gunner, this is a very fine farm you have here. No doubt, for say, a hundred and fifty thousand it would sell quickly. I bet someone would snatch it right up."

"So, the woman suggests Mr. Hubbard sell the farm for a fraction of its market value to pay the debt." Drexel raised an index finger, "But there is a problem. Continue watching and you'll learn what it is."

"The place belongs to the kid. It's what the will says. I can't touch it unless he leaves. And he won't leave. I've tried everything to get him to. No matter how bad I treat him or how bad I beat him he just continues to stay."

"Ladies and gentlemen of the jury, Mr. Hubbard was telling the truth. According to the will, the farm did belong to Lane Masterson at the time because he lived there."

Drexel Reece walked to his table. His assistant pulled a document from her briefcase and handed it to him. Reece held it up. "Here's the will and it plainly states that the farm could not be sold as long as Mr. Masterson was living there. Furthermore, it states that it could be deeded over to Mr. Masterson when he turned nineteen, which is what happened. You heard the chancery clerk's testimony." Drexel handed the will back to his assistant and walked to the jury box. "And by Mr. Hubbard's own mouth we know that his relationship with his stepson, Mr. Masterson, was strained and he's the one who strained it. He brutalized Mr. Masterson for the purpose of driving Mr. Masterson to leave the farm. Because if Mr. Masterson left, Mr. Hubbard could take possession, sell it and pay the woman the money so she wouldn't do whatever it was he knew she'd do. Probably kill him." Drexel put both hands on the rail of the jury box and leaned forward. "But . . . that's . . . not . . . all. There's more." He pulled the remote from his pocket again and started the video.

"Mr. Gunner, surely there must be some clause in the will that could work to your favor."

"There's not I tell you. I've even been to a lawyer. The only way would be for him to leave or deed it over to me and he won't do either."

"I see. What if something were to happen to the kid?"

"If something were to happen . . . like what?"

"Let's say for instance, the kid was to die."

"Then the place would come to me. He's my stepson. I adopted him a few years ago."

"Sounds like a very effective solution to your problem."

"You mean murder him?"

"No, Mr. Gunner. I never said, 'Murder.' But sometimes kids do have accidents. You know, they go hunting and a gun discharges unintentionally. They go swimming and the water is deeper than they thought. They go for a drive and the car has a malfunction. They feel sick and take too much medicine. The possibilities are endless."

The crowd continued to watch as the lady got back into the SUV and made her parting remarks to Gunner, remarks which the video did not pick up.

Drexel turned to the jury. "So, it is clear beyond question that Mr. Hubbard was a man under extreme emotional stress. He had to come up with one hundred thirty-five thousand dollars within ninety days or face whatever consequences the lady would've dealt him. Ladies and gentlemen of the jury, have you ever had financial stress?" Drexel paused and scanned their faces, giving them time to let his question settle in their minds. "If you are like me and most everyone else, the answer is yes. And, you know that it wakes up with you in the morning. It follows you throughout the day. It keeps you awake at night. That bill that's coming due that you don't have the money to pay, and, furthermore, you don't know where you're going to get the money. Imagine what Mr. Hubbard's state of mind, knowing that the bill of one hundred thirty-five thousand was coming due SOON. And if he couldn't pay it, he'd be tortured or killed. Can . . . you . . . imagine?"

Drexel walked back to his table. His assistant gave him three pieces of paper. Drexel turned to the jury again. "I have here in my hands three pieces of paper." He held up the one to the jury. "This first one is a hospital report. You see, some months ago, Mr. Masterson had to be taken to the hospital. It seems a coral snake, a very poisonous snake, the most poisonous snake native to the United States might I add, somehow found its way into Mr. Masterson's bed. It bit him and Mr. Masterson had to be rushed to the hospital. Turns out, it was a dry bite. A dry bite occurs when a poisonous snake bites without injecting venom. Doesn't happen often, but it happens. Luckily for Mr. Masterson, his case was one of those few."

Marvin Buckman yelled out. "Objection, Your Honor! Irrelevant!"

"Your Honor, it is relevant because Gunner Hubbard signed the report as Mr. Masterson's guardian."

Judge James Redford nodded. "Overruled."

Drexel Reece placed the report behind the other two and held up the second one. "This one is a hospital report. It seems that, less than a month later, Mr. Masterson was involved in an automobile accident. An unidentified truck rammed into the back of the truck Mr. Masterson was driving. It forced him off the road and into the Yallaboosa River. He'd probably be dead today if someone hadn't freed him from the submerged truck, drug him to the shore and performed CPR."

Buckman pushed his chair back and jumped to his feet. "Objection, Your Honor. This is absurd."

"Once again, Your Honor, Gunner Hubbard's signature is on the report as Mr. Masterson legal guardian."

"Overruled."

Dexter looked at Buckman, smiled and shrugged. He shuffled the documents and turned back to the jury. "This third one is a receipt from Mount Everest Insurance Company. It states that the premiums on a five hundred-thousand-dollar life insurance policy taken out on William Lane Masterson are paid up for the next three years. Remember what the lady said to Gunner Hubbard. Remember how the lady talked about accidents happening to kids. Hunting accidents. Swimming accidents. Et cetera."

Marvin Buckman's table slid on the floor a few inches as he stood up without pushing his chair back. "Objection, Your Honor. This is pure speculation."

"Your Honor, saying that my client, Lane Masterson, murdered Gunner Hubbard is pure speculation, as well. The defense simply asks for the same judicial liberty the prosecution enjoys."

Judge Redford tightened his jaw and pressed his lips. He pondered for a few seconds. To Lane it felt like an hour. He knew Drexel had Buckman on the ropes. If only the judge would overrule the objection!

"Overruled."

"When Gunner Hubbard adopted Lane Masterson, he became the beneficiary to the policy which means that if Mr. Masterson would've died from either the snake bite or the wreck, Mount Everest would have cut Gunner Hubbard a check for five hundred-thousand dollars."

"Objection, Your Honor," Buckman called out. "We're not here today because Gunner Hubbard attempted to murder Lane Masterson. We're here because the defendant is charged with murdering Mr. Hubbard."

Drexel looked at the judge and shrugged his shoulders. "Your Honor, I never alleged that Mr. Hubbard attempted to murder Mr. Masterson. I simply stated a fact. If Mr. Masterson had died from either the snake bite or the wreck, the insurance company would have paid the benefit to Mr. Hubbard."

"Overruled."

Marvin Buckman dropped back down in his chair and sighed so loudly that the entire room could hear him.

"Mr. Buckman, are you okay?" Judge Redford asked.

"Yes, Your Honor. I'm fine."

"Well, if you are, please act like it in my courtroom."

"Yes, Your Honor."

Drexel approached the witness stand. "Miss Weston, what did Mr. Hubbard do when Mr. Blade and the lady drove away?"

"He went back inside the house."

"And what did you do?"

"I came down from the barn loft and walked to the house."

"Your house or Mr. Masterson's house?"

"Mr. Masterson's."

"Why did you walk to Mr. Masterson's house?"

"Because I wanted to spy on Gunner Hubbard."

"And did you spy on Mr. Hubbard?"

"Yes."

"Would you tell the court what you saw?"

"I looked through his bedroom window and saw him looking through some papers."

"Do you know what papers he was looking at?"

"The will and the life insurance policy."

Drexel turned to the judge. "No further questions, Your Honor."

He walked to his table and sat down. Lane leaned over to him. "That was incredible," he whispered.

"Hang on. Buckman's not gonna go away without a fight."

"Mr. Buckman, your witness," Judge Redford said.

Marvin Buckman rose from his chair and walked to the witness stand with the confidence of a lion. "Miss Weston, it sounds like you and Mr. Masterson are quite fond of one another. Are you?"

"Yes, we are."

"Romantically?"

"Objection, Your Honor!" Drexel said. "Irrelevant."

"Sustained."

Buckman raised his palms in an apologetic gesture and smirked. "Pardon me. I was just trying to get acquainted. Miss Weston, you've got quite the flair for cinematography. Why did you decide to wait to the last minute to come forward?"

"You inspired me, Mr. Buckman."

Buckman cocked his head and drew down his brow. "How on earth did I inspire you?"

"I thought Mr. Masterson's innocence would be so apparent that what I recorded wouldn't be needed. But, when I watched the way you handled my dad and Mr. Pritchard, I realized I'd figured wrong."

Buckman turned to the crowd. "My, my, my. She certainly has a way with words. Doesn't she?"

The people chuckled.

Buckman turned back to Abigail. "Miss Weston. You testified that you saw Gunner Hubbard looking through some papers and that those papers were the will and the life insurance policy. Are you certain that those were the papers?"

"Yes."

Buckman grinned as if he'd won a prize of some sorts. "Well, Miss Weston, please enlighten us. How could you possibly tell that it was the will and the insurance policy that Gunner Hubbard was looking at? After all, you stated you were spying through the window."

"After he studied the papers, he put them back in the box he had them in. He slid the box back under the bed and then left the house. When he was gone, I checked the window, and it was unlocked. So, I raised it and went inside. I took the box from under the bed and looked through the contents."

"Hmm. A window that just happened to be unlocked. Now, I'm not saying you're lying, Miss Weston. But I am saying that your story sounds a little suspicious. How can we be sure you're not making things up?"

Abigail reached into her pocket and pulled out a slip of paper. She handed it to Buckman. "Because of this."

Buckman studied the paper. "It's a pawn shop receipt with various items listed and Gunner Hubbard's name on it. How does this validate your story?"

"Mr. Buckman, you'll notice that there is a record player and some vinyl records on the list. Those items belonged to Lane. Gunner Hubbard stole them and hocked them at a pawn shop over in Robinsonville where the casinos are. Almost a hundred miles away. The pawn receipt was in the box along with the will and the insurance policy. I kept the receipt. Mom and I drove over to Robinsonville to the pawn shop and I bought the record player and the records and gave them back to Lane on his birthday."

A collective "ah" rose in the courtroom.

"Miss Weston, how long have you known the defendant?"

"We met last July."

"So, less than a year?"

"Yes."

"How well did you know Gunner Hubbard?"

"Hardly at all. We had contact on a few occasions. That was about the extent of it."

"Did you ever observe Gunner Hubbard verbally abuse Mr. Masterson?"

"No."

"Did you ever observe Gunner Hubbard physically abuse Mr. Masterson?"

"I saw WHAT he did, and I saw what he did it WITH. But I wasn't there when he did it. So, no."

"Did Lane Masterson ever tell you that he hated Gunner Hubbard?"

"Yes."

"Did he ever tell you that he wanted to kill Gunner Hubbard?"

"Yes"

"Did that not prompt you to tell someone that Gunner Hubbard's life might be in danger in light of Lane Masterson's sentiments?"

"No."

"And why not?"

"Because I knew that Lane was just talking. He was hurt and venting his frustration. Gunner Hubbard was abusive to him. Beat him black and blue with a leather strap from an old saddle."

Buckman huffed. "Your Honor, the state moves to have Miss Weston's last two statement stricken from the record."

"Motion granted, Mr. Buckman."

Buckman turned his attention back to Abigail. "Just answer my questions, Miss Weston. No ad-libbing, please."

"Well, I swore to tell the whole truth."

Laughter filled the courtroom. Buckman shook his head, his jaw clinched. He inhaled and exhaled through his nostrils. "Your Honor, the state moves to strike Miss Weston's comment."

"Motion denied, Counselor. There's nothing out of order about the witness reminding the court of the oath she took."

Lane leaned over to Drexel Reece. "She's doing good. Isn't she?"

"She's matching him punch for punch so far," Reece replied.

Buckman's facial expression turned hard. He looked Abigail in the eyes and motioned to the projection screen. "Miss Weston, why didn't you go to the authorities and show them your recordings? If you had, it might have prevented Gunner Hubbard's death, you know."

"Objection, Your Honor. Badgering the witness!" Drexel Reece said.

"Overruled. I want to hear this," Redford replied. He looked down at Abigail. "Answer the question."

"Because I didn't trust them. Didn't think they'd do anything."

Buckman cocked his head. "Miss Weston, that sounds absurd. Why wouldn't you trust law enforcement?"

"Because I believe the sheriff has some kind of personal relationship with the man known as Mr. Blade."

Buckman lifted opened palms. "Oh, so you're trying to convince the court that the sheriff of Huntsville County is corrupt?"

Abigail didn't flinch. "I didn't say that."

Buckman put his hands on his hips and began pacing. "Well, surely, Miss Weston you must have some reason to distrust the sheriff's department," he said, his words saturated with sarcasm. "Please enlighten us."

"I'd originally planned to turn the pictures and the video footage over to the sheriff. My cousin drove me to the sheriff's department. When we arrived, my cousin stayed in his Jeep and I went inside. I told the lady at the front desk that I wanted to speak to the sheriff. She said the sheriff had someone in his office but that a deputy was available. I told her I'd wait. She told me to have a seat, so I did. After several minutes, the sheriff came out. Mr. Blade was with him. He was the one the sheriff had been meeting with evidently. They were talking and carrying on like they were close friends."

"What were they talking about?"

"About the bear hunting trip in Alaska they and the Locust Fork police chief were planning on taking together in April."

A loud sigh filled the courtroom. Judge Redford pounded his gavel and called for order. The courtroom quieted.

"Well, Miss Weston, there are higher ranks of law enforcement. The Mississippi State Attorney's office. The FBI. Did you think about contacting either of them? I'm sure you could've found someone somewhere who wasn't going on the hunting trip."

"I thought about it but didn't. It was clear to me that time was of the essence. Lane could be killed at any moment. His life was in jeopardy."

"What about Gunner Hubbard's life? It appeared to be in jeopardy as well. Didn't you care for his well-being?"

Abigail shook her head. "No. It wouldn't have mattered to me if Mr. Blade had cut his finger off or if the lady would've killed him. I had no sympathy for Gunner Hubbard. As a matter of fact, I hated him."

"Why did you hate him? You said you hardly knew him!"

Abigail leered at Buckman like she'd fight him if need be. "Because he was brutal to the man I love!"

The court room erupted. Judge Redford pounded the gavel. "Order! Order!"

Abigail looked at Lane. She'd said the word first. Lane had planned to say it first, but she'd beat him to it. And she'd done it publicly and passionately and before a room full of people. I love you too, Lane mouthed.

"No further questions, Your Honor," Buckman said and walked back to his seat.

"Mr. Reece, would you like to call another witness?"

"No, Your Honor."

"Mr. Buckman, does the prosecution rest its case?"

"The prosecution rests it case, Your Honor."

Drexel Reece stood to his feet. "We make a motion to dismiss, Your Honor."

"On the basis of what grounds?"

"On the grounds that the evidence the prosecution has presented did not prove guilt beyond a reasonable doubt."

"Motion denied. That's for the jury to decide. The court will hear closing arguments first thing in the morning. Court dismissed until 9 AM tomorrow."

James Redford rapped his gavel.

CHAPTER TWENTY-FOUR

Lane and Abigail sat on the floor of the treehouse, hand in hand, their backs leaned against a wall.

"Abigail, if they declare me guilty, I'm either going to prison or getting the death penalty."

"Don't say that."

"It's the truth and I just want to say that these months we've been together have been the best times of my life." Lane eased his head back and looked around. "You like this old treehouse, don't you?"

"I LOVE this old treehouse. I've got some future plans for it."

"Like what?"

She bumped their joined hands on the top of Lane's thigh. "It's a surprise. You'll just have to wait and see."

"You talk as if I'm going to be around to see."

"You will. I'm sure of it."

"Well, I want you to know that I'm telling Drexel, if I get life or the needle, it's all yours. The house, the farm—everything. So, you take this old treehouse and do whatever you want with it."

Abigail reached her free hand to Lane's chin and turned his face toward hers. "You're going to be alright. Trust me. You're not going to prison and you're not getting the death penalty."

Lane raised his brow and cocked his head. "I hope and pray you're right. But you heard what Drexel said. It doesn't look good. Buckman's got the evidence on his side. All I have are two character witnesses—your dad and Desi. And Buckman did his best to make them both look questionable to the jury."

"Don't forget my videos."

Lane pushed up one side of his upper lip with his bottom lip and nodded. "Yup. And they're tremendous, for sure. They definitely prove that Gunner owed a bunch of money to that Japanese lady and that he could get the money to pay her back by killing me. But they don't prove that I didn't murder him."

"In the end, the truth will prevail. That's what I believe."

•   •   •

As with any small town, Locust Fork's grapevine thrived with a vigilance. Talk of the sudden suspicious death of Gunner Hubbard circulated like news of a free money giveaway. People filled the inside of the courtroom. Those who hadn't arrived early enough to get a seat crowded inside the courthouse corridor. With cameras and microphones in the ready position, news crews lurked outside the courthouse like pelicans around a freshly docked deep sea fishing boat.

Judge James Redford declared the court in session and gave Marvin Buckman the floor. Buckman stood from his seat, performed his usual ritual on his suit lapels and necktie, then strolled to the jury box. He placed both hands on the rail. "Ladies and gentlemen of the jury, imagine, if you will, a large balance scale. A ton of iron on one side, a single copper penny on the other. An odd illustration, you might say. But such is the difference between the evidence put forth by the State of Mississippi as opposed to that put forth by the defense. Your job will be relatively easy and most likely, quick. Let me begin with the defendant's character since the defense has made it of such significance in this case. Mr. Reece called two witnesses to the stand, both of which testified of Mr. Masterson's fine character." Buckman took a few steps back and lifted a hand toward Lane. "He's an honest man, they said. According to them, a young man of his word. So, I say, let's agree with them. Let's all say, 'Yes, Mr. Masterson is a man whose word is good. He doesn't lie and what he says he will do, he will indeed do.' That means when Mr. Masterson says he's going to do something, it's prophetic. It's a given and just a matter of time before he lives up to what he has said. Well, there is police report evidence in this case where Mr. Masterson is quoted as telling Gunner Hubbard and I quote, 'I hate you and I'll kill you.' Words which were confirmed to be true by none other than Dr. Will Weston, the pastor of Soulshine Church. A Bible teacher and a man highly respected in this town." Buckman clinched his fists and hammered them in the air. "A real man of God!" The seasoned prosecutor walked back to the jury box rail and leaned on it with one arm. "So, what we have is a declaration by Mr. Masterson of what he would do—kill Gunner Hubbard. And we have a credible witness in Dr. Weston to the fact that Mr. Masterson is honest and therefore can be trusted to do exactly what he says. Therefore, we have a prophetic declaration on the part of Mr. Masterson and a respectable affirmation on the part of Dr. Weston. But wait, there's more. We heard the testimony of Miss Blassengame. A woman, I might add, who had ab-so-lute-ly nothing to gain by coming and testifying in this case. She did so simply because of the affection she had for her friend, the deceased Mr. Hubbard. She informed us of the fact that Mr. Hubbard feared for his life. No doubt, the fear Mr. Hubbard experienced was due to the violent threat of Mr. Masterson. Afterall, Lane Masterson had already sent him to the hospital once. Surely, Mr. Hubbard feared that Lane Masterson would send him to the morgue next." Buckman straighten himself and raised an index finger. "But wait, we still have more. We have physical evidence—antifreeze in the kitchen." He put his hands on his hips. "Have you ever known anyone to store antifreeze under the kitchen sink? Of course not. And then there was antifreeze in Mr. Hubbard's tea pitcher. AND Mr. Masterson's fingerprints on that tea pitcher. A drinking glass in the sink with antifreeze residue. Mr. Masterson's fingerprints on it as well. And just how did Gunner Hubbard die? Antifreeze poisoning." Buckman shrugged his shoulders and turned up his opened palms. "And how did the antifreeze get into his body?" He put his hands on the rail again and leaned forward. "The day before Gunner

Hubbard died, Mr. Masterson went to the barn. Got the jug of antifreeze. Placed it under the kitchen sink. Then, late that night or very early in the morning, when he knew Mr. Hubbard was sound asleep, he got out of his bed. He walked to the kitchen. Took Gunner Hubbard's tea pitcher out of the refrigerator. Opened the cabinet door under the sink. Took out the jug of antifreeze. Poured some of the antifreeze into the tea pitcher. Placed it back in the refrigerator. Put the remainder of the antifreeze back under the sink. Walked back to his bedroom. Laid down and went to sleep, hoping that Gunner Hubbard would drink a glass of tea before leaving for work the next morning. Mr. Hubbard did just that. And by 8:30 AM the antifreeze had gone from his stomach to his blood stream causing him to be incapacitated at work. His co-worker called 9-1-1. When the ambulance arrived on the scene, Mr. Hubbard was writhing in pain as the antifreeze was ravaging his heart and lungs. He was rushed to the hospital and in less than twelve hours, Gunner Hubbard was dead!" Buckman twisted in his shoes and pointed an index finger to Lane while keeping his eyes on the jury. "Ladies and gentlemen, that man, Lane Masterson, hated Gunner Hubbard! That man, Lane Masterson, assaulted Gunner Hubbard! That man, Lane Masterson, threatened Gunner Hubbard! And finally, with premeditated depravity, that man, Lane Masterson, MURDERED Gunner Hubbard!" Marvin Buckman relaxed the tension in his shoulders and began speaking to the jurors as if he were Mr. Rogers talking to a group of youngsters. "Ladies and gentlemen, you have a civic duty as honest, responsible citizens of this great country to find Lane Masterson guilty of murder in the first degree. Anything less and justice will be averted. Consider the weight of evidence and let your conscience guide you. A guilty verdict will not bring Gunner Hubbard back, but it will hold Lane Masterson accountable for the devilish scheme he planned and enacted."

Buckman took a few seconds and looked each jury dead in the eyes. Then, he walked back to his table. His assistant looked at him almost worshipfully. Buckman gave her a confident grin and took his seat next to her.

Drexel Reece pushed his chair back, stood to his feet and walked to the jury box. "To find Lane Masterson guilty, all twelve of you will have to vote that he did as Mr. Buckman just stated. I bet some of you aren't certain because there's not a single witness that saw Mr. Masterson do what Mr. Buckman says he did. It may look like Mr. Masterson did it, but you can't be certain. What you do know, based on the evidence you have seen and heard, is that Lane Masterson is well thought of by those who know him best, one of which is his own pastor. Ladies and gentlemen of the jury, my client did say that he hated Gunner Hubbard and that he wanted to kill him. Have you ever made a brash statement in a time of anger?" Drexel Reece paused, scanned the face of the jurors then began pacing in front of them. "The evidence we've presented makes it clear beyond a doubt that Gunner Hubbard was a man at the end of his rope. He owed a small fortune to someone devoid of conscience. Someone who encouraged him to kill his own stepson in order to get the money to pay his debt. You saw it on the video. You also saw the stress and anxiety of Gunner Hubbard's demeanor during the exchanges he had with the woman dressed in red and her enforcer whom she referred to as Mr. Blade. You saw how horrified Gunner Hubbard was at the suggestion of killing Lane Masterson. He even raised a question for clarity because he was so stunned by it. Gunner Hubbard didn't have a criminal record. He was not a hardened criminal and the thought of killing his stepson paralyzed him. So much so that he chose to take his own life. Yes, my client's fingerprints were on the jug of antifreeze and on the tea pitcher and on the drinking glass. But so were Gunner Hubbard's. Which of us has not moved some things around in our refrigerators? Which of us has not adjusted dirty dishes in the sink? There's no more evidence to show that Lane Masterson poisoned Gunner Hubbard than there is to show that Gunner Hubbard poisoned himself. Are you ready to send a man who just recently turned nineteen to prison or to his execution based on the subjective speculations the prosecution has presented?" Reece came back to the rail and looked at the jurors through compassionate eyes. "What if it was your teenage son or grandson who was on trial today? Would you believe that he did, in fact, commit murder or would you believe that he simply MIGHT HAVE committed murder? If it's only MIGHT HAVE then you can't vote to convict Lane Masterson. You have to vote in favor of his innocence. I trust that you will do exactly what Mr. Buckman recommended. Consider the weight of the evidence and let your conscience be your guide."

Drexel Reece walked back to his table and sat down. Judge Redford gave the jury some instructions, rapped his gavel and declared the court adjourned until a verdict was reached.

•   •   •

Drexel Reece's cell phone chirped at 3:48 PM. In less than five hours of deliberation the jury had reached a decision. Court would reconvene at 4:15. Word spread like a tornado warning. It was standing room only when Redford entered his courtroom. The crowd sat down in unison and Redford began.

"There will be complete silence as the verdict is read." He turned to the jury. "Has the jury reached a verdict?"

A mid-thirties man dressed in black slacks and a blue pin-striped, buttoned-down-collared oxford stood from his chair. "Yes, Your Honor."

Redford looked toward the defense table. "Would the defendant please rise and face the jury as the verdict is read?"

Lane and Drexel Reece stood to their feet.

"Mr. Foreman, would you please read the verdict?" Redford said.

"We, the jury, find Lane Masterson guilty of murder in the first degree."

Voices erupted. Lane rounded his shoulders, lowered his chin to his chest and began slowly shaking his head. James Redford pounded his gavel. "Order! Order in this court, I say."

The room stilled. The judge focused his attention on Lane. "Lane Masterson, you are hereby sentenced to spend the rest of your life in the Mississippi State Penitentiary without the possibility of parole."

Abigail jumped to her feet. "He's innocent! It was me! I poisoned Gunner Hubbard! I did it!"

The courtroom exploded. Like a machine, Judge Redford hammered his gavel as he issued full-throated commands for order. The triggered, unrelenting crowd ignored him.

•   •   •

The next morning, thirty minutes before his regularly scheduled docket was to begin, Judge Redford entered the courtroom. Abigail's confession the day before had lit up Locust Fork like a Roman candle tossed into a pile of gasoline doused pine needles. All the national news media outlets had picked up the story and were on it with political scandal fervor. In little more than eighteen hours, Locust Fork had become the most famous small town in America. Judge Redford's wisdom told him to expedite Abigail's hearing for the sake of the town. His personal opportunism told him to do it for the sake of his own notoriety and advancement. Perhaps the governor would tap him for the Mississippi Supreme Court. Or, heck, maybe the president was keeping up with the story and would appoint him to a district seat. At the very least it would help him at ballot box in the next election cycle. The iron was hot, and Redford aimed to strike.

Redford took the bench. Drexel Reece stood behind his table, dressed like a million bucks. To his left , wearing an orange jumpsuit, stood Abigail.

"Counselor," Redford said, his eyes locked onto Drexel Reece's. "The state of Mississippi is charging your client, Abigail Sophia Weston, as an adult for the crime of murder in the first degree. How does your client plea?"

"Not guilty, Your Honor."

"Very well. Trial is set for thirty days from today."

"Your Honor, we would like to request that a bond be set that is lower than normal. Afterall, Ms. Weston is only seventeen. She still lives at home with her parents and she poses no threat whatsoever to the public."

"Your request is duly noted, Mr. Reece. Bond is set for two hundred thousand dollars."

•   •   •

In an investigation room at the Huntsville County Jail, Drexel Reece and his new female assistant, Lacey Higgins, sat across the stainless-steel table from Abigail, Lane next to her. Drexel pushed a button on a mini recorder.

"The testimony of Abigail Weston," he said and noted the date and time. He gave Abigail a nod and she began.

"First of all, I knew Gunner had been abusing Lane. I saw the bruises on Lane's back. I hung around after I made the video. I watched through Gunner's bedroom window and saw him looking through some papers in a box under his bed. He left the house, and I checked the bedroom window. It was unlocked so I raised it and climbed into his bedroom. I looked in the box and found the receipt where Gunner had pawned Lane's stuff. That's how I was able to get his record player and albums back. I also found his mom's will and the insurance policy she'd taken out on him. I knew that, with Lane dead, Gunner would get a half million dollars and the farm. I figured if I went to law enforcement, they wouldn't do anything. Afterall, the sheriff of Huntsville County and the police chief of Locust Fork are hunting partners with Mr. Blade. When Lane was bitten by the snake in his sleep, I knew that Gunner was behind it. The most poisonous snake in the US just happens to crawl into Lane's bed. Come on, I'm not stupid. When the truck forced Lane off the road and into the Yallaboosa River, I realized Gunner was not going to quit until Lane was dead. So, I came up with a plan to protect Lane. After the wreck, when the hospital sent Lane home, I went home with him. While at his house, I unlocked his bedroom window so I could get in and out. I'd been making preserves and jelly for Lane and Gunner. I'd make two jars. One for Lane. One for Gunner. He really liked what I made because he was going through a jar about every two weeks. I'd put their names on the jars because Gunner would go ballistic and beat Lane if he ever ate any of Gunner's food. I made a jar of preserves and mixed antifreeze in it. I put Gunner's name on the jar and went to Lane's house. I climbed in through his bedroom window and put the jar in Gunner's cabinet. I figured he would eat it at breakfast or put it on a sandwich for his lunch at work. Each day I'd go back to the house and check the jar to see if he'd eaten any of it. After a few days, I saw where he had. So, I went out to the barn and got the jug of antifreeze. I knew it was there because Lane had used some of it in the company truck that Mr. Banks had let Lane drive as a daily driver. I poured some of it into Gunner's tea pitcher and sloshed some around in a glass. I put the glass in the sink, the pitcher back in the refrigerator and the jug under the sink. I did all that to make it look like a suicide. Later that day, we found out that Gunner Hubbard had died. I knew my plan had worked. I wore gloves so that my fingerprints wouldn't be on anything."

Drexel Reece pushed the button again and stopped the recorder. He pushed back in his chair and raised his opened hands in front of his chest. "Absolutely amazing."

Lane turned to Abigail's profile. "You did all that for me?"

Abigail turned and looked him dead in the eyes. "I sure did, and I'd do it again. I'll always have your back."

"If, by some miracle, we get her out of this, you better marry this girl," Drexel said.

"I plan to," said Lane.

Abigail leaned her head toward his and they shared a quick kiss.

"We can argue the protector angle." Lacey Higgins said. "That, given the dire urgency of the situation, Abigail HAD to kill Gunner in order to save Lane's life. Think about it. The eradication of an evil person so that an innocent person might live. It's both righteous and heroic. Like right out of a Hollywood movie. A jury will eat . . . it . . . up."

"They will," Drexel said. "But we need more than just Abigail's word to make it stick." He interlocked his fingers behind his head and stretched out on his chair. "Something that ties Gunner Hubbard to the coral snake or to the driver of the black truck."

"I'll go back through Hubbard's phone records," Lacey said. "Maybe there's something there we didn't see the first time."

"Let me do that, Lacey. You pay Freda Blassengame a visit," Drexel added. "You're a woman. Maybe she'll talk to you."

"Got it."

Lane, however, had a plan too.

CHAPTER TWENTY-FIVE

Lacey Higgins purposely arrived at Crawdaddy's Keg early in the afternoon so as to beat the end-of-the-workday, blue collar patrons. Convinced that Freda Blassengame knew something that'd help Abigail's defense; Lacey meant to get it out of her. And the last thing she wanted was for her and Freda to be continually interrupted by new walk-ins and "I'll have anothers," not to mention the lewd comments and come-ons females have to endure at the mouths of men emboldened by alcohol. To Lacey's delight, only one car was parked in front of the establishment. She hoped it was Freda's. When Lacey walked in, the inside of the drinking joint greeted her with dim lighting and the sound of a heated argument. Freda sat on a stool at the bar watching a reality television show where a man and woman were having a knock-down drag-out over whether or not he was the baby's father. Freda muted the sound and looked back at Lacey. "Afternoon," she said and slid from the stool and onto her feet. She walked around the end of the counter and took her place in front of the wide variety of liquor bottles that set under the long mirror behind the bar.

"I'll have a bottle of Perrier if you have it," Lacey said.

"You must still be on the clock," Freda said with a grin and pulled one from a small refrigerator.

"A girl's gotta eat."

Freda twisted open the bottle and set it down in front of Lacey. "Four bucks. What do you do for a living?"

Lacey pulled a five from her purse and handed it to Freda. "My job changes all the time. Right now I'm trying to keep a teenage girl from going to prison or worse."

"Lawyering for that Weston girl, huh?"

Lacey turned up the green bottle, took a drink and set it down on the counter. "Yeah. Actually, I dropped in to see you. I've got some questions about Gunner Hubbard."

Friendliness vacated Freda's demeanor. "Gunner and me, we had some plans. We were gonna head out west and see if we could start a life together. Then she went and poisoned him."

"Trust me, there's a story behind it all."

"I don't' care what the story is. She poisoned him. That's what matters to me."

"What if she did it to—?"

Freda cut her off. "He's dead. She confessed to killing him. It's all over TV. I don't care what she says was her reason. She deserves whatever she gets."

"Even if it's the needle?"

Freda placed both her hands on the edge of the bar, looked away, inhaled then exhaled. She began shaking her head, a defiant smirk on her face.

"A seventeen-year-old girl executed by lethal injection. And you're okay with that?" Lacey said.

Freda cut her attention back to Lacey. "Listen," she said, her eyes venomous. "They can give that little heifer the electric chair for all I care. Now, why don't you take your sparkling water and your misplaced sympathy and leave."

•　　•　　•

Drexel Reece chomped on a crawfish po' boy and swigged on an RC Cola. He'd been parked on the shoulder of the blacktop since before daybreak. It was now close to 1 PM. To just pull up in the driveway unannounced could prove hazardous. Drexel was familiar with the personality type. Such people didn't like strangers, especially on their property. People like that were reclusive, always packing, and had secrets—secrets they meant to protect even if it required the use of lethal force. Drexel had done a drive-by of the house the day before. He knew the man drove a fully restored 1995 black Chevrolet Suburban. Drexel ran the license plate. The desirable truck had come back registered to a Yullis Touissant. No criminal record. Drexel had called a lawyer friend in Baton Rouge who, in turn, reached out to a contact at the Louisiana Bureau of Investigation. As it turned out, Yullis Touissant hadn't reported any taxable income for the previous three years and had no current place of employment. The man fit the black-market modus operandi to a tee. As Drexel stuffed the last bit of the po'boy into his mouth, the Suburban pulled onto the pavement. Yullis Touissant was on the move. Touissant traveled north for just over an hour. Drexel glanced to his right and to his left from time to time, taking note of the bayou scenery. Shanty homes with nice, late model vehicles in their driveways. Herons and cranes perched on dead logs, flanked by box turtles and river cooters. A dead nutria here and there. Billboard advertisements for restaurants, night clubs, gambling venues, ambulance-chasing law firms, etc.—all further up the road in New Orleans. Within an hour they entered the town of Barataria. Touissant made a few turns in the small, backwater town and finally pulled into the parking lot of a well-kept single-story facility. The sign read Lafitte Retirement Home. Touissant parked near the entrance door, got out of his vehicle and went inside. Drexel figured the man of questionable business dealings had stopped in to visit an ailing relative, so he decided to wait and catch Touissant in the parking lot when he came out. He parked his car next to the Suburban leaving one vacant parking space between them. Reece watched as a middle-aged man pushed an elderly woman in a wheelchair along the concrete sidewalk that ran the length of the front of the building. Off to one side, a woman and two children sat at a cedar picnic table with a man Reece guessed to be a late octogenarian. They shared a bucket of chicken from KFC and drank soda from cans. On one end of the table was a chocolate cake with a single candle in its center. A man dressed in a green work uniform trimmed the hedges and raked the clippings in the facility's landscape beds.

The front door opened and out walked Yullis Touissant. Reece opened his car door and got out. He walked around the back of it and met Touissant in the empty parking space that separated their vehicles.

"Mr. Touissant," Reece said and offered him a business card.

Touissant gave a cool expression and said nothing. He took the card, looked at it and offered it back. "I don't need a lawyer." He reached for the door handle of his truck.

"I'd like to ask you some questions."

Touissant didn't look back at Drexel. "I have nothing to say," he said and opened the door.

"A young woman's freedom's at stake. I'd appreciate your help."

Touissant climbed into the husky SUV and sat down in the driver's seat. "Sorry. It's not my problem." He slammed the door and fired up the engine.

Drexel Reece pulled open the door. "Mr. Touissant, here's the deal. I know you sold a coral snake to a man. The man's dead and a teenage girl is going to trial."

Yullis Touissant looked at Reece with fiery eyes. "Get your hands off my truck and leave me alone or I'll scrub the parking lot with your face." He reached to pull the door shut but Reece stepped in and held it open with his body. He looked at Touissant like a lion looking at its prey. "Mr. Touissant, I know all about you. I know what you do. I know where you live. All I have to do is make one phone call to the attorney general's office in Baton Rouge and a SWAT team will descend on your little compound before you can get back home to unlock the door for them. Now, do you want to talk to me or shall I dial the number?"

Touissant looked through his windshield. He shut his eyes as he inhaled and exhaled through his nostrils. He paused for a moment then shut off the engine.

"Good. Good," Reece said. "Let's talk across the hood of your truck."

Touissant got out and slammed the door hard.

Reece stood back and studied the truck. "This is a nice girl you have here. Highly desirable. You ought to be a little nicer to her."

Touissant looked at Reece and rolled his eyes. "Ask your questions so I can get going."

Drexel walked to the front of the Suburban and put one foot on the bumper. He pulled a picture of Gunner Hubbard from a shirt pocket and placed it on the hood. "Remember this guy?"

Touissant tightened his jaw and nodded.

"Yeah. I know you do," Reece said. "I need you to come tell the court about the little business transaction the two of you made."

"Listen, Man, I ain't going nowhere. The dude bought a snake from me. It ain't illegal in Louisiana, you know. You got any questions—" Touissant jabbed an index finger on the hood of his truck. "You ask 'em right here right now. I'll answer them and then we don't ever see each other again."

Reece smiled. "If only life were that easy, Yullis. That's your first name. Isn't it?"

Touissant shot Reece a look.

"You're a man with a temper. That's alright. I've talked to lots of men with tempers. See it all the time in my profession."

Touissant curled up one side of his upper lip.

Reece smiled and nodded. "Okay, okay. I'll ask my first question. Do you have a computer in your house?"

Touissant shut his eyes and huffed. "Yeah. I got a computer in my house."

"Nothing unusual about that. Most everybody does. Got anything on it that you wouldn't want anybody to know about?" Reece lowered his head a little and drew down his brow. "Show some manners. Look at me when I'm talking to you, Yullis."

Like an irritated schoolboy, Touissant looked at Reece.

Reece smiled. "That's better. I was asking about your computer. Got anything on it that you'd like to keep a secret? You know. Correspondence? Pictures?"

Touissant grimaced.

"Ah, I see. You've got some pictures on it, don't you?"

Touissant pressed his lips and looked down.

"Angola Prison is a tough place to call home. I hear the neighbors can be socially awkward to say the least," Reece commented. "Well, here's my next question. Which would you prefer to be? A witness in a courtroom in Mississippi or a defendant in a courtroom in Louisiana?"

•   •   •

It was Saturday. Lane had cut and edged three yards since his day began. The remainder of his day would be taken up with weeding and mulching the beds at Michael Berilli's sprawling estate. Lane pulled into the parking lot of Miguel's Cantina and shut off the engine. The place was hopping with business. It was Lane's lunch hour, and he was hungry, but he had a much greater motivation for stopping in. He walked in and sat down in a booth that needed busing. A man with a gray plastic tray approached him. "Afternoon, Amigo," he said and began removing the used dishes from the table.

"Good afternoon," Lane said. "Would Berto happen to be in today?"

"Si," the man said. "You need see him?"

"Yes, please."

The man began wiping down the table with a bar towel. "I tell him. Your server be here soon."

The man walked away leaving behind a clean tabletop for Lane. A waitress walked up. She looked to be in her mid-thirties. The name badge below her left shoulder read "Rosalita." Her black hair was pulled back tightly and gathered into a bun on the back of her head. She set a basket of chips and a small bowl of salsa down on the table and placed a menu in front of Lane. "Welcome. What can I get you to drink?" she said with a smile, her English as American as Lane's.

"I'll have water with lemon."

"Coming right up."

She walked away and Lane began scanning the crowd. Lane recognized four boys who sat at a table toward the back of the dining area. Classmates from school. Lane's eyes met those of one of the boys. Jack Landers. Jack raised his chin a bit as a hello gesture. Lane responded in like fashion. Lane saw Mike lean in a bit and comment to his friends. A gossip session, Lane guessed. Huntsville County High School was buzzing with talk of Abigail's case. Her looks had enabled her to overcome much of the stigma and she'd made friends with some of the girls. The guys knew the arrowhead necklace meant she was off limits to anyone other than Lane. Overall, the kids were nice to her, but the running joke being whispered throughout the school was, "If the new girl from Texas offers you a peanut butter and jelly sandwich, run!" Erica encouraged Abigail to walk away from it all and finish her senior year as a homeschooler. Abigail, however, would not be deterred. She was determined to walk with the graduating class of Huntsville County High, her gown accessorized with the honors regalia she'd rightfully earned.

Rosalita returned with Lane's water, three lemons perched on the rim of the large plastic drinking cup. She set it on the table. "Have you decided?"

"I'll have a lunch number four."

"Hard or soft shell on the tacos?"

"Hard, please."

"Got it," she said. "It'll be out shortly."

As she walked away, Lane cut his eyes to Jack Landers and his friends. One said something to make the other three laugh. The peanut butter and jelly sandwich joke, no doubt.

"Amigo, you wanted to see me?"

Lane looked up. The man wore a white apron that bore witness to the fact that he'd been busy in the kitchen. He had a green star tattooed under one eye. Thick black hair and prominent eyebrows.

"Are you, Berto?"

"Si."

"I'm looking for Mill. He told me you'd know how to reach him."

The man raised his brow. "Ah! Okay, Amigo."

He pulled his cell phone from his pocket and sat down in the seat across from Lane. He swiped the screen, touched it and placed it to one ear. He spoke some Spanish words, none of which Lane understood except one—gringo. He looked into Lane's eyes. "Name?"

"Lane."

"Lane," Berto said and began nodding, acknowledging the words of the person he was talking to. "Si. Si. I'll tell him. Adios." He ended the call and set the phone down on the table. Rosalita approached and set a plate of hot food down in front of Lane. "If you need anything else, just let me know."

Lane looked up at her and smiled. "Thank you."

Rosalita moved on the next booth.

"Alright, Amigo," Berto said. "Do you know where Flores Transmission Shop is?"

"Next to the railroad track on Magnolia Street?"

"Si."

Berto motioned to a man at the cash register. The man responded promptly and walked over. Berto pointed to Lane's meal. "He'll need a to-go box for this. Quickly."

The man hustled away.

Berto looked at Lane. "Mill will meet you there in twenty minutes."

Lane reached for his wallet.

"No. No. Amigo. No pay," Berto replied, shaking his head and slicing the air with one hand. "You're Mill's friend."

•　　　•　　　•

Back in the day the building was the Greyhound bus station for Locust Fork. Though lime green and no longer the familiar classic gray, the structure still generated the vintage aura of its mid-twentieth century history. Over the years different businesses had opened and closed at the location. However, the original red, white and blue sign with a greyhound stretched out in a sprint had remained fastened to the side of the building, untouched as if it were a historical land marker. Vehicles crowded around the place like strewn dominoes. Lane parked on the shoulder of the street and snaked his way through the numerous cars and trucks. He walked in through one of the raised roll-up doors.

A short man wearing a blue shop uniform and covered in grease greeted Lane from underneath a lifted Nissan Altima. "Hello. What can we do for you today?"

"I'm here to see Mill."

Without removing either of his hands from the breaker bar he worked with, the man motioned with his head. "He's back in the office."

Lane proceeded toward the back of the shop, stepping over tools and automobile parts as if they were land mines. A placard attached to a door read "Office." Lane pushed it open and walked in. A black Cane Corso lay on the concrete floor in front of a desk. Lane froze.

"He's fine. Don't worry," the man sitting behind the desk said. "You here to see Mill?"

Lane relaxed. "Yeah."

"He's with someone. Have a seat. He'll be here when he's finished. Shouldn't be long."

"Okay. No problem."

Lane took a seat against one wall and began surveying the office. A Mexican flag. Several pictures of Mexican boxers, all signed and personalized to Mill. A large sombrero. An oil painting of a Mexican pastoral scene. A Corona beer sign. The back door of the office opened and in walked a Mexican man. He wore jeans, a teal blue western shirt and black cowboy boots with silver toe tips. The man shot Lane a big smile and stretched out his arms. "Lane, my friend. How's it going?"

Lane stood from his seat and welcomed Mill's embrace. They clapped each other on the back a few times, then let go.

"Let's sit down," Mill said.

"I'm hoping you can help, Mill. My girl's in a situation."

"I'll do my best. What's going on?"

Lane hesitated and glanced at the other man.

"It's okay," Mill said and motioned toward the man. "This is Rico. He's my brother. You can say anything."

"Absolutely," Rico said.

Lane and the man shook hands and exchanged pleasantries. Lane turned his attention back to Mill. "My stepfather tried to kill me two times. My girlfriend poisoned him to protect me."

Mill hammered a fist on the arm of his chair and grinned. "Excellent! You have a loyal lioness." He cut a look to Rico who was laughing. "What do you think, Rico?"

"Bueno! Bueno!"

"Go on, Little Brother," Mill said.

"There's this woman. Her name's Freda Blassengame. She works at this bar called Crawdaddy's Keg. It's out on Highway 7 right before you cross over into Lafayette County."

"I know the place you're talking about."

"Me too," Rico added.

"Well, the lawyer thinks she knows some things—things that could help my girlfriend, Abigail. The trial is coming up soon. She's being tried for murder. As it turns out, the woman had a thing for my stepdad and so she refuses to talk. Says she hopes Abigail gets the death penalty. Do you think you could get her to talk?"

Mill looked at Rico. With a cool expression, Rico nodded. The two of them engaged in some back and forth in Spanish.

Mill turned back to Lane. "I will have some people talk to her. Trust me, she will tell them everything she knows."

CHAPTER TWENTY-SIX

Freda raised her heavy eyelids enough to see the time on the digital clock. 10:46 AM. Two factors had caused her shift to stretch out two hours later than scheduled: Liz Stutz's no-call no-show and Corkscrew, a unique sounding Memphis-based progressive rock trio. The three men were Rhodes College dropouts, musical prodigies with a knack for online marketing. In less than a year they'd amassed a consequential following throughout Alabama, Tennessee and Mississippi, especially among college students. A last-minute cancellation at an Oxford auditorium, due to a plumbing problem, presented an opportunity for another nearby venue. The owner of Crawdaddy's Keg got wind of the news and successfully booked the trending band. The happenstance Friday night concert pulled in over two hundred faithful fans from Ole Miss. The hearty partiers pressed inside the drinking joint like passengers in a subway train at five o'clock. Crawdaddy's Keg more than doubled its previous beverage sales record. The seasoned bartender arrived home just after 3 AM worn to a frazzle and four hundred dollars the richer in tip money.

Freda Blassengame managed to throw back the covers and sit up on the side of her bed. She coughed the tickle out of her throat and rubbed the mop of her head. A cup of coffee and a Marlboro would complete her resuscitation.

"Good morning, Señorita," came a male voice.

Forget the coffee and the Marlboro. Freda Blassengame was suddenly birddog alert. In horror, she cut her attention toward the voice. A man and woman stood just inside her bedroom door. "What are you doing here and how did you get in!"

The two of them smiled. "We mean you no harm," the man said. "We simply want to talk to you."

"About what?"

"You look like you could use a cup of coffee. We'll be waiting for you in the kitchen," the lady said.

Freda looked to her nightstand expecting to see her cell phone.

"It's right here," the man said.

Freda turned her attention back to them. The man held up her cell phone and maintained the same friendly smile.

"You take cream and sugar?" the lady asked.

"Just sugar. No cream."

"Great," the lady replied. "We brought donuts also. I hope you like plain glazed."

The two of them turned and walked out of Freda's bedroom. She pulled on her robe and slid her feet inside her house shoes. As she walked to the kitchen, she was startled further by a man that stood guard at her entry door. He gave her a big smile. "Good morning. Did you rest well?"

"Uh . . . yeah. Who are you people?"

"Friends, Señorita. We are your friends."

Freda felt her stomach churn. She felt that, at any moment, she might soil her panties.

"Here you go. Sugar. No cream," the lady said and held out a tall cup with a donut shop logo on it.

Freda reached and took the cup, her eyes rounded. The lady lifted open the top of the box of donuts. "Please," the lady said.

"I'm good. What do you want from me? I don't have much money."

"No, no, Señorita. We are not here for money. We only want to talk. You see, we work for a very important man. He has lots of money." The man pulled a banded block of twenty-dollar bills from one of his jacket pockets.

He thumbed one end of the cash. "One thousand dollars. He wants you to have it in exchange for something."

Freda wrinkled her brow and curled one side of her mouth. "For what?"

"He has a friend, a very special friend. This friend of his is in a very difficult situation. You can help his friend. This money is his way of saying thank you for your help."

"How can I help?"

"By telling us all that you knew about Gunner Hubbard."

"So that's what this is all about!"

"Yes."

"And what if I don't want to talk about him?"

"Why be so foolish? He's dead."

Freda paused, her eyes fixed on the man's. Then, she looked at the woman. The woman nodded. "It's true. One thousand bucks. Just tell us what you know."

Freda's stomach began to settle. She took a sip of the coffee and leaned her back against the refrigerator. "Okay, I knew him. We weren't really a thing, but we talked about a future together."

"Very good. Keep talking," the man said and extended the cash to her. She took it and stuck it in a pocket of her robe. "He was scared. Told me his life was in danger. That's about it."

"Are you sure?"

Freda gave an unconvincing nod.

The man pulled another banded stack of twenties from his other jacket pocket. Freda's eyes telegraphed her lust for it.

"My boss's friend was forced off the road by a man in a black truck. Give me the man's name and you'll have two thousand."

"I tell you that and I'm dead."

The man scanned the kitchen. "You own this place?"

"Rent."

The man shrugged his shoulder and turned up a palm. "Then why not just take the money and leave town?"

"Got nowhere to go. Besides, my car is a rag."

"Yeah. I've been watching you. That car you drive is a real piece of junk."

The man motioned to the man standing guard at the back door. The man at the door reached into a back pocket, pulled out an envelope and handed it to the first man.

"Pen," the first man said.

The man at the door produced a pen from inside his jacket. The first man opened the envelope, took out a document and placed it on the counter for Freda to see. "This is the title to the Ford Fusion parked right outside your back door. Check it out."

Freda pulled back the curtains above the sink and looked through the window. "It's nice," she said and looked back at the man.

"It is," the man said. "Only has seventy-three thousand miles on it. You'll have no problems getting to Houston. There's a really nice club on the west side called The Acapulco. I'm talking first class. The owner's looking for a good bartender like yourself. You could make two grand a week easy. My boss makes a phone call and the job is yours."

The man's facial expression turned solemn. He held up the brick of money. "You give me the name and number of the guy who drove the black truck and I'll give you this plus I'll sign the car title over to you. You can say goodbye to this place and never look back."

Freda shook her head. "He'll find me. He's that kind of guy."

"Think about it, Freda. We've never met before." The man motioned to the man at the back door and to the woman. "The first time you meet us is right here in your house. We stopped in for a visit and let ourselves in without a key and without waking you. We showed up with money and a nice car for you. What kind of people does that make us?"

Freda thought about it for a few seconds, then nodded.

The man raised one hand and placed the other over his heart. "I promise you on my mother's grave, you'll never see him again for the rest of your life."

•   •   •

In the shop behind his house, Rayburn Slide sat on a mechanic stool and whaled away with a big ball peen hammer at the truck's seized-up brake rotor. The canvas bag slipped over his head and the drawstring tightened snug around his neck. Two men forced him to the floor and zip-tied his wrists behind his back. They jerked him up to his feet and ushered him out of the shop to their car. Rayburn heard the trunk pop open. The men shoved him down inside it. Things went black when they slammed the lid shut. The gravel cracked under the tires as the car rolled down the driveway and took to the paved road. The driver's aggressive turns tossed Rayburn back and forth inside the trunk. His abrupt stops and restarts threw Rayburn forward and backward. The car came to a stop. Rayburn heard the car's four doors open and shut and voices speaking Spanish. The trunk popped open again. Four hands lifted him out and stood him up on his feet. He felt their strong hands against his triceps as they made him walk. They shoved him down hard onto a chair.

"Hello, Mr. Slide. I'm glad you could give us some of your valuable time," came a voice in slightly broken English.

"Who are you? What do you want with me?"

The speaker patted Rayburn on one knee. "Relax, My Friend. No need to get so excited. You can call me John. We brought you here to have a professional conversation."

"Uh . . . okay. I'm listening."

"Good. Very good. Some months ago, you had a conversation with a gringo named Gunner Hubbard. He hired you to do something. What exactly?"

"I don't know what you're talking about."

"No. No, My Friend. Don't lie to me. It's not professional."

Rayburn Slide jerked at the blast of a shotgun discharge just feet from him. He felt the end of the gun's barrel press against his crotch.

"Okay. Let's try again. As I was saying, some months ago, you had a conversation with a gringo named Gunner Hubbard. He hired you to do something. What exactly?"

"I ain't saying nothing!"

John clicked his tongue three times. "He thinks you won't pull the trigger. Blow off one of his feet."

Rayburn felt the end of the barrel move from his groin to his right foot.

"Okay! Okay! He hired me to off someone!"

"Ah! Cooperation. That's professional," John said. "Who did he hire you to kill?"

Rayburn Slide paused. The bag over his head contracted and expanded as he inhaled and exhaled nervous breaths. He felt the barrel move from his foot back to his crotch and heard whoever held the gun pump the action to chamber another shell.

"Ah, Man! It was some high school kid!"

"How did you do the job?"

"Ran him off the road. He crashed into Yallaboosa River. Didn't die though. The kid survived somehow."

"You used a black truck? Si?"

"Yes. A black truck."

"Where is the black truck? We saw only a blue one at your house."

"The black paint was washable. I sprayed it off after I wrecked the kid."

"Okay. Listen very carefully, My Friend. There is a court case coming up soon. You are going to tell this story to the court."

"Man, if I do that, they'll send me back to prison. I can't do no more time."

"Mr. Slide, you will not go to prison. No matter what. I promise. You have my word. Once I give my word, you can take it to your grave."

"Your word? What does that mean? You're not a lawyer or a judge, are you?"

"You could say I'm a little bit of both."

The men accompanying John began to laugh.

"Do you have a cell phone?"

"Yeah. It's in my pocket."

"Stand him up," John said.

Two hands reached under Rayburn's arm and lifted him to his feet. Rayburn felt another hand go into his pocket and retrieve his phone.

"I am dialing a number," John said. "The man on the other end of the line is an attorney. I want you to tell him what you just told me and how he can reach you. Comprendes?"

"Yes."

Rayburn felt the phone against his ear. On the second ring Drexel Reece answered.

●   ●   ●

The twelve jurors filed back into the courtroom and took their seats in the box. They'd been out less than two hours. James Redford declared the court in session. He turned to the jury foreman. "Has the jury reached a verdict?"

A man stood to his feet. "We have, Your Honor."

Redford turned to Abigail and Drexel. "The defendant will rise for the reading of the verdict. Abigail stood up, Drexel at her side.

"We, the jury, find the defendant, Abigail Weston, not guilty."

The courtroom erupted. Redford hammered his gavel and called for order. The crowd quieted.

"Miss Weston, you are free to go," the judge announced.

Lane and the Westons rushed to the table. Will, Erica and Brodie embraced Abigail.

Drexel Reece stepped across the aisle to Marvin Buckman. "Buckman. I'm two for four. And you're two for four. We're even . . . until next time."

Buckman cocked his head and narrowed his eyes. "It's two for five. Remember?"

Drexel Reece pressed his lips and shook his head. "A guilty verdict overturned as soon as it's read, doesn't count. We're both two for four."

Buckman nodded and grinned. "Fair enough, Drexel. Fair enough."

After the Weston's affectionate celebration, it was Lane's turn. He kissed Abigail and pulled her in tight. "Abigail, you're the most amazing girl in the world. I love you," he said, his mouth against her ear.

"I told you that you wouldn't go to prison. I love you too, Lane. With all my heart."

●   ●   ●

Rayburn Slide's testimony did two things. First, it swayed the jury to acquit Abigail; Yullis Touissant's reinforced them in their decision. Second, it landed him in jail as it prompted the State of Mississippi to charge him on two accounts: conspiracy to commit murder and attempted murder. State prosecutor, Marvin Buckman, looked forward to the trial with bated breath. Rayburn Slide stared thirty-three years at Parchman Farm square in the face. James Redford set bail at one hundred thousand dollars. Slide bonded out and was given an ankle monitor as a door prize.

Two months before his trial was to begin, in the shop behind his double-wide, Rayburn Slide lay under the chassis of a 1973 Ford Ranchero. A few years prior, he'd found the inoperable vehicle in a junkyard in nearby Byhalia. The car had a caved-in driver's side quarter panel and no wheels. An eyesore to look at to say the least, but money in the pocket for someone of knowledge. And Rayburn Slide's knowledge of cars was scholarly. To his good fortune, the junkyard's owner had failed to examine the car thoroughly. Had he done so, he would've discovered the car's great worth—the factory 351 Cleveland engine under its hood. Due to the junkyard owner's negligence, Slide all but stole the roller project for a mere $1500. When fully restored, the Ranchero would fetch $60,000 minimum with ease. Slide, however, wouldn't be selling car. Instead, he'd be handing it over in exchange for services rendered to Carl "Highball" Anderson, north Mississippi's most noted defense attorney. No one from Batesville to Southaven was more effective at garnering acquittals than Highball Anderson. The case against Rayburn Slide seemed to be open/shut. But with Highball representing him, Slide's chances of walking were better than 50/50. The savvy courtroom spinster's services didn't come cheap, however. More than Slide could afford, for sure. But an agreement had been reached. Highball would work his magic on Slide's behalf. And Slide, for his part, would pay him with the Ranchero fully restored in car show condition.

Slide was draining the classic car's oil pan when he heard footsteps on the shop's concrete floor. As he lay on his back, he turned his head to look. Two pairs of cowboy boots made their way to the front of the car. One pair was black with silver toe tips.

"Hello, Amigo," one of the men said, his voice hauntingly familiar to Rayburn Slide. Slide adjusted his body to emerge from under the car.

"No, no, Amigo," the man said. "Don't let us interrupt you. Keep working. I just came by to reassure you of the promise I made. No need to worry. You will not go to prison."

"I certainly hope you are right," Slide said, his voice shaky.

The man stooped down and made eye contact with Slide. "You have my word," he said, his broad smile displaying his gold capped teeth. "And as I told you, once I give my word, you can take it to your grave."

Later that afternoon, the Huntsville County Sheriff Department received an anonymous phone call from an untraceable phone. The caller reported an accident at Rayburn Slide's residence. When emergency officials arrived, they found a disengaged floor jack positioned under the front of the car's chassis. Slide's lifeless body lay pinned under the Ranchero, his skull crushed under the car's engine.

CHAPTER TWENTY-SEVEN

Nine months later

Dr. Will Weston lifted the veil from his daughter's face then resumed his position. He looked at Lane and smiled. "Lane, you may kiss your bride."

Lane leaned in close to Abigail's face and gave her an extended kiss. The two of them then turned and faced the congregation.

The pastor raised his voice. "Ladies and gentlemen, I present to you Mr. and Mrs. Lane Masterson!"

The organist launched into Mendelssohn's Wedding March. Lane and Abigail headed down the aisle and exited Soulshine Church's worship center. Falling in behind them were the best man and the matron of honor: Desi and Becky Pritchard. After Brodie escorted both his grandmothers and Erica out, the wedding attendees exited and convened in the fellowship hall. As they were enjoying hors d'oeuvres, cake and punch, Big Pop announced, "And now, I invite the newlyweds to center of the floor for their first dance as husband and wife."

Lane and Abigail walked hand and hand to the open area in the middle of the large room. Piano music began to play over the sound system. The couple began moving to the beat of the tune. A young boy walked up the platform steps and strolled to the microphone. He wore a white one-piece polyester jumpsuit. It had flared legs. Its dominant collar lay open exposing the boy's bare chest. The suit's numerous rhinestone studs matched those on the wide white belt that fit snug around his narrow waste. A bright red scarf hung loosely around his neck. Donnie Newhouse took the microphone from its stand and bellowed out the words, "Welcome to my world. Won't you come on in. Miracles, I guess, still happen now and then."

Two hours later, the crowd assembled along the walkway that led to the entrance of the fellowship hall. The entry doors opened. Lane and Abigail stood before the crowd dressed in jeans, western shirts and western boots. The crowd cheered and tossed birdseed at the couple as the two of them walked. At the end of the sidewalk, Big Pop held Sundown's reigns. Lane placed a foot in one of the saddle's stirrups, pulled himself up and swung his other leg over the beautiful horse's back. He reached a hand down to Abigail and lifted her up on Sundown's rump. Big Pop gave Lane the reins and off the newlyweds rode. Abigail held her arms tightly around Lane's midsection as Sundown cantered across the back lawn of the church's property and into the tree line where the couple's property began. They made their way through the woods and came to the bend in the creek where they'd often swam.

"Can we stop for a minute?" Abigail asked.

"Of course," Lane said and pulled on Sundown's reigns. The great animal stopped.

"What do you want to do?"

Abigail leaned her head against the back of Lane's shoulders. "Nothing. I just want to look at it. It's so beautiful."

"It sure is."

"Let's postpone our trip to Branson for one day and come back here for lunch tomorrow."

"Sure. Whatever you want to do, Sweetheart."

"Okay. We can go now," Abigail said.

Lane nudged Sundown with his heels, and they continued into the woods. Lights appeared through the trees. "You see those lights?" Lane said.

"I do."

"I wonder what's going on."

"You'll see," Abigail said.

Sundown walked on. The scene became more apparent. The tree house had been transformed. It gleamed like a decorated Christmas tree. A small portable generator hummed as it gave power to the lights that trimmed the newly constructed ladder, the roof and the paned windows.

"Wow! Did you do all this?" Lane said with his eyes rounded and a broad grin of excitement on his face.

"Yup. Mom and Dad helped."

Lane stopped the horse and he and Abigail dismounted. He tied Sundown to the small tree where there set a bucket of water and a pan of sweet feed.

"Me first this time," Abigail said and began ascending the ladder. She climbed to the floor of the treehouse and flung opened the trap door. She turned and looked down at Lane. "Alright, Mr. Masterson, I'm ready for a honeymoon. What about you?"

"Amen to that," he said and headed up the ladder.

Abigail pulled herself up into the tree house and waited for her husband. The inside of the treehouse was no longer a rudimentary haven for a young boy. It was a storybook dwelling. A table for two with chairs. A small Adirondack loveseat and matching coffee table. A mini refrigerator. A bearskin rug. On the walls were framed photographs of Lane and Abigail and various scenes from around the farm. A pair of binoculars on the seal of the window that faced Ole Miss. A bookshelf with the books neatly arranged. A lamp. And a pallet bed with pillows.

Abigail spread her hands apart and raised her brow. "So, what do you think?"

"What do I think? Baby, I think this is the most beautiful place I've ever seen in my life."

"When I told you I had plans for this place. I wasn't JUST talking about all this. I was talking about this night. OUR night."

Abigail laid down on the bed and looked at Lane. "And now, here we are. Just like I dreamed."

Lane laid down on the bed next to her. He pulled her close and gave her a passionate kiss, then gazed into her eyes.

"I'm all yours, Lane Masterson. Always," Abigail said. "Just one rule though."

Lane drew back his chin and pulled down his brow. "And what's that?"

Abigail reached inside the neck of her shirt and lifted out the arrowhead, the light reflecting off the gold chain that bound it. "This," she said, her eyes locked onto his. "Never comes off . . . ever."

THE END

ACKNOWLEDGEMENTS

Tons of appreciation to Patricia Bradley, ECPA, Parable and USA Today Best-Selling Author. Thank you for reading my work and giving your valued, seasoned input.

A special thanks to my incredible first readers: Monica King, Jayne Vinzetta, Bill Bolton, Dawn Story, and Clay Miller. Your enthusiasm for my work is more encouraging than you'll ever know.

I am truly grateful to attorney Ryan Baker for providing input on legal proceedings and courtroom protocol. Thank you for being a friend and always just a phone call away.

A big shout out to the Black Rose Writing team for bringing the story to the marketplace. Thank you for being easy to work with and for being so prompt to respond when questions arise.

ABOUT THE AUTHOR

Levi Bronze is an Alabama native and resides in the Memphis, Tennessee area with his wife and son. He is the author of the YA fantasy, *The Red Brick Road* and the southern thriller, *Two Yellow Cabooses*. He loves college football season, the outdoors, barbeque, and traveling with his family.

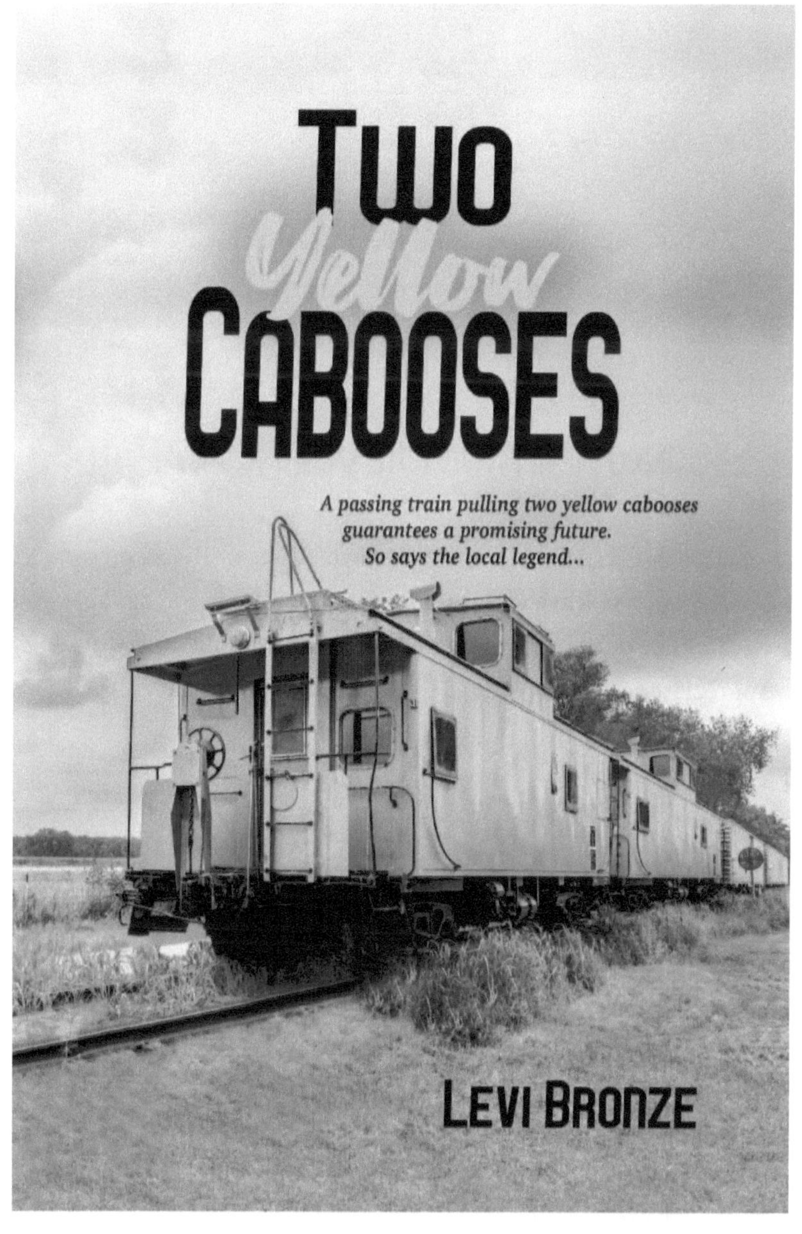
Two
Yellow
Cabooses
A passing train pulling two yellow cabooses
guarantees a promising future.
So says the local legend...
Levi Bronze

NOTE FROM LEVI BRONZE

Word-of-mouth is crucial for any author to succeed. If you enjoyed *Blood Runs Crooked*, please leave a review online—anywhere you are able. Even if it's just a sentence or two. It would make all the difference and would be very much appreciated.

Thanks!
Levi Bronze

We hope you enjoyed reading this title from:

www.blackrosewriting.com

Subscribe to our mailing list – *The Rosevine* – and receive **FREE** books, daily deals, and stay current with news about upcoming releases and our hottest authors.
Scan the QR code below to sign up.

Already a subscriber? Please accept a sincere thank you for being a fan of Black Rose Writing authors.

View other Black Rose Writing titles at www.blackrosewriting.com/books and use promo code **PRINT** to receive a **20% discount** when purchasing.